She grabbed her gun with both hands, took a stance. At the same time, I heard someone run up behind me.

"This time, Jack, I'm putting you out of commission." She all but snarled it.

I wished myself out of the room.

Neola fired. Twice.

I felt something pass through what should've been my right shoulder. I fell on my knees and watched my body reassemble itself. Something warm trickled down my arm. Blood dripped through my cuff onto the back of my hand to the tips of my fingers. Neola's legs appeared in front of me. I hadn't left the room, probably because of the super-conjugator.

"What's the matter, Jack, having problems with your telecarb? That's too bad. You're staining the carpet, but I imagine a little more blood won't make a difference. Since this wound isn't life-threatening, I'll remedy that." She raised the gun to my temple.

ALSO BY M. D. BENOIT

Metered Space
Humanity's Music (2006)
Meter Destiny (2006)

A JACK METER CASEFILE

METER MADE

BY

M. D. BENOIT

ZUMAYA OTHERWORLDS GARIBALDI HIGHLANDS BC
2005

This book is a work of fiction. Names, characters, places and incidents are products of the author's imagination or are used fictitiously. Any resemblance to actual persons or events is purely coincidental.

METER MADE

ISBN 13: 978-1-55410-302-7
ISBN 10: 1-55410-302-9
Cover art and design by Martine Jardin

Look for us online at http://www.zumayapublications.com

_ Library and Archives Canada Cataloguing in Publication

Benoit, M. D., 1957-
Meter made / M.D. Benoit.

(A Jack Meter casefile)
Also available in electronic format.
ISBN-13: 978-1-55410-302-7
ISBN-10: 1-55410-302-9

I. Title. II. Series.

PS8603.E56M465 2005 C813'.6 C2005-907070-6

ACKNOWLEDGEMENTS

This story is based on quantum physics brane theory, which is real and does explain the existence of eleven dimensions and parallel universes; any twisting or tweaking of it, of course, is strictly my doing and my responsibility.

The places and streets in this story are real, except for the Richmond Grill and the apartment block on Guigues street. All the characters, even though they might resemble living people, are completely fictional. The aliens, on the other hand, are real.

I would like to thank my friend Peggy Loyer, whose steadfast help has made this book, like all the others before it, a better read. To Daniel, my life companion, my biggest fan. Thank you for propping me up during dark times.

Dom

IN MEMORIAM

Donalda Bonin-Fournier (1911-2003)

CHAPTER ONE

"MY BUILDING IS GONE, MR. METER. I WANT YOU TO GET IT BACK."

The short, balding man in the gray pinstripe suit wrung his hands and waited. I tried not to groan while I thought of a way to let him down gently. I was a private investigator not a repo man.

I glanced at Peter Winston, the lawyer who shared the house where I had my office, and who was my landlord and friend. He leaned against the doorjamb pulling on his stogie and filling the room with blue smoke. He grinned then shrugged.

"I'll let you two gentlemen sort this out," he said. He closed the door softly behind him, leaving a pile of cigar ashes on the floor.

I cleared my throat, and swore he would pay for this one.

"I'm sorry for your loss, Mr. Garner, but—"

Garner made a cutting gesture and dumped his butt in the vinyl chair on the other side of my desk. His straggly white hair flew up then settled. Their oily tips touched his shoulders. Sour sweat and fried onions wafted toward me.

I studied my new potential client. His three-day-old beard grew in white patches over reddened skin that made him look like a dog with mange. He scratched his chin. White fluff snowed down on his jacket. The jacket itself had a cut that looked expensive, in a drab brown that showed several greasy stains.

"Winston told me you might be able to help me," he said. He swallowed visibly. "That you wouldn't laugh at me. He said you were used to the...unusual."

I frowned and pulled the sleeve of my sweater a little lower to hide one of those unusual things I was "used to." "I suppose that's true," I said, my tone soothing, "but—"

Garner scooted to the edge of the seat. "One day it was there then the next, poof! Gone. I want to know what happened to it."

Now I was confused. His building had exploded?

"You want me to find out who blew up your building?"

"What the hell are you talking about?"

"You said poof!"

"I mean poof! not boom!"

"Poof." I was going to kill Winston. "Okay, let's start from the top."

I made a big show of taking out a yellow legal pad and a pencil.

"Then you'll take the case?"

"I didn't say that. I'd like to know a bit more about you and your building first. Then I'll decide."

He stared at me for a moment, rubbed his bald pate with the palm of his hand then nodded.

"You know my name."

"Lambert Garner. You're a client of Winston's?"

"No, we're neighbors. I bought the house across from his fifteen years ago."

I nearly whistled in appreciation. Garner might look like a rummy, but if he could afford a house in New Edinburgh, he must have been doing well.

"Address?" I wrote down what he gave me so I could check it out for myself. Owning a house didn't mean you had the dough for the upkeep. For all I knew, the place was a dump, just like him.

"Occupation?" I'd already noticed the silver pinky ring, which meant he had some kind of engineering background.

"I'm in property management. I used to be a civil engineer, but one day I bought a building and I was hooked." His eyes shone. "I couldn't believe how easy it was. I got tenants, they paid for all my expenses, and I made a profit. I bought a second one then a third. Soon after, I had to incorporate. I never looked back."

I suddenly made the connection. "You mean you're Garner Properties Inc.?"

"That's me. Of course, now it's not only me. There's a whole infrastructure set up. The corporation practically runs itself." He frowned, as if puzzled by his own success. "The company's assets are in the billions."

I closed my eyes then opened them again, hoping they had deceived me and the man sitting in front of me would look better, or richer. He didn't.

"So, you're claiming one of your buildings has disappeared."

"Yes, Mr. Meter, that's what I'm saying." His whiskers rasped under his fingers. His nails were long, broken in places, and far from clean. "Even though I don't have as much time as I used to, I like to do spot checks on the buildings I own, to make sure they're well maintained, that the people who work for me do their jobs. I pride myself on well-maintained buildings." He coughed. "Could I have a glass of water?"

"Sorry." I got up and pointed to the coffeepot. "Would you prefer coffee?"

He nodded, and I poured. After the usual ceremonies—"one cream, three sugars, please"—he slurped, smacked his lips then continued.

"I picked up the file on the building I wanted. What I usually do is, I go into my secretary's office, open a file cabinet drawer then pick out a file at random."

"I would've thought you'd have all that info on the computer."

"Oh, I do. But there's nothing like the feel of paper, isn't it? I suppose I'm old-fashioned. Besides, there are always pieces of papers that must be signed, contracts, leases, etc. We have electronic copies, but the originals must be on paper." He slurped some more coffee syrup then set the cup down, splashing a dollop of liquid on the desktop. Jesus, the guy was a slob.

I tamped down my irritation, reminding myself I wasn't Mr. Clean either. I yanked a tissue from the box in my drawer and set it under

Garner's cup.

"So," he continued, "I took out a file folder with the name of the building on the tab. When I opened it, it was empty." He stopped, looking at me as if he'd said something significant.

"Empty," I repeated. "Your secretary must have misplaced the papers."

"That's what I thought, although Inga's been with me for fifteen years and she's never misplaced so much as a parking stub. I asked her to call up the file from the computer and print me the documents. She couldn't find the file."

"The file folder must have been stuffed in the drawer by mistake then."

"That's impossible."

"Everybody makes mistakes, Mr. Garner, even faithful secretaries."

"Granted, but in this case, Inga didn't make a mistake. You see, I'd picked up the file of the first building I ever bought."

"So you sold it, never removed the file folder."

"It has great sentimental value for me, Mr. Meter. I'll keep that building until it falls to the ground on its own." He frowned. "At least, I will if you can find it again."

I wasn't sure I wanted to go there yet.

"What did you do next?"

"I was greatly puzzled, but Inga assured me it was only a glitch in the system, and that she'd find the missing papers. I decided to check out the building anyway. I know the address, of course. When I got there, it was gone. There was no such building."

"Someone dug it out and left with it?" I said, grinning.

He glared then picked up his cup.

"You don't understand. There wasn't a hole there, or another building. On one side of my building is a bank, on the other side a restaurant with an apartment above. Now they're side-by-side. The entire space occupied by my building is gone."

* * *

I followed Garner into the back of a silver Mercedes 450SL. After he gave the driver the directions, he picked up a cell phone and began to make some calls. His driver wove smoothly through traffic in the direction of Richmond Road, where Garner's building supposedly had been.

I tuned him out, trying to decide if I believed him, or if he was just a kook stringing me along. A rich kook, maybe, but a kook nonetheless.

The thing was, if he'd come to see me a year ago, even if I'd been in good-enough shape to listen to him, I'd have sent him packing with a referral letter to my old warden at the Royal Ottawa, recommending a nice padded cell for an indeterminate time. But after what had happened last fall, I wasn't so sure that vanishing buildings were an impossibility.

I pulled up my sleeve and peeked at the swirling colors of my telecarb. For a reason that neither the Thrittene nor I understood, it had resisted extraction, so I was stuck with it. I couldn't use it anymore, though, unless I wanted to live the rest of my days as a Thrittene, a fate I'd rather avoid.

In the last three weeks since I'd whacked Mueller, I'd tried to get back to a more normal life, if there could be any kind of normal without Annie, tried to forget that I was wearing a piece of alien technology. It was far from easy, especially since memories I'd rather not revisit filled my dreams.

Through the car window I watched as the Ottawa River, flat and gray under the late-October sky, passed by. A few joggers ran on the bicycle path, the tip of their noses red and an expression of pain on their faces.

I'd done nothing in the last three weeks except lounge around and shop for a few clothes and some new toys for the office. I had to admit, normal was boring. I couldn't even drink myself into oblivion anymore, as much because the telecarb wouldn't let me as because I'd lost the need to forget. Maybe that was why, as wacky as I thought Garner was, I'd felt the faint pitter-patter of thrill walking up my spine when I heard his story.

The driver stopped across the street from the bank and the restaurant. Sure enough, there wasn't even space for a toothpick between the two.

"There," Garner said, "that's where my building was."

"Did your building have a name?"

"The Carlisle."

How original.

"Okay, wait here." I crossed the street and went into the bank. "Excuse me," I said to the pink-faced man at the information desk, "I'm looking for a building called the Carlisle. I was told it was around here."

He looked at me with a confused air then said, "Does this have to do with a banking problem, sir?"

"No, I'm looking for a building."

"I can only help you with banking matters."

I raised my eyes to the big sign above his head with INFORMATION printed on it.

"That's what I want."

He perked up. "Would you like to sign up for a bank card?"

I turned on my heels and tried the restaurant next door. As soon as I stepped inside, the skin around my telecarb tingled. I stopped, astonished. It was sending me little shocks, a bit like static electricity, which meant something potentially dangerous to my health was going on and I should pay attention. I knew I wasn't in mortal danger because it would have whisked me out of there faster than I could blink, but it was warning me.

I nodded at the hostess, who was waiting for me with a big smile and an overlarge menu clutched to her chest.

"Smoking or non-smoking, sir? We have a heated patio in the back."

My throat constricted, thinking of my beloved Gitanes. I still missed the pungent sticks of death with smoke that caressed the throat and loose tobacco that burned holes in all my clothes. I shook my head.

"I'm not here to eat; I'm looking for a building. The Carlisle?"

Her grin slipped, and she looked down at her menu then back at me through her eyelashes.

"I'm sorry, sir, I've never heard of that building."

Was she lying, or did she look sly every time people said they weren't here to eat?

"Are you sure? I was told it was around here. I'm supposed to meet someone there."

Her head shot up. "Really? I'm sorry, I can't help you." She looked past me. "Hello. Smoking or non-smoking?"

I took that as my cue to leave. My telecarb stopped tingling as soon as I stepped outside.

Back in Garner's car, I noticed the addresses. The restaurant was at 2091, the bank at 2095. There should have been a 2093 in between.

"So?" Garner said.

I glanced at him and his anxious eyes, red skin and dandruff. I'd never seen a sorrier-looking millionaire. I didn't need his money, but he'd caught my interest. I stared across the street at the restaurant façade.

"I'll take the case."

CHAPTER TWO

I STOOD ON THE SIDEWALK IN THE POURING RAIN, LOOKING UP AT WHAT USED TO BE my apartment. Half of the brick at that level had crumbled, windows had shattered, steel had melted in the blast. Since I'd lived on the top floor, Mueller's bomb hadn't started a fire or weakened the structure. That was fortunate—if you call it fortunate that the explosion had pulverized Johnson, my janitor. All tenants were back in their apartments now except me.

Rain changed into sleet; it stung my face and collected on my beard in a thin sheet of ice that crackled when I opened my mouth. I shivered inside my leather jacket, the only piece of relatively warm clothing I had left.

I felt like a moron standing there, people flowing around me like water around a rock; but I needed to see the apartment for myself and maybe send a message to Johnson that I'd got his own back, since he couldn't do it for himself. I didn't believe in ghosts, but I figured I'd hedge my bets. If anyone had a right to haunt a place, it was Johnson.

So I sent a thought up—Mueller had paid, in full; he was now a soulless, mindless, half-dead guest of the Binaries, who wanted to study biological entities.

I turned around and headed for my current favorite café, the Moulin de Provence, thinking I should start hunting for an apartment soon. Winter was coming on, and I couldn't live in my office indefinitely. For the moment, though, I had a case, although I was damned if I knew where to start.

I stopped in the entrance, absorbing the smells of sweet pastry, fresh bread and coffee. The café was full and noisy, as usual around ten o'clock in the morning. Ottawa's a government town, after all, and coffee breaks are sacred.

I didn't need to pounce on a seat—Terry Parczek was already seated near the window, a cup of coffee in front of him. I waved to him, ordered an espresso and walked to the table with the small cup in hand.

"Hey," I said.

"Jesus Murphy, Jack, you could've picked a better day to drag me all the way downtown for a friggin' coffee. I nearly froze my ears, and I'm wet through crossing the street from the parking lot."

"Don't you own a coat?"

Terry grunted. "It was nice this morning when I left home."

I sipped my coffee and grinned at him. His olive-green tweed jacket had darkened over the shoulders from the rain and smelled like wet wool. Rain had also spotted his blue shirt and brown tie.

"It's nearly November, Terry. In the fall, it rains."

"Tell me about it." He took a sip. "Haven't seen you in a while. How've you been doing?"

"Fine."

He peered at me, eyes half-closed. "I called a couple of times. No answer."

"I must've been out."

"I left messages."

"I'll have to talk to my service."

"Yeah, why don't you do that." He sniffed.

I'd pissed him off. I sighed.

"Listen, I needed time, okay? I'm fine, now. All I need is an apartment." I grasped for a change of subject. "Have you heard from Claire?"

"I've been keeping an eye on her, just in case. She's been cleared of the guard's murder, even though the only witness was you."

"She's not exactly the killer type."

"I didn't know there was a type," he said, grinning. "Anyhoo, she'll be back at work at the end of the month. Went nuts for a little while there, but she's a tough gal."

I laughed, wondering how Claire would react at being described that way.

"She is," I said.

"She sure had some words about you." He paused then smiled. "Not what I'd call friendly words."

"Claire and I understand each other."

He pointed at my wrist. "That thing giving you any trouble?"

"The telecarb? Funny you should mention it."

"You haven't tried to use it."

"I have no interest in mutating into white goop."

"You should get it removed."

"Can't. But the Thrittene asked me to go back to their world for a while so they could try to fix it."

"I take it you declined."

I shrugged. "I'll have to go, eventually."

Terry nodded. We fell silent, looked around us at the café patrons, oblivious to everything but their companions and their croissants. It felt good to be in this place with a friend. Terry was the only one, apart from Claire, who was aware of everything that had happened. He knew the real story behind Mueller, who'd been stealing, blowing up buildings and killing humans and aliens alike so he could build himself a universal soldier that just happened to look like my Annie. In the process, that sonofabitch had almost destroyed the universe, which is a lot bigger and weirder than anyone could imagine, and had unwittingly forced me to live with a piece of alien matter melded to my arm.

All-in-all, a very joyous experience.

"So," Terry said, looking back at me, "your telecarb's been acting up."

"Sort of." I finished my coffee. "I have a case."

"About time. Lazing about just makes the brain go mushy."

"You look more relieved than you should be."

"Betty has been after me for two weeks now, telling me I should talk to you."

"That's what you're doing now."

"No." He gestured with his hand, stretched his neck forward. "*Talk* to you. She's worried."

"Oh. You can tell her to stop worrying then."

"I'll do that." He sat back as the situation dawned on him. "You avoid me like the plague for three weeks then you call me up, all buddy-buddy. I must be slipping. What's your case?"

"This guy claims his building disappeared."

"As in vanished."

"Yeah. Poof. We drove to the site of his building, and there was a restaurant in its place."

"Maybe the building was never there."

"That's what I was leaning toward, but the addresses didn't match up. Like a chunk of Earth had been removed and the two buildings on each side took up the space. When I went into the restaurant, my telecarb acted up."

"It indicated to you the place was dangerous."

I nodded.

"Could it be malfunctioning?"

"Don't think so. As soon as I got out, the tingling stopped."

"Hmm. Give me the address. I'll check it out."

"That's not exactly what I'd like you to do for me." When he raised an eyebrow, I continued. "You have access to SETI databases and the like, don't you? You could do a search on disappearing buildings."

"You're kidding me, right?"

I grinned. "Hey, I figure if my telecarb is acting up, there could be some extraterrestrial involved."

He narrowed his eyes. "Is this client for real?"

"Have you ever heard of Lambert Garner?"

"Of Garner Property Management?" Terry whistled. "Holy shit."

I didn't say anything, let him process the information. With him, it was always better to wait than to pressure. I knew I'd get him to help me eventually—it was just a matter of letting him catch up to me.

"If I didn't know you," he said, "I'd laugh my head off. Buildings just don't disappear like that. Poof, my ass."

"It gets weirder. Garner claims that all the information pertaining to the building has also disappeared. The paperwork, building permits, leases, maintenance logs—everything."

Terry grimaced. "Garner needs the address of your shrink."

I leaned toward him. "Maybe, but do you want to take the risk that he's just a flake and let it go at that? According to Garner, there were fourteen apartments in the building. He thinks he had full occupancy. He doesn't remember the names of the tenants, of course, and the paperwork's gone, but even if there was only one person per apartment, that's still fourteen people unaccounted for at minimum. Gone."

"That's impossible. We'd have heard if that many went missing at the same time. People go to work, have families, kids go to school. If we hadn't been on it, the media sure would have, and they would've raised hell."

"My gut tells me there won't be any reports."

"How'd you figure that?"

"Right beside the restaurant is a bank. No one inside the two buildings remembers that the Carlisle was there."

Terry shook his head. "Man, how d'you get these weirdo cases?"

"I've got Winston to thank for this one. Apparently, he and Garner are neighbors." I got up, went back to the counter for two refills, one to go, which I set in front of Terry.

He looked up at me then shook his head.

"Okay, okay. I'll check the databases, get back to you." He stood, picked up his paper cup and nodded. "Thanks for the coffee."

I sat back down at the table and stared into my cup. The chances that a report of anyone claiming their house or building had disappeared would appear in a legitimate, controlled databank were slim to none. There were the chat rooms for conspiracy theorists, general warmongers and neo-Nazis that the Mounties monitored, but I doubted "disappearance of building" were keywords for info retrieval.

I rubbed my sleeve over the telecarb. At least fourteen missing people, all of them gone without a trace. Terry was right—people didn't live in a vacuum. Even I, with my limited social life, would eventually be missed should I vanish. There was my sister, Terry, Winston, a couple others who would wonder what had happened to me after a while.

I realized that, even though Garner's story had stepped over the line of weird to go into ludicrous, I believed him. I thought about that restaurant. I'd have to go back, maybe when there weren't so many people around.

The telecarb would be useless to me on this case. I'd have to use the good old standard methods of detecting, like breaking and entering. The idea had some appeal.

I glanced outside. Funny, I'd forgotten the rain.

CHAPTER THREE

THE FREEZING RAIN ADDED TO THE USUAL DOWNTOWN CHAOS. PEDESTRIANS slipped and slid around cars stopped halfway through intersections, their tires unable to grip the icy pavement. Horns blared when lights changed, trying to encourage forward movement, but they didn't seem to have much of an effect.

My dark-skinned cab driver stoically picked up the prayer beads that hung from the rearview mirror and began to mumble.

I thought about death. I didn't have the support of faith, like my driver, or the belief in an afterlife. I'd seen what was beyond Earth, and it wasn't Heaven. For two years, all I'd wanted was to die. At least I'd thought so, but it had come to me at one point that I'd been kidding myself. Even through the greatest depths of my grief for Annie, I hadn't thought about suicide.

How would I have done it? I hated guns; I hadn't taken a pill in my life except for aspirin; I didn't use a razor. I could've thrown myself off a building or a cliff, but it sounded too messy. Wasn't it Nietzsche who'd said it was always consoling to think of suicide because it helped you through the bad nights? It might've been true for me. Or maybe I'd only needed some kind of ending, a sense of completion, to think about living again.

Traffic started moving. My driver hung up his beads, put the car in gear. He glanced at me in the rearview mirror.

"Would you believe this weather?" he said. "I hope we don't have another ice storm like the one in '98."

"I'm with you," I said, relieved he yanked me from my brooding mood. I chatted him up for the rest of the trip, discarding the gloomy thoughts like a candy wrapper.

I waved to the cab driver and nearly broke my neck crossing the sidewalk to the door. I was about to run up the stairs to my office when I changed my mind and veered toward Winston's instead.

Charlotte St. Clair, Winston's secretary, scowled at me down her narrow, pointy nose and over lips pressed together tighter than a virgin's thighs. She was dressed in a severely ugly purple suit and a white shirt buttoned up to her scrawny neck.

"Hey, Charlie, howya doin'? Still madly in love with me?"

"Your sense of humor, if that's what it is, is more pitiful than usual. It must be the weather."

"If I knew how gracious you were going to be today I would've dropped in earlier."

"I'm so glad you restrained yourself."

I sent her my most charming grin. "Is Winston in?"

Charlotte huffed, picked up the phone and punched in a number.

"Mr. Meter is here to see you, sir." She peered owlishly at me and jerked her head at a closed door. "Go on in."

Winston's office looked very Churchillian—huge desk, recessed bookcases full of impressive tomes, blood-red leather chairs, and the smell of cigar smoke permeating the entire room. Winston stood behind his desk stuffing papers in a briefcase.

"You'll have to make it quick, Jack; I've got court in thirty minutes. Judging by the state of the roads, it's going to take me that long to get to the courthouse."

"You'll probably be the only who made it. The roads are wicked."

"The judge is there. I need to talk to him anyway." He snapped his briefcase closed. "So, what's up?"

"Garner," I said.

"You took the case then."

"You knew I would. Is he really your neighbor?"

"Sure is. Great house, too. He has a thing for buildings."

"Did he tell you what it was about?"

"Not really, just that something weird was happening, and he couldn't go to the police. Naturally, I thought of you, seeing as we share this house and I know for a fact you've some time on your hands."

"I've been busy."

"Yeah? I haven't seen too many clients rush up the stairs these past few weeks."

I shrugged. "You know I don't need clients."

"Sure you do. What else are you going to do with yourself?" He pushed by me and strode to the door. He opened it, turned and smiled thinly. "By the way, I'm getting sick of hearing you snore up there," he said. "I suggest you get an apartment. Otherwise, I'll have to revoke the lease on your office."

"I don't snore," I called out to his retreating back.

Charlie snickered.

I went up the stairs, deeply miffed. Maybe I hadn't been searching that hard for a new apartment, but my last case had taken its toll. I needed the rest.

I considered myself a simple guy, with simple tastes. All I needed was a place to crash, a full bathroom, small fridge, hot plate and coffeemaker. I had all of that here.

True, the office wasn't the best place. That old leather sofa sagged so much it looked depressed. The smell of Winston's cigars mixed with a whiff of stale pizza and dirty laundry because the windows had been painted shut for so long I'd have to break a pane to get in some fresh air. The cleaning staff had left little piles of accumulated dust in the corners that looked like dead mice under the fluorescent lights.

It would be nice to sleep in a real bed. A TV would be good, too, and a sound system so I could listen to my opera again. A full kitchen. Hmm. I hadn't cooked a full meal in a while. I missed that.

I looked around again, decided Winston was right. I'd take some time from the case and look for an apartment.

That decision out of the way, I sat down at my desk and fired up my computer. Now that Winston had vouched for Garner, I wanted to do a check on him—holdings, financials, security, even state of health. The Internet was a great tool to dig up that kind of information, especially if you subscribed to search engines that weren't available to every Joe on the street.

A couple of hours later, I had a clearer picture of my client, although he was pretty much whom he purported to be—a civil engineer turned property manager. Unassuming as he looked, Garner owned about a third of the National Capital Region. He preferred small apartment blocks, condominiums in upper-crust neighborhoods, corner stores. In fact, he owned the building with my ex-apartment. He was divorced, had two adult sons—one worked as an engineer in Toronto, the other was a film producer in Victoria.

Garner's ex-wife had remarried after a hefty settlement.

He had bought the house he now lived in fifteen years previously when he was still married. He looked to be in good shape financially, if being worth forty million meant you were comfortable. I'd even found a family picture in an archived *Citizen* article.

So Garner was who he said he was. Whether he was functioning with all of his brain cells was another matter entirely.

I got up to stretch, walked to the window. Across the street, on the corner, the convenience store owner had hung a lighted plastic pumpkin in his window beside a cardboard skeleton. The rain had abated, changed into a mist. City trucks had spread a mixture of salt and sand, and traffic seemed to flow a little better. It was barely three o'clock, but the gray skies made it appear later. I thought about going back to Richmond Road and checking that restaurant again. Nah. Tomorrow would be soon enough.

I'd check on the missing persons instead. I picked up the phone to call my pal at the police station.

At that moment, the air in front of me shivered like heat above hot pavement. I dropped the receiver back in its cradle. My telecarb warmed up, but not in the regular way that warned me of danger. It was cozier, like a hot toddy with plenty of whiskey in it.

In about five seconds, the air solidified into a woman, on the short side, with a tight body wrapped into a black jumpsuit, rich whiskey eyes and a full mouth that ate up the space of her pixie face. Black, jaw-length hair, parted in the middle, shining silver under the fluorescent light. She held a small box the size of a PDA in one of her hands.

I said nothing while she peered around her with curiosity.

"I expected something classier," she said. Her voice, in contrast with her small body, was deep and rich.

"I'm sorry it disappoints you," I said.

"You don't seem surprised to see me."

"Oh, I'm surprised."

She waited. When I said nothing, she raised an eyebrow. She glanced at the chair across from my desk, sat down, crossed her legs. She wore black leather ankle boots with three-inch spike heels.

"My name is Neola Durwin. I believe you stumbled into one of my cases."

She still held that metal box in her hand.

"If that's a weapon, I have to warn you, I don't respond well to them."

She looked down at the box and smiled. Her finger moved over it and the box shrank into a pin, which she attached to her suit, right above her left breast.

"It's my Universal System Integrator. USI for short. Gets me from one corner of the universe to the other."

A mechanical telecarb, I thought. Why couldn't the Thrittene have thought of that?

"So, where do you come from?"

She laughed. "Minnesota."

"I thought I detected an accent."

She uncrossed and re-crossed her legs, sinking deeper into the chair. "So, what do you have so far?"

"Ms. Durwin—"

"Neola."

"Neola then. It depends on what you want."

She frowned. "You triggered one of the alarms. I thought that was deliberate. You have a reputation across the universe, Jack Meter. Don't tell me we're not on the same photon."

"We're not even on the same light beam."

"Oh." She rose, unfolded her USI. "So long then."

And she wasn't there anymore.

Hmm. On the scale of weird, that was right up there. I also didn't like coincidences. As soon as I get a case that could delight my shrink if I had the notion of talking to him about it, Miss Neola appears. If she and I were working on the same case, she seemed to have a bit of an advantage—she sounded like she knew what it was about, even if she'd said less than nothing.

That was how the whole Thrittene gig started—they'd lured me with a few half-truths and mostly lies, and I ended up hip deep in caca. Maybe she'd come here as bait, sent by someone else who wanted me involved.

If that was the goal, it was working.

* * *

"How many MPs have you had in the past week?"

I heard the clicking of keys on a keyboard, tried to imagine BB's stubby fingers dancing over the little squares, but the picture couldn't quite form. They didn't call him Big Bruiser for nothing. He had fists like sledgehammers, and they went with the rest of his body.

"The usual," he said. "One or two, both recovered within twenty-four. What've you got?"

"I'm just following up on a lead, BB. You know if I have something I'll tag you."

"Yeah, you're good for it."

"If you start to get a rash of reports, let me know, will you?"

He agreed, and I hung up. My stomach growled, reminding me I'd skipped lunch. I got up, walked to the fridge. As I passed over the spot where Neola had stood, the room temperature dropped, and my telecarb warmed around my wrist for a fraction of a second. I backed up until I felt the slight chill again. I wondered if the effect was only the residue of Neola's device or if I could follow her trail somehow.

I blinked, and I was somewhere I didn't know. My first reaction was panic. Without wanting to, I'd used my telecarb. The last time I'd used it I'd almost ended up permanently looking like a Thrittene. I examined my hands; I had all my fingers. My body was all there, too. No sign of any white matter, except for the telecarb, which glowed faintly.

Okay, how was that possible? Maybe it had to do with Neola, or possibly her USI. This meant that I might not be able to go back to the office on my own steam.

I glanced around curiously. A lamp on a table beside a red loveseat lighted the place, a small glass tower from the look of it. A powerful telescope stood on a tripod on the other side. I approached a window, made a hood out of my hands and peered into the dark outside. Snow. Wide expanses of it, with the stark outline of peaks in the distance. Somehow my telecarb had brought me here, which I knew couldn't be Minnesota.

I followed a set of stairs going down and found myself in a large living room. Bare planks covered the floor, ceiling and walls. The furniture, rustic and well used, clustered around a fireplace so large I could've crawled into it and taken a snooze.

Across from me, on the other side of the room, I heard rustling coming from beyond one of two half-opened doors. I tiptoed to it, pushed it slowly opened, and there was Neola. Her back was to me as she worked some figures on a computer.

I leaned against the doorjamb. "That was very rude, leaving like that."

She jumped and turned around. "Christ, how the hell did you get here?"

I smiled. "Nice place you have. Where is it, exactly?"

"Colorado."

"I thought you said you were from Minnesota."

She got up and moved toward me. The top of her head fit just below my chin and I had a couple dozen kilos over her, but she looked like she wanted to deck me anyway.

"Get out of my way, pal," she said.

I waited a few seconds more then moved aside. Her gaze swept the living room; then she rushed up the stairs to check the tower. She came back down a little more slowly.

"You're alone."

"Were you expecting a squad?"

"I wasn't expecting you, that's for sure."

She'd changed into tight-fitting jeans and a yellow T-shirt. Her feet were bare. She wore no jewelry except for that pin that changed into the USI—that was still above her breast. A nicely rounded breast, currently without a bra.

I sat down on the arm of one of the sofas.

"Listen, sweetheart, why don't we stop playing games here? Maybe you messed up when you came to visit me, or you did it on purpose. No matter. Whether you like it or not, you're stuck with me for a while until I figure out how you jive with the case I've just agreed to work on."

She glared. "You call me sweetheart again, I'll bust your balls."

I grinned. She had spunk, I had to say that for her.

She turned her back on me and moved to a recessed area I hadn't noticed when I arrived. A kitchen, complete with a small table. Neola poured herself a cup of coffee.

"I wouldn't mind one of those," I said.

She threw a glance over her shoulder, took down a second cup from the cupboard and filled it. She pushed the cup so it slid over the counter toward me. I nipped it before it fell to the floor, took a sip. It had the consistency of sludge and tasted like liquefied blood pudding. I made an effort not to gag.

"So, you *are* working on a case," she said.

"Just started. I wondered if you're competition. So I came to visit."

She stared at me for a long moment. Bravely, I took another sip of sludge and schooled my face not to wince.

"Are you as good as they say you are, Jack Meter?"

"Probably not."

Her lips curved, but the motion had nothing to do with a smile.

"Then you'd better have luck on your side." She went back to the living room and sat down in one of the overstuffed chairs set in front of a bay window. She said nothing more, just stared at her reflection.

"I'm not leaving until you give me some answers," I said softly. I decided not to tell her I had absolutely no clue how I'd get back to my office.

"Tell me about this case you have," she said, her eyes still averted.

I shrugged and sat down across from her.

"My client is a property developer who lost a building. Apparently, it disappeared into thin air."

"And?"

"I took the case. That's it."

"Why?"

"Because I haven't had time to do any investigating."

She made an impatient gesture.

"Not that. Why did you take the case? Your obvious conclusion should've been that the guy was nuts." Understanding dawned on her face. "Your telecarb reacted to the alarms. That's why you believed him."

"Give the woman a cigar."

"Why didn't you just tell me?"

"You were in a hurry. I didn't get the chance."

She flushed slightly. "I suppose I was a bit rude."

"I forgive you." I made myself more comfortable in the chair. "How about you give me what you have now."

She barked a laugh. "This is my case. I'll take care of your client. You stay away from him."

Before she could react, I leaned over and swiped her pin.

"You may have the case, but without your USI, you're stranded here." I grinned, knowing I looked brash and arrogant.

I had to admire her restraint. She didn't jump up or try to get the pin back from me. She just sat there, hands fisted, knuckles white.

"The device won't work for you," she said through clenched teeth.

"Oh, I don't intend to use it, just to prevent you from using it yourself."

"Are you always this much of a jackass?"

I lost the grin and looked straight into her eyes.

"My client hired me to find his building. Frankly, I really don't give a shit about a bunch of bricks. But there were at least fourteen people living in that building, and they're gone, too. I'm not going to let this go, Neola. With or without you, I'll do what I have to do to get those people back. It may take me longer if we don't work together, but I can get there on my own."

She looked at me soberly. "I work alone."

"Too bad."

She took a deep breath and let it out very slowly.

"All right. I don't like it, but I'll give you what I have. Maybe we can work this from different angles and meet in the middle."

I smiled. "Sounds like a plan."

She smiled back, extended her hand, palm up. I dropped the pin into it. Before I could say "Let's shake on it," she was gone.

CHAPTER FOUR

I SWORE THEN LAUGHED ALOUD. I SHOULD'VE KNOWN BETTER, SINCE SHE'D rabbited once before. I passed my hand over the space where she'd been sitting and felt the same chill …

I landed in a purple desert, on top of a purple sand dune, its crest tinged with green from a rising or setting sun—I couldn't tell. Stifling heat made me gasp; I thought longingly of the freezing rain I'd left back home.

Footprints led to a round structure nestled in a dip in the sand. I followed them. The door was ajar, and I pushed it opened. Neola leaned on the edge of a clear counter, her arms crossed below her breasts, a small smile on her face.

"I guess I'm stuck with you," she said.

"Wherever you go, I go." I glanced around. Recessed in the walls were panels with blinking lights and strange characters. "What's this place?"

"Not so fast, buster. I showed you mine, you show me yours."

"Darling, I didn't know you felt like that about me."

She simply raised her eyebrows.

"Okay, okay." I pulled my sleeve up and showed her the telecarb.

She pushed away from the counter and approached me, obviously fascinated by the swirling colors.

"Wow. Incredible." She looked up, beaming. Something twisted in my stomach. She was beautiful like that, her eyes bright, her mouth smiling. "It's interfaced with your own neural system, isn't it?" she continued, oblivious to my reaction. "I'd heard that was the way the

Thrittene did it."

"Yeah, that's the way. I'm stuck with it now."

"Why would you want to remove it? This way it can't be lost." She sent me a telling look. "Or stolen. But I'd also heard that using the device was morphing your cells into their substance. I didn't know the Thrittene had fixed it."

I said nothing, not wanting to go there yet. I simply gestured with my head in a noncommittal way.

"How does it work?"

I shrugged. "I just think where I want to go and I'm there." I didn't mention the little detail that any person I was following had to have vacated the arrival point for me to follow. "Now that the niceties have been covered, are you going to tell me where we are?"

She moved to the left wall, tapped a few lighted pads, and the door behind me snapped shut.

"We're in a universal way station." She gestured at the right wall. "On that side is the comm equipment." She tapped a few more pads. "This side is the control station, to program the next leg of our journey."

"This is like your USI only bigger."

She threw a smile over her shoulder. "Something like that. We're here."

I hadn't felt anything, not even the slight chill or the warming of my telecarb. She tapped the pads in reverse order and the door opened.

"Let's go."

"After you," I said.

She grinned and stepped through the door. I followed her, curious to see where we'd landed.

The way station had set—if, indeed, it had moved at all—on the onyx-black grassy shoulder of a cobbled road that, straight and flat, stretched to a dot on the horizon in either direction. Sequoia-like trees, with bark resembling polished black marble, flanked each side, their branches jutting out at forty-five-degree angles and strewn with clumps of blue-green leaves that made me think of carved jade. There was a whole forest of them, its floor this same onyx-black grass.

There were no bird cries, no rustling from animals or wind, and no sunshine, either, only a strong, sharp light as if reflected from a mirror. The temperature was cooler here than on the purple sand planet, but it still was warm. I was glad of it, since I'd left my leather jacket at the office.

Neola started down the road. She was barefoot, but the unevenness of the cobblestones didn't seem to bother her. Even as I shortened my stride to match hers, the trees zipped by as if they were moving the other way. We walked in silence for about five minutes. I had begun to get bored when a house materialized in front of us. At least, I assumed it was a house, since there was a door, windows and a roof. That was it, though—no walls, no floor, no frames. The door stood at an angle, the windows floated in the air in a scattered way on two levels.

"I brought you Jack Meter," Neola said in English to the door. "He stumbled onto my case."

The windows on the second level dipped down as if they were looking at me. "Where?"

To my ears, the single word sounded like the opening of a door in dire need of WD-40. It was a good thing the Thrittene had installed a universal translator in a previously unused portion of my brain so I understood what it said. Neola must've had something similar.

"Earth," she said.

"They are reaching far."

"Yes. His telecarb triggered the alarm I'd set. He wants to get involved."

"You have told him of our problem?"

"I have not. I wished to consult with you first." She gestured at me with her thumb. "He tagged along."

The door turned toward me.

"How is it, Jack Meter, since the Thrittene have not repaired your telecarb, that you have been able to follow Neola Durwin and stay whole?"

Neola turned on me. "You said it had been."

"I didn't say anything, sweetheart. You assumed."

"Don't call me sweetheart," she said through clenched teeth. "If you say it one more time, I won't answer for my actions."

I looked down. "I'm really scared."

"Jack Meter," the house boomed, "answer the question."

I winced and turned to it. "I have no idea. There's some interaction between Neola's USI and my telecarb. The USI seems to leave an energy residue the telecarb is using."

"You must go back to Thrittene."

"Yeah, yeah," I muttered. "Everybody's very big at giving me advice."

"The Thrittene have advanced their research considerably."

"I'll think about it."

"You may bring Jack Meter up-to-date on the circumstances, Neola Durwin."

Neola gave a short nod, turned on her heel and started back the way we'd come.

"Your client is a house," I said. "No wonder you didn't want to talk about your case."

She entered the way station, engaged the lock behind me, tapped the launch sequence then turned back to me.

"It would've been interesting to find out if you could follow the station the same way you followed me."

"I don't particularly want to try it."

Suddenly, she smiled, all genial-like.

"You're stuck on Earth without me. Or anywhere else, for that matter."

I sighed. She was too sharp not to have got there eventually.

"That's why I'll be sticking to you like glue, sweetheart."

She sauntered close to me, a flirtatious look on her face. Slowly, she raised her hands to my chest.

"I told you," she said as she grabbed my shirt. Pain exploded. "Don't call me sweetheart."

I crumpled to my knees, hands to my crotch, black spots in my eyes. I lost it for a few seconds while I tried not to puke. When I came back up, my breath wheezing, she was gone.

I staggered up, searched for the chill, followed. I was back in her cabin in Colorado. I took a deep breath and followed the sounds coming from the kitchen, going down the stairs very painfully.

"Damn, woman, you fight dirty."

She kept her back to me, took out a can of coffee.

"I start as I mean to go on."

I grabbed her arm, whipped her around. "Let me tell you something, sweetheart."

Her eyes darkened.

"You'd better start over." I grabbed the coffee can and set it on the counter then pushed her ahead of me toward the living room. I tried not to limp. The cutting pain was now a low throb, but it still pissed me off.

I whipped her around, planted myself in front of her. There was no fear in her eyes, just annoyance. Despite myself, I started to feel amused.

"You've been a pain in the ass since I laid eyes on you. You're arrogant, sneaky and untrustworthy. You'd better readjust that attitude of yours real fast."

"Or what?" She crossed her arms below her breasts. "You can't move around the universe without me, you have no information, no clues. Basically, you have no case." She smirked. "And I bet you can't even make it back to that dingy office of yours in one piece so you can tell your client you haven't got a hope in hell of solving his problem."

I took a deep breath, concentrated on keeping my hands to my sides instead of clamping them around her neck. She was absolutely right. I knew it, and she knew that I knew it. Time to change tactics.

"Damn," I said, as I plopped on the couch.

She waited a few seconds then sat beside me and patted my knee. I glared.

"Sorry," she said. I could tell she was trying to hide a grin. "You want coffee?"

"Yeah, but I'll make it. I'm not drinking that slime you make." I checked my watch. It was nearly suppertime, and I still hadn't had anything to eat. "How about some grub while we're at it? Breakfast's a long way away."

Neola declared she didn't cook, which didn't surprise me, considering how she could mangle coffee. Her pantry was nearly bare, but I managed a cheese omelet and toast.

"Hmm," she said on her last bite. "I'll keep you around if you continue cooking like this."

"I'll have to go back to the office eventually." I sat back, took a last slug of coffee. "Time's up, Neola. You've had your fun. You hold all the cards right now, but there are ways of equalizing that."

"Why haven't you gone back to Thrittene to get the telecarb fixed?"

I shrugged. "Didn't see the reason for it. I didn't anticipate I might need it again."

"But if it worked, you could go anywhere in the universe, visit any planet."

"Regardless of where you go, life's pretty much the same."

She looked at me doubtfully, as if my answers didn't satisfy her. They were the truth, though. I'd found that, regardless of where I went in the universe, one principle held for everyone: self-preservation at all costs. I'd rather deal with that on my own planet. At least the liars and the cheats looked familiar.

"Are you going to get it repaired now?" she said.

"Why, when I have you and your USI?"

"We could split up, be twice as efficient."

"Uh-uh. I'll stay close for a while. See how you operate."

She got up, fixed us each a brandy.

"Okay, let's play it this way," she said as she handed me the snifter. "I'll tell you what it's all about, as far as I know it, and we'll try to make it a go as a team. If it doesn't work out, you let me finish it by myself."

"If it doesn't work out, we finish it separately."

"Now why did I know you were going to say that?" She sat back down, nodded. "How much do you know about astronomy?"

"The basics, I suppose."

"You know about the theory that the universe is expanding?"

"Since the Big Bang. It's slowly going outwards."

"Soon the astronomers are going to find the opposite. The universe is shrinking, and fast. Too fast."

"Parts of it are disappearing, just like my client's building?"

She nodded. "We don't know who or what is responsible. In some cases, at the edge of the galaxy, stars just wink out. In other galaxies, chunks of planets are vaporizing. In most cases, barely anyone notices."

That made me think. "My client noticed."

"As I said, it's quite rare, but it happens, once in a while. That's how I got involved."

"You're a scientist then."

"No, an investigator."

"You think someone is responsible for the universe shrinking?"

"I think someone is doing some cut-and-paste. Unfortunately, we know about the cut part but not where the stuff's going."

I got to my feet and strolled over to the window to look into the night.

"You realize what you're saying? Someone is steadily stealing pieces of our universe."

"Sounds more than farfetched, doesn't it?"

"Do you have any leads?"

"Not really. Our first goal has been to determine the rates of shrinkage. I've been placing alarms all over the universe—I can explain to you how they work later on. Once we correlate the disappearances, we might be able to pinpoint the source."

"If they don't make you disappear before you do."

"That's always been a risk." She hesitated. "I'm the fifth agent assigned to this case. All the others have disappeared."

"Agent?"

"I belong to an organization called the Intergalactic Agency, IGA for short. A sort of Interpol for the universe."

I threw up my hands. "Why not. So, whoever is responsible for shrinking the universe is on to you."

"Is aware that IGA agents are involved, yes."

"I've always liked those kinds of odds."

"There's still time to step out, let us do the job."

"Not on your life, sister. Tell me—"

The "Dive! Dive!" siren of a submarine blasted through the cabin. Neola jumped up, snapped off her pin.

"They've triggered another alarm." She checked her device. "I'll see you there."

With those words, she vanished.

I stepped on the spot where she'd stood, felt the chill, wished myself with her.

My telecarb tingled and left me where I was. I backed away and tried again, with the same results.

"Damn you," I said to my telecarb, "follow her."

In answer, it sent a sharp jolt to my wrist, and I still stood exactly were I was.

I swore again. Wherever Neola had gone, she'd landed right in mortal danger.

CHAPTER FIVE

I HAD TWO CHOICES—EITHER I WAITED FOR HER TO COME BACK, WHICH MIGHT never happen, or I found a way to follow her. There might be another USI in the house, but Neola had said hers only worked for her, so I assumed any other one lying around would have the same properties. Regardless, I had no idea how to operate one, or where she'd gone, so it was pointless.

I glanced at my telecarb, totally frustrated, and summed up my situation. I didn't know why the telecarb could follow Neola's USI without side effects on my body, although it had obviously kept its protective failsafe and refused to send me where I could be damaged beyond repair. I didn't dare go back to the office, for two reasons. First, I wasn't sure I wouldn't be transformed into a Thrittene—seemingly, the telecarb didn't consider that fate as permanent impairment. Second, wherever she'd gone, no way would I let Neola fend for herself. I knew that her trail would stay warm for a few hours. I had to find a way to follow her, and the only solution I could see didn't make me sing with joy.

I had to go back to Thrittene.

I strode to the small bar in the corner and checked out Neola's stash. No scotch, but a decent brandy. I poured myself a healthy slug and gulped it down. Heat spread from throat to gut and made me calmer. I poured myself another shot and thought about the answer I'd come up with.

What if all this was only an elaborate scheme to get me back to Thrittene? I didn't want to feel paranoid, but a certain amount of healthy suspicion when it came to those blobs of white matter had saved my life once. The only catch was that I couldn't see how they'd have enrolled Garner in their scheme. They had no way to communicate with humans, and the only reason they'd been able to kidnap me was because of my connection with Annie and the pickled state of my brain.

Regardless, I had to admit defeat—I was stuck here unless I went back to the office the normal way, by plane. I stared outside at the night. Neola had said the cabin was somewhere in Colorado, but where...that was still a mystery.

Defeated by my own logic, I wished myself on Thrittene.

*　　　*　　　*

The place hadn't changed—it was still as boringly white as before. I stood where I landed, knowing I stepped on all of the Thrittene at the same time, which meant I didn't need to advertise my presence. I'd done the equivalent of jumping on their backs.

A white column rose from the floor and slowly shaped itself into a human figure. This time Trebor's face was normal. I kind of missed the mouth on the forehead. Leinad split from him and stepped to the side.

"Jack Meter," Leinad said, turning purple. "Finally."

A multitude of sounds swirled around me and made me wince. I'd never gotten used to their way of expressing emotions, with a mix of color and sounds. In this case, their relief, exasperation and excitement, multiplied by the total of all the Thrittene, were enough to blast my eardrums.

"All right, all right," I shouted above the noise. "Keep it down, will you?"

The screeches abated, but they remained in the background, making my teeth ache.

"We expected you earlier," Trebor said, reproach in his voice.

"Yeah, well, I had things to do, places to see. I'm not here to shoot the breeze, Trebor. I want you to fix my telecarb so I don't change into one of you every time I use it."

Leinad approached, pulled up my sleeve and touched the device on my wrist. Colors swirled happily.

"I thought you understood, Jack Meter. We cannot repair the telecarb, because there is nothing wrong with it. It is part of us. The problem is with your body."

"My body's just fine, thank you. Except for the parts you tampered with."

"Leinad has been working apace on a solution," Trebor said. "The problem is difficult. Now that you are here, he will be able to perform some tests."

"How long is that going to take?"

"As long as needs be, Jack Meter."

"Uh-uh. I need you to fix it now."

Trebor gestured with impatience. Sounds around me increased.

"Then obviously you will have to accept Leinad's solution. He will have to change your cellular configuration."

"Oh, no. Forget it."

Both Thrittene watched me without a word. Even the sounds clammed up. That made me extremely nervous.

"You guys have been tinkering with my body for your own amusement. Well, that's it. You have to remember something—it's my body." I sounded petulant, even to my own ears. Disgusted, I turned my back on them. I didn't do petulant. Surly, morose, snarly—yes. Petulant, no.

I gave up.

"Have you even tried this before?"

Happy sounds swirled around me.

"We have made very precise calculations," a pink Leinad said. "I am quite certain it will work."

"That means you know squat, as usual." Right at that point, I noticed one of the Three Stooges was missing. "Hey, where's Nasus?"

They both stared at me, uncomprehending.

"You know—female, well-stacked, voice like she's just come out of bed?"

They still looked blank.

"Okay, let's take it one step at a time. You remember Annie?" They nodded. "Mueller?" Yes again. "Ener?"

Screeches.

"He is dead, gone from us," Trebor boomed.

"That's right. But you don't remember Nasus."

They both shook their heads.

"Shit."

There was only one explanation—the Cut-and-Paste Gang had struck again. Not good. I had a bit of a crush on Nasus, even if she was the most twisted of the lot. Now I had two people to recover.

"After you reconfigure my cells," I said to Leinad, "that'll do it, right?"

He hesitated.

"You will be able to live anywhere you wish."

"But?"

"You may have to come back to Thrittene regularly for adjustment."

"I'm not a goddamn carburetor."

"I tried to find the optimum solution, in the very short time I had," he said in an offended tone. "You are quite an impatient man, Jack Meter. I had to do all my research without you helping out. Now you come here, and you want perfect results. It is just not possible."

Now *he* was starting to whine.

"Okay, okay. Don't get your knickers in a twist. Is this a temporary solution? I mean, if you can change my body one way, surely you can change it back?"

"Probably."

I sighed. "Just keep working on refining this thing, will you? In the meantime, I'll take what you have."

The floor moved up and slanted at the same time, so I found myself lying down. I should've been used to it by this time, but I still didn't like this feeling of weightlessness I had when I lay down on their repair table.

"No restraints this time, you hear me?"

"I do," Leinad told me, as strips of white matter strapped me to the table. "However, this procedure is delicate. It is important that you do not move. I will keep you conscious, however, so you may ask questions of the procedure."

Before I could start swearing at him, Trebor's face jutted out of the low ceiling.

"What is this matter of urgency for which you need the use of your telecarb, Jack Meter?"

The table began moving forward, Leinad beside it, his body like a wave with me riding on its crest. When we reached the wall, we simply melted into it, Trebor's face still following overhead.

Beyond was another room, halfway between a lab and an operating room. Claire had told me the Thrittene were well equipped technologically, but what she hadn't said was that all the trappings were also made of Thrittene material. There were long and short rods, disks of various shapes, a form that started out as a cube and ended up with too many sides to count. I gained new respect for Claire's brain. She'd worked with those devices, or some other similar weird stuff, to make the conjugator that vaporized Annie's clone.

I decided I really didn't want to know what Leinad was doing. To distract myself, I thought I'd do a bit of probing.

"Have you ever heard of the IGA?" I said to Trebor.

He beamed. "Has the agency recruited you? Congratulations. You will be a fine addition."

"They haven't. I'm involved in a case with one of their agents. Hey, Leinad, do you know what a USI is?

"A Universal System Integrator," he said from somewhere behind my head. "A crude but effective traveling device."

"Whatever. Here's something I bet you don't know. The telecarb can sense its trail and follow it."

Leinad's face appeared in front of my eyes.

"Without ill effects to you? Fascinating. I will have to obtain one and study its relationship with our matter."

"Which doesn't help me right now." I took his silence as agreement. "What do you know about the IGA, Trebor?"

"Not as much as any of us would like to." His cheeks became rosy, and the tone of the noise around me sounded very much like embarrassment. "Obviously, we couldn't go to them when we had our little problem."

"If you call the imminent destruction of the universe a little problem."

"Yes, but our involvement in it..." Trebor sighed. "Fortunately, you were available. We made a good choice with you, Jack Meter."

"The agency, Trebor?"

"Ah, yes. It is a multi-species investigative agency."

"They're not cops then."

"Cops?"

"Police. The agent I met said they were like international police."

"They do specialize in global threats, and on some worlds, they have jurisdiction over the local constabulary."

"I thought you guys were the only ones who had developed a device to travel around the universe."

"Up until a short time ago—time being relative, of course—that was true. IGA agents worked mainly locally, unless their off-world investigation occurred close to home, like a neighboring planet. They have a sophisticated communications network. The IGA formed a consortium to devise a means of intergalactic travel. We participated, of course, gave them the benefit of our expertise."

"Looks like they came up with a gizmo that works." I glared at Leinad. "And they don't have to donate a chunk of their bodies to use it."

"I am certain their device has limitations you have not identified yet," Leinad said, unfazed.

"Do you have any agents with the IGA?"

Trebor shook his head. "We are one."

I kept forgetting there was no separation between the Thrittene world and the Thrittene themselves. They'd parted with a few pieces of themselves, like my telecarb, but it was reportedly a painful process.

Now, though, someone had chopped off a chunk of them—Nasus included—and they hadn't even noticed. I thought about Neola and wondered if she'd suffered the same fate.

"Aren't you finished yet?" I said to Leinad. "I gotta go."

"Just finished now."

The restraints fell away. I sat up. The room melted, and we were back where we'd started.

Leinad slid in front of me.

"The restrictions still apply, Jack Meter. If you are following someone, it will bring you only to the place where that being was as long as that spot has been vacated. This is to prevent a juxtaposition of matter. However, I have been able to refine the process. Previously, there was also a proximity inhibitor, which prevented you from following the entity if that being had not left the area. I have been able to remove that constraint. Of course, the telecarb will not take you to a place where there is immediate danger to your life."

"I hoped you'd remove that."

He shook his head. "This self-preservation component is inherent to Thrittene matter."

"Anything else I should know about?"

Leinad hesitated. I knew I wasn't going to like what he was going to say.

"The problem with the use of the telecarb was that it was reconfiguring your cells into Thrittene matter every time you used it. I have enhanced this morphing process then programmed your cells to reverse it."

"Give it to me in English."

"Essentially, every time you use the telecarb, you will become Thrittene matter then change back into yourself. This means that anyone else you take with you will experience the same effect." He made a sound equivalent to a clearing of the throat. "I am not certain if the process will revert both forms to their original configuration."

"So I could end up with a piece of someone stuck to me."

"Essentially, yes."

"How do I know this is what's going to happen?"

Leinad turned a pukey shade of green. "You must try it."

"Great."

"I don't have all the answers, Jack Meter. If I'd had more time..."

"You're sounding like a scratched CD, Leinad." He looked so miserable, I relented. "Listen, bud, I appreciate you doing this, really. All I want, though, is for you to find a way to remove the telecarb. I don't have a problem living the rest of my life on Earth, following adulterers and finding lost pooches."

"You would abandon the friends you made throughout the universe?" Trebor said, a hint of censure in his voice.

"In a blink."

Sounds around me became mournful. White became gray. I could feel their regret under my skin.

I thought about the weeks I'd spent recharging before Garner had dropped his problem in my lap. I'd already admitted to myself I was bored. Now I had to concede maybe I'd also missed these flaky aliens.

I raised a hand to stop the sounds. "Okay, okay, I lied. But my body's not a sandbox; you can't play in it anymore. Understand?"

They both nodded.

"Good. Gotta go."

I tried to wish myself where Neola had gone. No dice. Okay, so I'd go back to the office, get a few things then head back to her house. Maybe I'd find a clue to where she'd gone—if she wasn't dead already. Going back to the office would also tell me how long I'd been on Thrittene. Time didn't work the same way here.

I wished myself in my office. The telecarb tingled around my wrist, but I stayed exactly where I was. I turned toward Leinad.

"Don't tell me I'm stuck here."

"I don't understand; it should be working." He cocked his head to the side. "Could there be danger where you want to go?"

I started to brush him off then stopped. Could there be someone intent on doing me harm in my office?

"Maybe," I said, more to myself than to answer Leinad.

I wished myself at the bottom of the stairs in front of Winston's office. My vision wavered. Time seemed to slow down, and I heard the millions of Thrittene voices calling to me. Then I felt as if my body split in two before it slammed together again.

I was facing Winston's door. Every cell in my body vibrated, making me tremble faster than I could perceive it, as if my atoms were going nuts. Less than ten seconds later, the sensation was gone. I took a deep breath, shook myself like a wet dog then patted myself all over. Everything seemed in order. The process wasn't altogether pleasant, but it was bearable.

I looked up and slowly climbed the stairs to my office. My telecarb stayed quiet, even when I placed my hand on the doorknob.

Since the last time I'd left wasn't through the door, it should be unlocked. I turned the knob and pushed. The office was empty. A fine coat of dust had settled everywhere, telling me I'd been away for a while. It also told me someone had been in, and that someone, according to the prints on the floor, wasn't human and was big.

I stepped inside, walked around, making sure no one was there. The bathroom was empty. As I passed in front of the couch, I felt the same chill I'd felt from Neola's device. Bigfoot had left here using a USI.

Curious about why my telecarb hadn't wanted to transport me here while my intruder roamed my office, I decided to follow him, if I could. Maybe he could give me a clue to Neola's whereabouts.

My coat was still on the hook where I'd left it. I picked it up, put it on and stepped through the chill, wishing me wherever the trail went.

I landed in a war zone.

Chapter Six

At least, it looked like a war zone from where I stood, on a high promontory overlooking a valley. A river, its water gray under a sky of roiling clouds, slashed across the flatland; and on either side hordes screamed and advanced toward each other, brandishing swords and lances. I squinted, trying to figure out who—or what—they were.

On the side of the river closer to me, the soldiers were as large as they were short, each a box-like form on legs, wrapped with some kind of shiny metal. They didn't appear to have heads, until I saw a few of them stick out a round, shiny bulb on a tube-like neck then retract it; like a turtle, they could sink their heads inside their bodies.

The soldiers on the other side of the river reminded me of Komodo dragons—low to the ground, ten feet long, scaly, with two clawed legs and three arms set perpendicular to the body. They arrived at the river first, slipped into it and quickly swam to the other bank. At the first clash, the lizards rose on their hind feet and, using their tail as a stabilizer, began to hack at the metal turtles.

The noise was indescribable. It rose in waves up to my vantage point—bellows and shrieks, chants and howls. Soon, the ground ran with green and silver blood, and the river changed from gray to brown. After a few minutes of slaughter, the Komodos stopped fighting, slipped back through the water to the other side and waited. The turtles didn't follow. I surmised they weren't able to swim.

Farther down, where the river narrowed, I noticed the turtles had started building a bridge. I wondered how they'd succeed in throwing it over the water.

On the other side of the flatland, a mountain range capped with snow scraped the clouds. Halfway up, something blue seemed to flutter in the wind. An ant line of soldiers moved up and down it.

I felt a movement behind my back. I whipped around to come face-to-face with three metal turtles holding very sharp lances. Their heads were out, so I figured I wasn't in immediate danger of being run through. I hoped.

Behind them was a round, candy-cane-striped tent with a long, triangular red banner floating in the wind above it. The turtles stepped aside, and one of them gestured with its lance toward the tent. I raised both hands in a pacific gesture and made my way across rocky terrain to the entrance. One of my guards prodded me in the back, and I went in.

The material of the tent, although opaque from the outside, was transparent from the inside. It afforded a perfect view of the valley below from, maybe, half a kilometer from the fray. A third of the way down, several red tents seemed to house more turtles.

A dozen of them worked frantically at a circular table in the center of the tent, on which several maps were scattered. The buzzing sound of whispering voices made a strange counterpoint to the cries of battle from down below.

A movement to my left caught my attention then held it.

Blood-red hair hung loose down a ramrod-straight back. A long white robe trimmed with red covered curvy hips and stopped just above trim ankles. She turned around to gaze at me.

Glittering red stones formed a crown and passed through a fleshy hump in her forehead. Delicate pink scales instead of eyebrows enhanced her red, slanted eyes. Thin lips and high cheekbones surrounded a sword-sharp nose. Her generous bosom matched the hips, although I had no yen to go peek at what was under the robe.

Her hands and feet were enclosed in red pouches. She was far from pretty, but her stance was regal and her eyes, for one moment, distressed. I bowed. I couldn't help it.

"Who is one, and what does one do here?" my telecarb translated for me.

"My name is Jack Meter. I was following someone who might want to do me harm."

"One usually puts oneself in dangerous situations?"

"Not really. It's just that I get into these situations, see. In this case, he might lead me to a friend who disappeared. She's in danger as well."

"How did one arrive here? Our attendants tell us one has appeared suddenly."

I didn't think it was a good idea to mention the telecarb.

"The being I'm following has a device that can transport him over great distances. I just followed."

"Where does one come from?"

"Earth."

"We do not know one's country." She paused. "But we have heard of another like one who was captured. Maybe one's friend. Was another female?"

"Yes."

"We have heard the female one is highly clever. Is one?"

I shrugged. "I seem to manage."

She stared at me, the pupils of her red eyes narrowing to vertical slits. After a moment, she nodded.

"We are Saurimo. As one can see, we are engaged in a war. One will provide ideas for a winning strategy."

"Hey, I'm Switzerland here." When she frowned, I added, "I'm neutral. All I want is to find my friend."

Saurimo pointed to the mountains across the valley.

"One's friend is held deep inside the mountain, well-guarded. One's likelihood of effecting rescue is remote, unless our battle is won."

I wished myself near Neola. My telecarb tingled and refused to budge, so it was still dangerous. Whether Neola was still alive was another question.

Following my intruder might've been a tactical mistake. I wondered where he'd disappeared to. I raised my hand to stop Saurimo from continuing.

"Let me verify something first. It may be important to your security."

She considered then inclined her head in assent. I'd noticed that, once I'd followed Neola, the energy trace the telecarb detected was gone, as if it had used up the residuals. I went back outside and, starting from the spot where I'd landed, walked back and forth from the edges of the rock, until I got to the tent. I repeated the process for the sides then the back. I couldn't feel a chill anywhere.

I went back inside the tent and motioned to Saurimo.

"You may have a spy in your ranks," I whispered. "Whoever I was following hasn't left."

"Would whoever have appeared the same way one did?"

"Pretty much, yes."

"Then whoever has not arrived. Our attendants did not advise us."

"It may be someone you already know, someone who had a good reason to be here, so your attendants wouldn't have questioned it."

Saurimo cocked her head; her eyes narrowed to slits and her hair changed to the white-red of fire. She then returned to her normal state. She remained silent and regal until the three metal turtles who had shepherded me into the tent entered, flanking a male of the same species as Saurimo.

His hair was short and he wore a tunic instead of a robe, and only a thin thread of metal passed through his metopic hump. When he saw me, the scales around his eyes darkened slightly.

I stepped closer to him. My telecarb warmed up around my wrist.

"We are told that Karoi was seen outside the tent a notahc ago," Saurimo said.

"Karoi wished to survey the troops," he said. I surmised he was talking about himself.

"When we had requested that Karoi oversee the dispatches at the foot of the valley?"

"Maybe Karoi was going to do a little dispatching of his own," I said. "When did Saurimo decide on the placement of her troops?" Now I was starting to speak like them.

Saurimo paused. "A notahc-and-a-half ago. The troops completed their maneuvers in one half-notahc."

I had absolutely no idea what that meant. Obviously, my translator had reached its limits.

"Karoi only wanted to ascertain the accuracy of the dispatches," he said.

"*We* determine the content of the dispatches." She tilted her head to the side. By that time, I'd figured out that when she did that she was listening to someone speaking to her. "We are told Karoi sent a dispatch across the valley when we had not requested that one be sent."

Karoi's hair and scales turned white.

"Saurimo will lose this war. Karoi is only a minor pawn in the game. Asela will prevail."

Saurimo's hair and scales were now also white, but they shone as if lighted from underneath. The red stones on her forehead gleamed until they became a solid band of scarlet. The metal band in Karoi's forehead turned black.

"Karoi has disappointed Saurimo," she said.

He grunted once then slumped on the floor.

Saurimo turned around. "Come, we must contain the damage. One will continue to help."

The turtles lifted Karoi, who appeared to be dead.

"Just one second," I said. I patted him down until I found a pouch sewn on the inside of his tunic. Inside were three stone discs the size of a mini-CD carved with what looked like runes, and a pin exactly like Neola's. I quickly pocketed the latter and brought the discs to Saurimo.

"I found those on Karoi. Maybe they'll help."

She stared at the disks, her hands moving behind her back, her scales and hair deepening to the color of blood.

"Do not move," she said.

"They're not dangerous," I said. "I'd know if they were."

"To one, they may not be," she whispered, "but to us...Karoi was more than a spy. Karoi sought to destroy us."

I glanced down at the innocuous-looking discs. "What are they?"

"Curses. If they had been thrown at us, they would have wrought havoc, although we do not know which kind."

"In my world, curses are words of magic, and they don't work very well." When she looked at me with disbelief, I shrugged. "What do you want me to do with these?"

"One could destroy them."

"Who is this Asela Karoi mentioned?"

Saurimo's stance straightened. "Ah. We knew as soon as we saw one that one would be useful to us. One will be our arm and weapon. One will throw Asela the curses."

Me and my big mouth. "Wait a minute, here. Because I mention the name of your enemy doesn't mean I volunteered for the mission. Surely, you have someone you trust who can do the job."

Saurimo's color faded to a pale pink. She was getting pissed.

"What did one put in one's pocket? We wager it is the traveling device one said Karoi used to return here. We could take it from one, but in exchange for allowing one to keep it, we will require one to perform this mission."

I didn't want to play tough, but I had no choice.

"It seems you have no bargaining power, here, Saurimo. I have the throwing arm and the weapon."

"If we must perish, we will not perish alone."

She glanced over my shoulder. When I turned my head, I saw three of the turtles pointing their lances at my back.

They didn't know my telecarb wouldn't allow me to die, of course, but they could be fast enough to shish-kebab me a couple of times. A poke from those lances would definitely hurt. Besides, I was curious about this Asela. I wasn't prepared to kill for Saurimo, but moving to the other side would get me closer to Neola.

I pocketed the curses. "Okay, I'll try to get close to this Asela. What are you two fighting about, anyway?"

"We have been grievously insulted," Saurimo said. "Asela insisted that our chroma offended the eye."

She was sending soldiers to be killed because the other guy didn't like her colors? I felt it prudent not to tell her she was nuts, just in case she took offence to that, too.

"I can see how that would be cause for war," I said.

"Well, Jack Meter?"

It was the first time she'd called me by my name. I thought of Karoi, and wasn't sure it was progress. I pocketed the disks.

"I can't promise anything, Saurimo, but I'll see what I can do."

She inclined her head. "Our attendants say that Asela is alone. Now is the time to go."

I bowed again—the situation seemed to call for it.

I wished myself in front of Asela. I felt the same disconnection and slamming of my molecules as previously; then I was standing in the middle of a blue-and-white-checkered tent, facing Saurimo's exact twin, except for her indigo color.

Her eyes widened, and two Komodos entered the tent. My telecarb tingled. I rushed closer to Asela, dug out the curses from my pocket and shoved them under her nose.

"I'd stop them right now, if I were you," I said.

The Komodos rose on their tails but didn't advance further.

"Where did one obtain these?" Asela asked.

"From Karoi. Unfortunately, he failed his mission."

"Ah. So our sister lives still."

These two were sisters. It figured. "Kicking and breathing. She sent me to throw these in your face."

"Why has one not done so?"

"I have no interest in your petty feud. I came to fetch my friend."

"One's friend would be Neola Durwin?"

"That's it, sister."

"That one has departed this life." She said it while her color changed to a pale blue. I didn't trust that answer.

"That's too bad then. Catch!" I made the motion to throw the disks but kept them in my hand.

Asela's color turned almost black. At least the sisters reacted the same way to fear.

"That was a warning, Asela. Next time, I will throw you the curses. Saurimo will have won."

She cocked her head in the same way as Saurimo. I heard the Komodos slither out then there was silence. I didn't break it, just waited, prepared to leave at the slightest sign of a threat.

I heard footsteps behind me.

"About time you made it here, Jack," Neola croaked.

I turned sideways so I could see both of them. Grime streaked Neola's yellow T-shirt, her left eye had a shiner that had turned purple-and-yellow and her lip was cut and bleeding.

"You've looked better," I said.

"Felt better, too."

I extended my hand. She took it. I could feel it tremble.

"Come on, let's get out of here."

"One moment," Asela said. "What of the curses?"

I made a face as if thinking about it.

"You know, I think I'll keep them. You two can find other ways to try to kill each other."

* * *

Neola crumpled on my sofa, leaned her head against the back, eyes closed.

"Where were they holding you?"

"In the caves. I had ten of those dragons guarding me at all times."

"That explains why I couldn't get to you."

"Mmmh?"

I could see she was going to zonk out soon.

"Hey, how about a bath," I said. "I think I have something for that lip, too."

"Bath? As in hot water up to the neck in a bathtub?"

"Yep." I motioned to the door of the bathroom. "Fully appointed."

"I wasn't going to move, but for a bath, I'd crawl."

She pushed herself up, hobbled inside and closed the door. I heard water run for a while then stop. A heartfelt groan made me smile.

"Don't fall asleep in the tub," I called. "I'd hate to have to fish you out."

She didn't answer but I heard splashing. It made me imagine a bubble-covered naked body, so I tried to tune out the sounds by busying myself with email.

Terry had sent me a couple of messages asking me where the hell I was then demanding that I call him as soon as I got in. There were two calls from Garner, asking me about progress. From the date on my computer, I'd been gone over a week, although for me it had seemed only a day.

I heard a noise and saw Neola in the doorway, wearing my robe. She'd washed her hair, too, and combed it back. It was still wet and shone under the light. She looked refreshed, making her black eye appear worse.

"I feel much better," she said with a smile. "Thanks."

She jumped at the knock on the door.

"Probably delivery," I said. "I called for pizza from this twenty-four-hour delivery place I know. It's pretty good, too."

She groaned. "Now that's three times you've saved my life."

She grabbed the box while I paid the pizza guy and was already eating before I closed the door.

"That's good. I needed that."

She wiped tomato sauce from the corner of her mouth with a finger. I watched as she licked it. My throat was suddenly too tight for swallowing.

She continued talking, unaware of my reaction. "We have a bigger problem than I thought."

That put me back on track. "Okay, I'll bite. What is it?"

"That place where we were? It's not in the known universe."

Chapter Seven

I DIGESTED THAT ALONG WITH MY PIZZA. "WHERE WERE WE, THEN?"
She shrugged then snatched the last piece from the cardboard box. "I have no idea."

"There have to be hundreds of galaxies in the universe. How could you tell?"

"I recognized the species. The lizard-like beings come from a planet called Kilosa. They have sentience, but they've barely come out of our equivalent of the Dark Ages. Neither have the Ank'lumtes—those are the armored 'turtles.' The Orapans—Asela and her sister—are more sophisticated, but their society is mainly agrarian and has no interest in space travel or colonization of other planets. The combination of all three on one world is an impossibility."

"You think that these beings were snatched from their own planets."

"It would make sense. When the alarm triggered, I followed, landed on Asela's side of the river and was captured."

I glanced at her bruises. "I was luckier than you. Saurimo decided to use me instead of beating the shit out of me."

"You'd think I'd be the one with the more trustworthy looks."

"It must be the beard that did it."

"The beard definitely has appeal," she said with a smile.

She leaned back against the armrest of the couch and extended her legs in front of her. The robe parted and revealed the creamy skin of her thighs. I cleared my throat, got up to throw the pizza box into the trash. When I turned back to her, she had covered herself. I ignored the amused look she sent me when I sat behind my desk.

"I can confirm at least one other disappearance," I said, concentrating on the topic at hand.

I told her about my stint on Thrittene and Nasus's disappearance, skimming over the fact that it felt like I was now half Thrittene.

"What bothers me the most is that nobody remembers those who disappear. No one filed a missing person report here; the Thrittene don't remember Nasus. Extracting Thrittene matter is very painful for them, they go into shock."

"Somebody wiped their memories."

"Do you realize what that leads to? Every race is different. The Thrittene are bright enough, but I'm not even sure they have a brain. What kind of equipment would you need to do that?"

Neola shrugged. Her robe parted slightly, showing me the curve of one breast. I forced myself not to wiggle in my chair.

"I stopped being surprised long ago," she said, oblivious to my discomfort. "As far as I'm concerned, if they can cut out chunks of universe, messing with your brain should be easy."

"I suppose. But there are other difficulties, too, like breathable atmosphere. They don't all breathe the same kind of air, do they?"

"I would imagine not. What about that Thrittene, Nasus?"

"They can't exist anywhere but on their own planet. I have to assume she didn't survive."

"You could use your telecarb to find out if she's reachable."

"The thought crossed my mind. Before I do that, though, I want a bit more to sink my teeth into. I don't want to land in something I can't control."

"You mean that we can't control."

"Right. One more reason not to rush things, since I'd have to drag you along."

"My main concern is to find who's responsible for this and stop him. Or her."

"There's one way we can do that."

She nodded. "If we find out why, we might find out who."

"Bingo."

Neola yawned. "God, I'm bushed. You wouldn't happen to have a cot or something I can crash on?"

"You're sitting on it."

"Oh. I meant at your apartment. Don't you have an extra bed?"

"My apartment's melted steel. I've been using the office."

She gave me an exaggerated blink.

"You're kidding. That's pathetic. How long has it been? Three weeks, a month since you tied up the Mueller case?"

"I was going to start looking." Even to my ears, I sounded belligerent.

"When?"

"Soon."

Silence settled. I went to the bathroom to wash the pizza grease off my hands. When I came back, Neola was sleeping, her head leaning against the armrest, one of her hands loose and pointing toward the floor. She was so small she should've looked like a kid sleeping like that, but her mouth was too full and her body way too tempting. She was also tough, intelligent, articulate. Despite her aggressive streak, I found I liked her. A lot.

Something like panic constricted my throat. I had to get out of there. I put on my jacket, shoved my hands into the pockets. In one of them was the device I'd taken from Karoi. I set it on the table in front of the couch then moved to the door. As I reached for the doorknob, I stopped.

"Damn," I muttered. I moved to the closet, pulled out the afghan I used as a blanket and covered Neola with it. She moaned, shifted, but didn't wake up. I tiptoed out and down the stairs.

Outside, the sky had turned a vivid, cloudless blue and the temperature had plummeted. There was a bit of dirty snow huddling against the wall of the house, but the sidewalks and roads were clear. I checked the time again and noticed my watch had stopped working. My computer had told me, though, that it was early afternoon. As to the date, I'd been gone for a week, Earth-time. Losing days like that always gave me a sense of dislocation, as if I'd slowed down while everyone else speeded up.

I breathed in the brisk air and instantly felt better. I'd go to the Market, I decided, grab a paper and a coffee, call Terry. Maybe I'd even start looking for an apartment.

Hopefully, when I came back to the office, Neola would be gone.

* * *

The sun was bright, but the weather was colder than when I'd left. I hailed a passing cab and directed the driver to the ByWard Market. The crackling of his mobile over the rock music from the radio made it impossible to chat, and that was fine with me. I parked my brain in neutral until I arrived at the café.

Once seated with a latte in front of me, I dug out my cell phone and called Terry at the office.

"Jesus Murphy," he said when I identified myself, "where the frig have you been? I've been trying to get ahold of you for almost a week."

"Here and there. As far as I'm concerned, though, I've been gone only a day, so lay off, will you?"

"Still on that loony case?"

"Yeah. Did you check those databanks?"

"Didn't find squat."

"It was a long shot."

"I did come across one weird thing while I was searching. A new cult cropped up a few weeks ago. It's catching recruits like a dog gets fleas. Three sub-sects have been set up so far; one of them's here. We're going to keep an eye on them."

"Goes to show you there's weird everywhere."

Terry grunted. "Hey, why don't you come to dinner tonight? Betty's making shepherd's pie. We could watch the game afterwards."

I shuddered at the idea of eating Betty's mixture of ground beef, creamed corn and lumpy mashed potatoes. I loved the woman, but she could not cook.

"Thanks, Terry, but I've got a few things I need to do. I'll take a rain check."

"That's your story and you're sticking to it, right?"

I laughed. "No, really. I've started looking for an apartment." Not quite true, but it would do if it saved me from Betty's shepherd's pie.

"About time. You know you can crash at our house until you find something."

"You live in the boonies, Terry. Besides, you'll want to keep an eye on me."

"You need a keeper."

"Bye, Terry," I said and ended the call. I knew he was referring to the fact that it had been two years since Annie, and I didn't want to go there. Two years wasn't such a long time.

The image of Neola sleeping on the couch made me blink. I couldn't deny she was the first woman since Annie who'd provoked a few twinges of lust. I wasn't sure how I felt about it, decided to ignore the problem.

I forgot all about my conversation with Terry as I checked the ads for an apartment. The pickings were more than slim, taking into account I wanted to stay downtown and I didn't want a condo. I made appointments for that same afternoon to visit two of them, which were walking distance from the Moulin de Provence.

The first one was a five-story apartment building near the corner of Dalhousie and Guigues. From the outside, it looked rundown, some of the metal, painted white, showing rust streaks. The security door was broken, and there was a stale smell of spices and oil in the air, mixed with wet dog and the rancid tinge of urine.

I knocked on the super's door. The woman who opened the door was still in her nightgown and robe, a lit cigarette dangling from her mouth making her squint. She looked me up and down.

"You the guy that called about the apartment?"

"Yes, but—"

"Too late, it's already rented." She made to shut the door.

I'd already decided I didn't want the apartment, but I didn't like her attitude. I planted my hand on the door to prevent it from closing.

"I called half an hour ago."

"You shoulda showed up instead of calling." She pulled on her cigarette and blew smoke in my face. "He ain't gonna be around long so come back if you don't find nothin'."

"I thought the lease was for a year."

"It is, but it's one of them new-agers who rented, you know." She cackled. "They're all going to disappear into thin air, and soon, is what he says."

That pricked my interest. This sounded too much like my case for me to ignore it.

"Where are they going to go?"

"How should I know? I ain't paid to listen; I'm paid to get leases signed. Now, go away."

I let her door slam in my face. It might be a good idea to visit this particular cultist, I decided.

I knew the apartment number from my phone call. The elevator was out-of-order so I took the stairs to the fourth floor. The carpet was frayed in the center, showing cracked linoleum; one out of two lights was off or broken. I wondered if Garner owned the building then decided not. As Winston had said, Garner had a thing for buildings. He wouldn't let one go like this.

I knocked on number four-sixteen. After a moment, I heard rustling from the other side of the door, the slide of a chain. The door opened a crack to show one brown eye.

"Yes?"

The voice was young, and male.

"Hi," I said, trying to sound cheerful. "The super downstairs told me you'd just rented this apartment. I'd called her to visit it, but you beat me to it."

"She said it's first-come, first-served."

"Sure, and I'm not here to convince you to give up the apartment to me. No, she mentioned you were a New Ager. I'd like to talk to you about that."

"Why?"

I took out a plasticized card from my wallet—Jack Meter, United Press. "I'm doing research for an in-depth article on New Age cults and I'd like to get the perspective from the ranks."

"I'm not interested."

"Come on. I won't mention your name if that's what you want. I respect my sources. Every good journalist does."

The eye turned vague for a moment then the door opened wide. I hid a grin of satisfaction. Few people could resist giving their opinion.

The eye belonged to a young man, maybe twenty years old. He was short, with doll's hands and feet. Dark, curly hair, cut short, revealed tiny ears. He wore a long tie-dye caftan.

"I don't have my furniture yet," he said, walking into the living room, "but I have a couple of cushions."

"That's fine." I planted my butt on a skimpy cushion. The large window, definitely the best feature in the place, put in relief the gouges in the parquetry floor and the unidentifiable stains on the walls. It must've been an elegant place when it was first built. I wondered if the landlord was into that thin-air theory and waiting for the building to disappear, saving him the costs of renovation.

"It's hard to find an apartment these days," I said.

"Yes. I won't be here for long, though, so you should keep an eye on it and grab it when I go."

"Where are you going?"

His face turned dreamy. "We will be brought to a place where the land is as pure as the air and we will start a new life there, unburdened from the worries and pains of our past."

He had raised his arms as he spoke, revealing several scars, some white and faded, some puckered and red. It looked like this young man had seen his share of pain, and I was prepared to bet it had been at the hands of a close relative. No wonder he wanted to escape.

"Who will take you there?"

"Ginir." His voice was reverential.

"Is he the one in charge of your cult?"

"Ginir is the true savior. Ginir has the power to move mountains, to dry up lakes, to uproot trees."

"Have you seen his power yourself?"

He shook his head. "I am only a novice. Even the initiates don't know how we are to be transported."

"Who's your leader here in Ottawa? Where do you usually meet?"

"Our High Sage is Abura. He is the only one who has direct contact with Ginir." He shoved his hands into his sleeves, Mandarin-style. "Only those who pass the initiation rites are allowed to know where Abura holds the nightly meetings."

"Where do I find this Abura?"

He shrugged and got up. "Abura finds you. I have to meditate now."

I followed him to the door.

"Don't bother showing me out," I said, "I know the way." I doubt the kid heard the sarcasm.

*   *   *

Because of the impromptu interview, I was too late to visit the second apartment. I walked past it and decided it wasn't what I wanted anyway—the ad hadn't mentioned the rental was in a house. I wanted the anonymity of a big building.

Night was falling fast, so there was nothing else to do but return to the office. I crept open the door and stuck my head inside, peeking left and right—empty. I went in with a sigh of relief. Neola was gone, the blanket carefully folded on the couch. I frowned when I noticed the USI still on the table. How had she left, then?

I heard a slight noise behind me.

"Oh, it's you," Neola said. "I wasn't sure who was coming in so I thought I'd make myself scarce."

"I thought you'd gone." She was wearing the yellow T-shirt and jeans again.

Her eyes narrowed. "Don't sound so broken up about it. I told you my device was destroyed."

"You couldn't reconfigure the one I left you?"

"Each device is coded for the bearer, in case they're stolen. It's useless to me. I'll have to go home and contact the IGA for a new one. I'll need your help, either to take me there or to lend me enough money to buy clothes and a plane ticket." She sat down and wiggled her toes. "Not exactly winter attire."

"I'll take you."

"Good. Might as well use my place as our HQ. We'd be cramped here."

"I'm coming back here."

"To what? Look around, pal, this ain't a model of comfort. You don't even have extra clothes."

"I do. They're at the cleaners." Even I could hear the note of defensiveness in my voice. I didn't like the tone of this conversation. Whichever way I went, I'd either lose the argument or sound like an ass.

Then I remembered Ginir.

"I found something interesting while you were snoozing the afternoon away."

I told her about the cults cropping up and my conversation with the novice, whose name I'd totally forgotten to ask.

"You're thinking we should follow him and have a chat with this Abura."

"He said they meet every night. I figure we got a couple of hours yet. I doubt they'd get together before six."

I took her hand and willed us to her house in Colorado. I felt my cells rearrange themselves then heard a muffled "whoa" from Neola. When the world righted itself, she was staring at me, eyes wide.

"What?"

"What did the Thrittene do to you?"

"They tinkered, as usual. Why?"

"For a moment, my hand melted into yours."

"Didn't feel a thing."

"Maybe you should go back there."

"Nah. This is par for the course." I grinned. "Don't worry, babe, if

you turn into Thrittene matter, I'll take you to them. You'll see—it's a nice, quiet place."

"Yeah, right. I'll go change. Oh, and Jack? 'Babe' isn't any better than 'sweetheart.' I'd watch your…." She glanced below my belt. "…language, if I were you."

CHAPTER EIGHT

"I CAN'T BELIEVE YOU DON'T OWN A CAR," NEOLA GROUSED.

"You look warm enough," I said.

"I'd be warmer sitting in front of a heater. I can't feel my toes anymore."

"Jump up and down a bit." I raised my collar against the wind. There was a definite smell of snow in the air.

Neola pushed away from a parked car and looked up at the lighted window on the fourth floor.

"We've been here for four hours. What can he be doing in there? You said the apartment was empty."

"He meditates."

"There's only so much meditation a body can—" She stopped. "He turned the light off. Maybe he's going to bed."

"We'll see."

As if we'd practiced the move, we backed up deeper into the shadows and waited in silence, side-by-side. A short figure stepped outside.

"Here we go," I murmured.

Our novice had switched from caftan to street clothes, although his windbreaker would be poor protection against the cold. He carried a knapsack over one shoulder. He quick-marched down Guigues away from the Market, then down Cumberland. Past a convenience store, he slipped into the alley between it and the next building. I motioned Neola behind me and followed him. We ended up in a poorly lit fenced courtyard, empty except for a couple of garbage bins. The kid had disappeared.

"Where did he go?" Neola whispered.

The wooden fence around the yard was more than two meters high—too high to jump, even for a kid. The back of the store had a door with a shiny new padlock, closed tight.

Neola peeked behind the garbage cans.

"Jack." She pointed at a hole in the fence, large enough for a man to slip through it. "Damn," she said. "He could be anywhere by now."

"He wasn't going far. Let's see what's on the other side."

I pushed through the fence, the hole a bit tight for me, Neola close behind me. Another fenced yard, this one belonging to a two-story house with carved trim around the eaves. Glass in several windows gleamed faintly—either no one was home or the windows had been blacked out. There was a door at ground level.

I prowled the perimeter, confirming that it was a completely enclosed courtyard and that the gate was locked from the outside.

"Unless our cultist locked us in," I said, "he went in there. We could always knock."

Neola grabbed my arm, suddenly tense.

"I heard it," I whispered.

Someone was coming into the yard. We melted into the shadows once again.

A dark shape passed us, stopped in front of the door. Three short knocks, two long. There was the sound of a door being unlocked.

"Back up," I whispered to Neola.

A beam of light spilled into the courtyard long enough for a murmured exchange of words and the newcomer's admittance.

"Did you get that?" At the shake of my head, she turned back to the door. "Me neither. We need that password."

"Or we could say we forgot it."

She pondered that for a moment.

"Too risky. If we spook them now, they may change meeting places. We may never know what they're all about."

"We could try to find out who this house belongs to first. Then we go interview the owner, check out what he knows."

"Let's come back when it's light, see who lives here." She went to the door of the courtyard. "Boost me up, will you? I'll check the address then meet you back on Guigues."

I could've grabbed her waist and pushed her up, but I didn't want to get my hands that close to her body. Instead, I joined my hands into a cradle, leaned my back against the fence door. She backed up a couple of steps, took a run up and vaulted over.

I didn't have time to straighten before another cultist arrived. He saw me right away.

"Hey, what are you doing there?"

"Change of plans," I muttered and wished myself inside the house. My telecarb tingled. I stayed where I was. "Damn thing never works when I want it to." I pushed away from the fence. "I came to see Abura," I said to the guy in front of me. What the hell, might as well stay in character. "I'm a journalist."

"Abura doesn't speak to reporters."

"Why don't you let him decide himself?"

"Only the Chosen are allowed inside during the ritual."

"I'll wait here." I could sense him hesitate. "Look, why don't you go ask him. If he says no, I'll leave."

"I suppose I could do that, but I'll stay here with you until we hear Abura's response."

"Fair enough."

He knocked with the appropriate code. The opening of the door revealed another young face. The gatekeeper listened for a moment, glanced at me, nodded then closed the door again. We waited in silence until it reopened and the murmuring started again.

The young man turned to me. "Abura declines to see you."

"Are those his exact words?"

"Yes. He wishes you Light and Peace in the next life."

"Yeah, same to him," I muttered before I slipped back through the hole in the fence.

* * *

"What took you so long?"

"Just a snag. Nothing major. You got the address?"

"As much as I could figure out—none of the buildings on that side have numbers. I got the one across the street, though, so we'll be able to pinpoint it fairly easily."

"Hmmm. I'll check it out tomorrow at city hall."

"Not tomorrow you won't. It's Saturday."

"Damn. That means two days' delay. How do you keep them straight?"

"Keep what straight?"

"The days."

"Practice. Plus a really good watch." Neola smiled then yawned. "I say we call it a night. How about taking me to my house?"

I thought of her asleep on my couch, and decided it was a good idea. I grabbed her arm and wished us to Colorado. The snapping sensation of my cells realigning felt more like a slingshot this time.

"You can let go of me, now," Neola said, her voice sober.

I looked at her, and for the first time, I saw something like fear in the back of her eyes.

I plucked my hand from her arm with difficulty—it seemed as if it had been Velcroed to her. She moved away, shedding her coat and gloves, her back turned to me.

"Leinad said that might happen," I said, more for conversation than for explanation.

"Leinad?"

"The Thrittene scientist who supposedly tuned my telecarb."

"Ah. I think it would be best if I got another USI."

"Don't you have an extra one for situations like this?"

"This is the second one I've lost. My boss won't be pleased."

"All in the line of duty, etcetera. How do you contact the IGA?"

She hesitated. "I have an emergency beacon. The problem is, it'll take several days, maybe a couple of weeks, before they respond."

"Not very efficient."

"It's a big universe."

"And you don't want to spend all that time melding into me."

"No offence, but I never planned to be a Siamese twin."

I grinned. "What's the other solution?"

"The way station. I have better communication equipment there."

"You want to risk another transport?"

"Do I really have a choice?"

"I could continue to investigate while you wait for a response from the IGA."

"No way." She took a deep breath. "Let's do it."

"I could go to the station alone. If you show me how to operate it, I could get another USI for you, explain the situation."

"Thanks, but I need to report in anyway. I have to let them know what we've learned so far."

"Which is damned little."

"Still, it's more than I had before."

She took off the heavy sweater she'd been wearing under her coat. This time, her T-shirt was red. I swallowed.

"Better take a few layers off," she said, still oblivious to the effect her peeling had on me. "You know how hot that purple sand planet is." She took off her boots.

Outside, a snowstorm battered the windows. I took off my gloves and leather jacket, dumped them on the couch. I followed suit with the heavy turtleneck, pleased I'd had the foresight to wear a muscle shirt underneath.

When I turned around, Neola was watching me, a slight smile on her face. Her eyes shifted to my wrist.

I'd always kept my telecarb covered before, even with Terry and Claire. With Neola, I hadn't even thought about it. I cleared my throat.

"Ready?"

She grimaced. "As I'll ever be."

I took her hand, and a second later we were on the purple sand planet. Neither of us mentioned the fact that it was even more difficult than before to separate from each other. For a few intense moments, I concentrated, visualized my cells splitting away from hers. It worked, but both of us were shiny with sweat when it was over.

"Hot here," I said. The green sun was high in the sky. "You never told me where this planet was."

"Somewhere in the Crab Nebula, I think." As soon as she entered the structure, she went to a cabinet under the counter, took out two bottles and pouches. She handed me one of each. "Here. It's not five-star food, but it'll fill you up and replenish our energy, since we're pulling an all-nighter."

There were no chairs in the station, so I sat down on the floor and took a sip from the bottle while Neola punched up a message on her communication system. The clear liquid had a slightly viscous texture, like maple syrup, and tasted between sweet and salty. There was some kind of powder in the pouch. Neola smiled down at me. "It works better if you mix them up."

I poured the liquid into the powder, sealed the pouch and shook. When I opened it again, the powder had changed into some kind of bread, and it was piping hot. I took a bite. It tasted like mashed potatoes and steak.

"Not bad," I said between bites.

Neola sat beside me and mixed up her own pouch. "It has a restorative in it as well so you'll feel as if you've had a good night's sleep when you're finished eating."

"How long do we have to wait for an answer?"

"A few minutes. It's faster from here, for some reason. They'll send instructions and coordinates for pickup."

We ate in silence. It was cool in the station, and I could feel the heat from Neola's arm. She leaned her head against the wall, eyes closed. My fingers itched to stroke the white column of her neck. I made a fist, turned my head, shifted slightly away.

"What made you get into this business?" I said, grabbing at the first subject I could think of.

"Same reason as you."

"You got abducted by aliens?"

She shook her head. "Some space thugs killed my husband."

I felt like I'd been sucker-punched. I fought not to see Annie lying in her own blood. I pushed to my feet, got out of the station. Heat wrapped around me, making it difficult to breathe. I walked a few steps, stopped. The pain in the center of my chest was back.

Annie.

"I'm sorry," Neola said behind me. "I didn't want to bring it all back." She placed a hand on my shoulder.

How the hell could I think of someone else, even for one second? I stared at the telecarb, its swirling colors changing under the green sun. There was a reminder. I didn't need anything else. I schooled my face and moved away from Neola's touch.

"And we go on living," I said.

"We do. Let's go back inside. It's too hot out here."

I followed her, sat back down against the wall. She hoisted herself onto the counter.

"I was a farm girl," she said, her voice low. "My father grew corn—our neighbors, too. I hated it, couldn't wait to get to the big city. In college, I met Michael, fell in love with him." She laughed softly. "It must've been love, because he was studying agri-business. All he wanted, apart from me, was to take over his father's farm and make something big out of it.

"Michael got his degree, we got married, and I went back to the farm with him. I still hated it, but as that kind of life goes, it was a good one, even though we didn't have a house of our own.

"He never expected me to do chores or help him. He knew how I felt, wanted me to be happy. One night, at the end of the summer when the corn was high and ready for harvest, Michael saw a light in one of the fields. We'd been having problems with protesters who didn't like it that we grew genetically modified corn. Michael got mad, jumped in his truck. I barely had time to get in before he was driving like a madman toward that field."

"It wasn't protesters, I take it," I said.

"Four Dowans—I learned what they were later—had landed. They were ugly mothers, their faces scarred and scabby. I don't know if Michael saw them before he jumped out of the truck but I did, and for some reason I knew they weren't wearing masks. I was scared shitless, tried to warn him. One of the Dowans saw him, blasted a hole the size of a soccer ball in his chest. I dove out of the truck, rolled under it. Came face-to-face with Michael. His eyes were opened. He looked so surprised.

"One of the Dowans approached the truck. I don't know what got into me. I got really pissed off, and I grabbed both his legs and yanked. When he fell backwards, I scrambled out, grabbed his rifle and shot the other three before they could even blink. I was about to blast the fourth one when an IGA agent arrived on the scene. He talked me down, took over, cleaned up the mess. Several months later, he offered me a job."

Her eyes were sad now, but her jaw was set.

"You took it."

She shrugged. "As I said, I hated the farm."

"Yeah, all that green. I'd take purple sand over it anytime."

"I have to say," she said with a slight smile, "this place leaves a bit to be desired." She frowned, checked her watch. "I should've received a message by now." She jumped from the counter, checked the equipment. "The message left, but it's been bouncing around. We might have lost a couple of stations."

"Why don't we go see your boss?"

"He changes coordinates regularly. I would need my USI to triangulate."

I dug into my pocket for the pin. "How about Karoi's?"

"I might be able to extract the data." She took the pin, unfolded it and studied it. With a few mutters, she punched in numbers and symbols on the station's console. "Here we go."

She walked to the door as it opened. The world outside was a blanket of fog.

"Ah, is this usual?"

"How should I know?"

My telecarb began tingling then gave me a shock.

"Let's get out of here."

Neola shook her head, opened her mouth to say something.

"Move!" I yelled.

I grabbed her hand and started running. I heard a kind of whistling, like the V-2s used by the Germans. Behind us, the world shattered. The force of the explosion threw us to the ground. Debris fell around us.

I raised my head. Fog, thick and clammy, rolled over the ground.

"Are you okay?"

Neola pushed into a sitting position, tapped the side of her head with the palm of her hand.

"I might never hear again from this ear."

I got up and headed toward the way station. The fog was so thick around us that I retraced my steps, grabbed her hand.

"Don't want you to get lost."

With this kind of limited vision, we nearly fell into the crater that used to be the station.

"Somebody really wanted to prevent us from going back," I said. "A bit overdone, don't you think?"

"If they wanted to piss me off, they've succeeded."

She sniffed. At the same time, I caught a musky scent that reminded me of flattened skunk.

"I have a feeling those coordinates you entered didn't take you where you wanted to go," I said.

"That's a safe bet," a voice said through the fog.

The mist parted. On the other side of the crater, the ugliest humanoid I'd ever met stood smiling. With two holes for a nose, his face looked like it had melted, shrunk, puckered. His eyes, round and bulging, gave him an astonished air until he blinked and reminded me of an owl. A wolf-sized yellow dog hugged his side.

"I'm Mariental," he said through a mouth without lips. His one-piece jumpsuit shimmered in the fog. The beast beside him shifted. "This is Mongo. I suggest we leave this site. They will come soon to search for your body."

"Optimistic bunch," I said. "Who are 'they'?"

Mariental's grin grew broader. It was scary.

"Why, the bounty hunters who want the price on your head, Jack Meter."

CHAPTER NINE

THE SOUND OF SEVERAL PAIRS OF SCURRYING FEET, MUTED BY THE blanket OF fog, kept me from asking more questions. I couldn't tell how close they were, but they were definitely coming our way. My telecarb tingled. Whether the threat came from behind or in front, I decided I'd rather take on one tall dude and his ugly dog than a gang of trigger-happy headhunters intent on ripping my hide from the rest of my body.

I tightened my grip on Neola's hand.

"Let's go," I whispered to Mariental.

At a signal from him, Mongo took up the rear and silently herded us. When I tried to veer from the path his master took, the dog moved swiftly, teeth bared in a silent growl. After we'd both done this a few times, Neola yanked her hand out of mine.

"Stop that," she hissed.

I grinned but quit teasing the dog.

We followed blindly for a long while until Mariental stopped. I bumped into him and Neola into me. The dog sat.

I took Neola's hand again. She frowned at me. I leaned close to her ear and whispered, "I may have to get out of here in a hurry. I don't want to leave you behind."

Mariental placed his hand over his chest and muttered something. A razor-thin vertical line slit the fog in front of him. At it expanded, it became a porthole large enough for us to pass through single file. Fog rushed into the opening, making it impossible for me to see what was on the other side.

Mariental looked behind him.

"Quick," he said, before he slipped through the hole.

Mongo pushed me with his nose. I stepped in, pulling Neola after me. As soon as Mongo was through, the hole closed, showing the same devastation all around.

It looked like hell had just been snuffed out. The heat was oppressive; my lungs burned from the fumes that rose from half-consumed logs. Here and there, thin plumes of greasy smoke rose lazily from charred branches. The roiling clouds shaped themselves into tormented faces that tore on the shards of the still-standing trees, but there was no wind at ground level. Nothing lived around here, except the silence.

Mariental seemed to take his bearings then stepped over a trunk reduced to charcoal.

"Hold it right there," I said, my voice hushed. "How about explaining that crack about bounty hunters before we go any further?"

"No time," Mariental said. "They're still in pursuit."

"We couldn't see in front of our noses in this fog. They couldn't follow us if they couldn't see us slipping in here."

"Obviously, they use something else than human eyes," Neola said impatiently. She moved ahead, following Mariental, who had ignored me and started walking. "Come on, Jack."

Mongo growled behind me. Mangy as he looked, he also came to my hip, and muscles rippled when he moved. I had no intention of going a round with him, so I followed.

I thought about using the telecarb to get us out of there, but we weren't in immediate danger right now and I was curious about our destination. Besides, Mariental had used just the right hook. Bounty hunters? A price on my head? It was farfetched enough to be true, even though I hadn't, to my knowledge, anyway, committed a crime. Plus, I'd been easy to find the last few weeks.

I didn't believe anyone did anything out of the goodness of their heart. There had to be something for Mariental in helping us, and I was curious to find out what it was. Maybe he was the real bounty hunter and had effectively captured me. I wondered if Neola had thought of that angle.

Mariental stopped in front of a nearly incinerated tree that was miraculously still standing. Again he placed his hand over his chest and muttered. He then grasped the edge of the tree and pulled it aside as if it were a tapestry. I didn't like what I saw at all.

Lightning streaked the sky. Gale-force winds carried thunder and the smell of ozone on their back. The sky was so alive it felt as if I was looking up at a black ocean. On the horizon, three tornadoes circled each other. Sheets of rain flew through the opening and drenched us.

"I didn't think it would be that bad," Mariental said above the noise. He slowly began to close off the curtain. "We'll take another way."

Mongo barked once, a low woof that made us turn around. Suddenly, I heard them—whistles and grunts, with a few clacks in between, and a lot of stomping and branches snapping. I counted four heads about half a kilometer away. At the same time, the motley gang saw us. With a cry, they began hurrying in our direction.

"I knew they'd find us," Mariental said. "Come."

He stepped into chaos. Fool that I was, I followed him and dragged Neola with me.

We could barely stand the wind was so strong. I looked behind me; instead of the bounty hunters, a huge tornado was bearing down on us.

"Let's get out of here," I yelled above the wind.

Mariental pointed to a mountain a dozen kilometers away. "We must get there to exit," he yelled back.

"Look," Neola said. She pointed to a building across a tilled field. Incongruously, someone had parked an ancient Oldsmobile Delta beside it.

We ran through mud, sliding and slipping, Mongo for once leading the way. I could feel the breath of the tornado behind me. Rain splattered around us in drops the size of golfballs—good thing it wasn't hail. Then a ball of ice hit me on the shoulder.

We arrived at the car, out of breath. I pulled on the driver's side handle.

"It's locked," I yelled. Hail stung my head. "Is there anyone in the house?"

"What difference does it make?" Neola said. "Move over." She dug in the back pocket of her jeans and took out a tool that stretched into a thin wire. She inserted it between window and door and pulled the lock. She got inside the car, popped the other locks. "Get in," she yelled.

We piled into the car, Mariental in the front with Neola, me in the back with the dog. That had not been my first choice.

"Why don't I drive?" I said.

Neola peered at me in the rearview mirror.

"I unlocked it, I drive it." She hot-wired the car and put it in gear in less than thirty seconds. I shouldn't have been surprised she had talents I didn't know about.

I glanced through the rear window. The tornado was gaining.

"You'd better floor it," I said, "or we'll end up in Kansas."

She did. The dirt road ahead twisted, turned, narrowed and slithered between gullies in which water was already gushing. The back of the car slid at every turn, pitching me against Mongo or him falling all over me. Neither of us liked it. I didn't complain, and neither did he, seeing that trees were beginning to crash around us.

"Turn here," Mariental said, pointing at an even narrower road.

With the skill of a NASCAR driver, Neola turned onto the lane. Branches and weeds brushed the sides, ruts and rocks jarred our teeth, but she didn't slow down.

I saw the tree that had fallen across the road a split second after she did. She'd already stomped on the brakes. I braced for impact. The car slid sideways, knocked against something hard, straightened then shuddered to a stop. I burst out and ran to the front. The distance between bumper and tree was barely a centimeter.

"Great driving," I yelled.

"Can you push it out of the way?"

I looked up then shook my head at her. "No time. We'd better start running."

"This way," Mariental said. He and Mongo jumped over the fallen tree and hurried forward only a few meters then stopped. I saw his lips moving. Another porthole formed in the middle of the brush, and he stepped through.

We followed. Just as the hole closed, I saw the car shudder then flip over and over before it rose in the air. With a sigh of relief, I turned around to survey the new world Mariental had brought us into.

We'd come out of the storm right in front of a four-story building. Above the door, carved into stone was its name: The Carlisle.

I'd just found Garner's building.

I did a slow three-sixty. Houses, buildings, huts—all jumbled together without plan or even streets—surrounded us. The ground appeared to be something like dried clay; there were no trees or grass, nothing that looked remotely like plant matter. A cloudless, metallic-blue sky made the ground appear even more desolate.

I sensed movement above me. I shielded my eyes against the brightness of the sun and raised my head; a face disappeared from one of the windows of the Carlisle. There are people living here, I realized, a bit stunned.

The question was, where was here?

"The tornadoes should give us some lead time," Mariental said. Before I could say anything else, he raised a hand. "I will explain everything, I promise, as soon as I feel you are safe."

"I didn't need to follow you here, Mariental."

"You're referring to your telecarb. Try it, if you wish."

That he knew about the device took me by surprise. I hooked Neola's hand and wished for my office. Nothing happened. Neola's cabin, then. Still nothing. Thrittene? The telecarb didn't budge.

Mariental was smiling slightly. It didn't improve his looks. He got into my face.

"There are only a few portals that will return you to Earth," he murmured, "and I'm the only one who knows where they are. I suggest you follow me, unless you both want to stay here." He glanced left and right. "I wouldn't advise it."

Beings of all sorts were coming out of their dwellings, and they didn't look friendly.

I glanced at Neola, who shrugged.

"Let's go," I said.

Mariental turned on his heel and followed what seemed like a random path between the structures. At every door their occupants, silently hostile, stood and watched us pass. I threw a glance behind me. A crowd followed us.

"We got groupies," I said to Neola under my breath.

"I saw them. Hopefully, they won't stampede."

"Do you recognize the species?"

"Most of them."

"They all seem to be able to share the same air."

"Oxygen breathers. Some of them look a little sick. The mix must be either too rich or too thin for them."

Now that she mentioned it, I felt a bit short of breath myself. Mariental didn't seem affected. He walked briskly, Mongo beside him.

"Do you figure Mariental's IGA?"

"He would've identified himself."

"Don't see why."

"It would give him more credibility."

"Only if we knew what he was talking about."

She smiled slightly. "You didn't when I first met you."

"You have a convincing way about you."

She grinned broadly at that. "We're stuck with him until you can use your telecarb then. I wish I had my USI. I'd bet all that mumbling he did is just good old-fashioned communications."

"Yeah, I figured he's in contact with someone who's helping him open portals to other worlds."

"Exactly." She got a strange look on her face.

"You know something."

"Hmmm. I just had an idea."

"Spit it out, sister."

"Not now. We're here."

Mariental stopped at a dwelling that looked halfway between a mud hut and a space station. It was square and brown, the size of a garden shed, with loopholes for windows and a thatched roof that an array of antennas and radar dishes used as a pincushion. A stainless steel door reflected sunlight and made me squint. He tapped a code on the keypad beside it; the door opened silently.

Through the opening, a wall full of instruments blinked at us. He gestured us in, locked the door after him.

Neola stepped to the instrument panels and peered at them curiously.

"You have an IPS?" I could hear awe in her voice. She turned to me, pointing to a panel that looked like a radar screen. On it were several intersecting lines in different colors. "That's an inter-dimensional positioning system," she said. "I thought they were still in the development stage."

"This is a prototype," Mariental said. "Although, I'm happy to say, most of the bibittes have been cleaned out."

"What does an IPS do?" I said.

"It provides your position on a particular dimension relative to your own universe."

"I see." I didn't see at all, but I suspected it was one of those cases where Trebor would say my brain was too small to get it.

"What is this place?" Neola wanted to know.

"This is similar to your way stations," Mariental said, "but somewhat more sophisticated."

She blinked, then her mouth fell open.

"You're from the AGES," she said, her tone reverential.

"You're losing me again," I said. "What are the ages?"

"The Agency for the Governance of Entities and Systems,"

Meriental said. "We're just like your basic government, except we manage the entire universe, not just one country."

"Oh, you're a bureaucrat," I said.

Mariental smiled. "If you want to look at it that way."

I took a breath in. "Nope," I said. "I'd say you might be in this for the money."

"Believe me, Jack Meter, I have no intention of delivering you to anyone. But you're right, there's a price for my helping you."

"There ain't no such thing as a free lunch, as they say."

"Exactly."

"I never pay for unsolicited services."

"Would you have preferred taking your chances with the bounty hunters?"

"You *said* they were bounty hunters. What I saw was a bunch of weirdoes running in our direction. For all I know, they were after you, not me."

"And why would you say that?"

"If someone wanted my skin they didn't have to look very far."

"That's assuming they could get to Earth."

"Why put a price on my head if no one can grab it?"

"Gentlemen," Neola interrupted, "would you mind setting the male hormones aside for a moment? This isn't getting us anywhere."

We both looked at her. There's nothing worse than being interrupted when the argument's getting good. Mariental's owlish eyes had taken on a dangerous glint, and I found myself frowning.

"There's no denying that we were a target, Jack," Neola continued, seemingly unfazed by our glares. "The way station is gone. Also, one person was able to get to you." She took Karoi's pin from her pocket. "Didn't you say he was in your office and that he wished you harm?"

"Yes. My telecarb sensed danger."

"You followed him and ended up with Saurimo," she said. "I followed one of the alarms and ended up in the same place, but on the other side of the conflict."

"So the person who triggered your alarm wasn't Karoi."

"There might be someone in Asela's camp who could give us some idea of what's going on."

"He's long gone," Mariental said.

"You know who it was?"

"No, but I picked up faint traces of plasma displacement indicating a fracture in the continuum."

"Now you sound like a bad *Star Trek* episode," I said.

"We have consulted on some of them."

I chose to ignore that. "Where did he go?"

"We don't know." His eyelids shuttered. "So far, they have been quite adept at covering their tracks. We still don't know who they are or what they want."

While we were talking, I'd been glancing at a screen that showed the outside of the building. The group that had followed us had milled around in front of the door for a few minutes. Now they were dispersing. Among a sprinkling of humans, Kilosans and Orapans as well as those turtle beings with the unpronounceable name and many other entities crawled, flew or hovered back, presumably, to their respective places of residence.

"There has to be a good reason for abducting all these beings and planting them here," I said. "Wherever here is."

"You disappoint me, Jack Meter," Mariental said. "We are in a parallel universe to yours, one that was created not long ago."

"I thought so," Neola said. "Asela's must be another one then. That's why my USI blew up." She dug out the one I'd taken from Karoi. "We'll have to find out why this one didn't."

Mariental extended his hand. "If you'll let me, I might be able to do that."

"Wait a minute," I said. "Back up. There are two words wrong here: *create* and *parallel.* As far as I know, there's no such thing as a parallel universe. Even if there were, how can you create one?"

"We're not quite sure," Mariental said. "However, whoever is responsible had help. From you, Jack."

CHAPTER TEN

THERE WAS ONLY ONE THING I HATED MORE THAN A WHAMMY—A DOUBLE whammy. I walked to a quartet of armchairs around a low table, sat down.

"You've had your fun, dropped your little bomb. How about you explain now, Mariental. I ain't playing your game anymore."

Neola sat beside me; black slashes underneath her eyes stressed her fatigue. I was beginning to feel frayed around the edges myself, and not only because we'd been running around parallel universes. I didn't want to admit that Mariental's last statement had rattled me. For some reason, it rang true, as impossible as it sounded. I thought of trying the telecarb again, but if I were successful, I might not be able to return. What I wanted more than a meal and a bed, right at that moment, were answers.

Mariental stepped up to us, remained standing, hands clasped in front of him. He looked like a crazy professor about to lecture unruly students. Mongo plopped down at his feet.

"Picture the universe we live in," he said in a didactic tone, "as a bubble. The membrane containing it is matter made of incalculably small strings.

"This bubble floats along the eleventh dimension in conjunction with an infinite number of other universes. For your benefit, imagine an endless string of pearls, each pearl being a universe."

"A string of pearls," I said. "Right. What does have that to do with me?"

He blinked owlishly. "I am coming to it. Regardless of what the

Thrittene might believe or tell you, they are at the edge of a tiny galaxy at the back of your universe, where nothing much happens. However, even if you throw a rock in water at the edge of a pond, some of the ripples will reach the other edge."

"And build into waves," Neola interjected, "if a wind picks up."

"Exactly," Mariental said. "The conjugator you used on your lover Annie—"

"She wasn't Annie."

Mongo raised his head and growled. Neola placed a hand on mine and squeezed.

"Easy," she whispered.

"Apologies," Mariental said. "On Annie Barnes's clone. The effects of the conjugator you used to break down the strings that held the segments of worlds Mueller had stolen acted as that wind Ms. Durwin mentioned. The ripples in the universe became a tsunami by the time they arrived at the other side of the membrane. A universe within ours formed then sliced itself off to form another stand-alone bubble along the eleventh dimension."

We'd switched from *Star Trek* to the *Twilight Zone.* Mariental's explanations would've been real hard to believe if it hadn't been for one tiny thing.

When I'd followed a fragment of Annie's clone with my eyes, just before it vanished, I'd seen something like a folding in space—a "ripple."

"You're saying I created a universe."

"Yes. This would not have been a problem if the universe had completely detached itself, but a connection remained. Realities mixed up. Matter exchanged."

"So buildings and people disappeared."

"Yes. You are now in the universe you created. By extracting matter from our universe, the new one grew, endangering other universes around it. We have determined that our own Big Bang was caused by two universes bumping into each other."

"You've proven this?" Neola said.

"We've been able to calculate the exact time, to the hundredth power, of the collision." He turned back to me. "We prevented the catastrophe by containing the flow and cutting the link."

"I'd love to know how you did that," Neola said, her tone excited. All her tiredness seemed to have evaporated.

"Just a sec," I said. "I sense a 'but' coming on."

"There is." Mariental rolled his shoulders. "Someone—we still don't know who—is using your technique to create *another* universe and is linking it to other universes. The ones we've passed through have all been linked. Fog, fire and tornadoes are not the usual for these worlds."

"If you tell me that this threatens to destabilize the eleventh dimension and will wipe out reality as we know it, I'm going home."

Mariental smiled. "Nothing as drastic as that, although, if the links remain, those who inhabit these universes may be greatly affected. For instance, with an infinite number of universes, it is quite possible that life in one bubble could mirror life in another, although events may take a different turn."

"In one of them, Hitler could have won the war," Neola said.

"Yes," Mariental said, serious again. "And in another, the dinosaurs might not have become extinct, or Dowa might rule."

I saw Neola blanch; I knew she was thinking of her husband and the Dowan thugs who'd killed him. I turned my hand palm up and linked my fingers with hers. She threw me a surprised glance but kept her hand in mine.

"We don't know what would happen if transfer were to occur both ways."

"I can see it now," I said. "Hitler's son invading Asia on a T-Rex."

"It sounds like a ludicrous possibility, even though it could become reality if the links can be kept open permanently."

"Why don't you just close off the links like you did the first time?"

Mariental shook his head. "As soon as we close off a link, another opens. In addition, we haven't been able to locate the new universe."

"Why would they want to link the universes?"

"We're not sure. All we know is that pieces have disappeared from each of them."

"And you can't locate the one where everything is going."

"No. They have it well camouflaged."

I pursed my mouth. "And you expect me to believe all this crap?"

Mariental blinked.

"How have you been traveling through the universes?"

He dug under the collar of his pantsuit and came up with a medallion on a chain. He took it off and passed it over to me. One side was smooth, like a mini LCD; the other had three small holes.

"This is an osmotic parser. It permits me to go through the membranes—or branes—of the bubbles."

"Does it also function as a USI?" Neola brought her face close to mine to examine the medallion. I passed it to her for a closer look.

"It does. We used reverse engineering, if you wish, to develop the OP. As far as my legitimacy as an AGES representative, I cannot prove it to you, Jack Meter. Anything I show you could be counterfeit." He made an impatient gesture. "Besides, proving I'm who I am is the least of my concerns. Right now, we have someone who is systematically linking to and cutting off chunks of alternate worlds." He paused. "I said that we didn't know who was responsible for linking universes, but one name has come up again and again."

"Mine."

Mariental inclined his head. I took that for a yes.

"Shit. No wonder I've got bounty hunters on my ass."

Neola laughed, a rich sound that echoed around the room.

"Sorry, Jack. That 'someone' is clever and has a sense of humor."

"Yeah. While I spend my time dodging bombs and whatever else these guys are throwing at me, I can't look for him."

"That's why we want you to go back to Earth—your Earth—and stay there," Mariental said. "We'll take care of tracking him down."

"You have as much hope I'd agree to that as you have of being hit with a snowstorm in hell."

"We could take you into custody until this affair is over."

I leaned back and extended my legs, crossed my hands over my chest.

"Sure, why don't you?"

I'd just decided I'd had it with him and it was time to split. Since we were in something like a way station, I was fairly sure my telecarb would work. I grabbed Neola's hand.

"Time to go, sweetheart."

* * *

"What the hell did you do that for?" Neola said after she'd unstuck her hand from mine.

"I needed a time-out."

"You just didn't want to listen to reason."

"Telling me to stay out of this isn't reasonable."

"It is if you want to stay alive."

I thought about the past two years, when I'd wished I could die every day.

"My survival instincts are well-honed."

"We're out of our league."

"Maybe you are, but I've got a couple of tricks left in my pocket. I seem to recall we had a few leads before we were detoured into alternate realities. Remember Ginir and Abura and the house off Guigues?"

"At this point, I doubt they're connected."

"We won't know until we investigate, will we?"

She bit her lip. "I suppose. I still don't have a USI, though."

"No, but you have an OP." I lifted the hand in which she still help Mariental's medallion.

"Oh." Holding it by the chain, she raised it to eye level. "I have no idea how it works."

"Just put it on and you'll see."

"This is alien technology. It could have strange effects on me."

"You don't have to tell me that."

She glanced at my telecarb.

"I suppose not." With a deep breath, she slipped the medallion over her head, the LCD screen out. "Now what?"

"Try to go somewhere. To the fog world."

She closed her eyes, waited, opened them again.

"We're obviously missing something."

"Mariental had the medallion under his clothes. Maybe it needs to touch your skin."

She nodded, slipped it under her T-shirt. She gasped, stepped backward then grunted as if she'd been punched in the stomach. She folded in two, took a deep breath, straightened.

"That thing attached itself to my breastbone. Something came out of those three holes and just punched through."

"Does it hurt?"

She threw me a sardonic glance. "Thanks for asking."

"Try to take it off."

She fished under her shirt, pulled, shook her head.

"Nope. I'll have to ask Mariental about it if we ever see him."

Then she disappeared. I stepped over where she'd been but didn't feel that faint chill I'd felt when she'd used her own device.

"Well," she said behind me, "it works for me."

"Where were you?"

"Fog world. That missile made a big hole." She sat down. "God, I'm tired. That thing takes some getting used to. It's as if I had this computer in my brain that calculates vectors and parsing degrees almost instantaneously. I actually felt my body fragment into strings that flowed through the brane and reconfigured themselves on the other side."

"Mariental didn't become string cheese when he moved us from one universe to the other."

"I didn't try it, but I think that once I'm in a linked universe I probably can find and open the links between other bubbles. It requires immense calculations. I think that's what Mariental was mumbling."

The sound of two pairs of feet lumbering up the stairs outside my office put us both on alert. I gestured for Neola to hide in the bathroom as the doorknob turned. Winston appeared in the doorway.

"I thought I heard the pitter-pat of your heels," he said. "I brought someone who's anxious to see you." He moved to reveal Garner.

"Mr. Meter," he said, stepping into the office. "I've left numerous voice and emails for you. You haven't bothered answering me in over a month."

I was shocked. Had it been that long since we'd left?

"What's the day, today?"

"December fifteenth," Winston provided. "Only ten days to get your Christmas shopping done."

"Never mind that, Winston," Garner said. Despite his rundown appearance, he was obviously used to giving orders. "I want a report, Meter. Have you found my building?"

"I have some good leads, Mr. Garner. These things take time."

"We're not talking about a pet dog. How difficult is it to locate something that big? I'm losing money here."

I sat on the edge of my desk, crossed my arms.

"I'd imagine that the people inside the Carlisle are of much concern to you and that in your anxiety you're mixing property value with potential loss of life."

He blinked, at a loss for a moment, then had the grace to flush.

"Of course, I'm concerned for my tenants." He stopped there, but I found his choice of words interesting.

"All I can tell you is that I'm working on it." I smirked. "And since I haven't asked you for a cent yet, I wouldn't worry too much about it."

"Yes, there's that, but what if you don't find it?"

"Then I hope you have insurance for Acts of God and Monsters."

Garner shook his head furiously; dandruff flew like snowflakes in a storm. His chest puffed up, showing a spot of grease on his tie.

Winston placed a hand on his shoulder. "Don't go saying something you might regret, Lambert. How many investigators might be prepared to work on this case?"

Garner was silent for a minute. His eyes bulged, as if he'd blow up if he held in whatever he wanted to say. Then, with a gust of breath, he swiveled and tore out the door.

Winston grinned, plucked a cigar from his inside pocket. "Don't think I'll come to your rescue every time he has a hankering to bash your brains in."

"He can hanker all he wants." Winston knew I could take care of myself, so I was certain he had ulterior motives for accompanying Garner. "What can I do for you, Winston?"

"Didn't fool you, huh?" he said around his cigar. "I was just curious about the other pitter-patter I heard along with yours."

He turned toward the bathroom. Neola stood leaning against the doorjamb, an amused smile on her face.

"Well, hel*lo*," Winston said, a croon in his voice. "What have we here?"

"Neola Durwin," I said, "meet Peter Winston, a.k.a. Winnie the Pooh."

Winston barked a laugh. "People call me that only once. Enchanté," he said in broken French. "Call me Winston, Ms. Durwin."

"Neola." She slinked toward him, hand extended. "I'm pleased to meet one of Jack's friends."

Winston took the hand and kissed her fingers. Her smile broadened.

"Especially since there aren't many of us around," he said.

"Okay, wise guy, you've met her now. How about you go back to putting bad guys where they belong?"

Winston ignored me. "What brings you to rub shoulders with this reprobate?"

"Mutual interests," Neola said.

"Business," I said at the same time.

Winston raised an eyebrow. "Then I'd better let you take care of those. If you get tired of this lout's company, Neola, come downstairs and visit. It'll be my pleasure." He clamped his unlit cigar between his teeth, nodded at me and opened the door. "Oh, by the way," he said over his shoulder, "if you plan to go out I'd put on some more clothes. It's well below zero out there."

Neola stared at the door then at me, her lips pursed.

"Jack, I wonder. Did you ever show your telecarb to Winston?"

I looked down at my bare arms. My telecarb glowed faintly on the left forearm.

"He knew about it, but I never showed it to him. Why?"

"He didn't comment on it."

"Maybe he didn't notice it."

"Oh, he saw it all right. I was watching him. That's all he was looking at when you were talking to your client. I wonder why he didn't comment on it."

I shrugged. "Maybe he thought the timing was wrong."

"Or maybe Peter Winston is a little more than what he appears to be."

CHAPTER ELEVEN

I WOKE UP IN A BED FOR THE FIRST TIME IN MORE THAN A MONTH. I'D forgotten what it was like to slip between cool sheets, lay my head on a soft pillow and sink into sleep. Which I'd done, like a brick through water, out of sheer exhaustion. Bright light snuck through the slats in the blinds so I assumed it was morning. The house was silent, except for a few creaks and the moaning of the wind against the window.

I got up, intent on making coffee before Neola got to it. I pulled on my jeans, shoved arms and head through a sweater and padded barefoot into the kitchen. I found the tin of coffee and was counting spoons into the basket when I heard shuffling behind me.

"Coffee'll be ready in a couple of minutes," I said.

She only grunted. I opened the fridge. There was nothing in it except moldy bagels.

"You need to go grocery shopping."

"This from the man who owns one pair of pants and two sweaters."

I raised an arm and sniffed under my armpit. "Not ripe yet."

"I'm so glad you shared that." She yawned, glanced at the clock-radio on the counter. "God, ten o'clock. I never sleep that late." She sat down at the kitchen table.

"Universe-hopping can be tiring." I cut the green stuff from a bagel, sliced it in two and slipped it in the toaster.

Neola's eyes were at half-mast. I gave her a cup of coffee before she fell asleep again. She sipped it, grimaced.

"This tastes like dishwater."

Since I'd made the coffee twice as strong as I usually did, I ignored her comment. There was also a bit of cream cheese left, so I smeared the bagel halves with that and passed one of them to her. For the next few minutes, the only sounds in the room were crunches and slurps. When I got up to pour a second cup, Neola looked awake.

"It occurs to me," I said, "that your job is finished. I'll be leaving after breakfast."

"My job isn't finished."

"Sure it is. You were hired to find out why the universe was shrinking. You did. End of story."

"Tell that to the IGA agents who disappeared. If they're not dead, they're stuck somewhere. I want to find them."

"I'll give you the same advice you gave me—leave that to the AGES reps. I'm sure they're working on restoring our universe to its pristine condition."

"Is that what you're going to do? Leave it to Mariental?"

"What I do or not isn't relevant here."

She crossed her arms under her breasts and tapped her foot. "You want me out of the way. Why?"

Bull's-eye. Except I didn't know how to respond to that question because I wasn't sure of the answer.

As a partner, Neola fit the bill. She was tough, bright, fearless when needed, with an ego that didn't interfere with the job. I stared at her, trying to find an acceptable reason. Her eyes were still sleepy, her hair tousled. She looked small, delicate in her chenille robe. I swallowed.

Something moved across her face; then her eyes narrowed.

"It's because of Annie, isn't it?"

I forced myself to stay seated when all I wanted was to do was jump up and pace.

"Leave Annie out of it."

"It's obvious you can't." She took a breath, let it out in an exasperated sigh. "There's this attraction between us, Jack. I feel it, and I know you have, too. And it makes you feel shitty because for moments at a time you forget Annie."

This time I rose, set the cup on the table before I could throw it against the wall, looked down at her.

"I told you, leave Annie out of this."

"I can't. She's between us." There was pity in her eyes. "I forget about Michael, too. But I realize it has nothing to do with you. It has to do with going on with my life."

I strode into the living room. "Two years isn't long enough to forget."

"You're not forgetting, you're just living."

"Without her." I rubbed my face, trying to bring back some of the blood that had left it. "I didn't think I could."

Neola came to face me. Her chin rose and she glared.

"I'll tell you something else, Jack. Just because I feel attracted to you doesn't mean I'm going to jump your bones. I have priorities, and right now, they don't include wasting time coddling you. You feel guilty, fine. Deal with it. I'll be damned if it'll interfere with the job. The deal stands—we're partners until we finish this." She poked me in the chest. "If not, I swear I'll go back to Mariental and I'll drag you along with me. After the disappearing stunt you pulled, he'll definitely put you in a cage until it's over." She backed away a step. "Now, I'm going to take a shower, get dressed. You do the same then we can discuss what we want to do next."

I watched her disappear into the bathroom, torn between the need to wring her neck or to grab her on my way to her bedroom.

I'd spent two years steeped in grief for Annie, until I'd realized that a lot of my grief had been anger. Damn it, I was still pissed at her. She knew she was going to die and just accepted it. If it had been me in her place, I'd have fought in any way I could to stay alive. To stay with me. Maybe that's why I couldn't get over it—she hadn't loved me enough.

I marched to Neola's office, picked up pen and paper and

scratched her a note. A minute later, I was back in my office.

*   *   *

"Jack, I'm talking about Christmas-frigging-Eve. You're not spending it alone. Betty always makes a turkey big enough to feed the entire state of New York."

"I don't celebrate Christmas, Terry, you know that."

"Well, we do, and you're coming over. Laura will be there."

"You can tell her hi for me."

"She's dying to see you again."

"Betty put you up to this, didn't she?"

Terry cleared his throat. "Inviting you over for Christmas Eve dinner was my idea."

I suddenly had a thought. "I'll come, and I'll bring a friend, if that's okay with you."

"A female friend?"

"Yeah." There was a stunned silence at the other end of the line. "What's the matter, Terry, it's okay for you to fix me up with your sister-in-law, but I can't make friends on my own?"

"No, I just thought…"

"We're working on a case together," I said to relieve his anxiety. "I don't think she has any family either."

"Sure, sure, bring her. The more the merrier. How's the case going, by the way?"

"It's more complicated than I thought."

"Does it involve your alien friends again?"

"In a roundabout way, yes."

My door opened, and Garner came in. He looked mutinous.

"Listen, I've got to go. Hi to Betty."

"You don't have Winston to run interference for you, this time," Garner said. He plunked himself in the chair across from my desk. He smelled like fried bologna and sour milk. "I want an update."

I leaned back in my chair. "What if I told you your building is in another universe?"

He leaned forward, his face eager. "You found it?"

"You don't seem that surprised."

"When a building disappears into thin air, including the land, and nobody pays it a nevermind, you know something out of the ordinary is going on. Another universe, you say."

"Somewhere along the eleventh dimension."

Garner harrumphed. "Well?"

"Well what?"

"How are you going to get it back?"

"You hired me to find your building, not to get it back for you. I'll send you a bill."

"I only have your word that you found it, don't I?" He got up, walked to the door. "Get it back for me, Mr. Meter. You're not getting paid otherwise."

"If you'd done your research, Garner, you'd know I don't need your money." The man miffed me.

"Oh, I've looked you up, Meter." He looked crafty, now. "I know you're in need of an apartment. It so happens that I own the Daly site." He opened the door. "If you get me my building back, you can have your pick of condominiums at half the selling price. You'll have a prime location, forever yours, for less than a hundred-and-fifty grand. Good day to you."

I could see how Garner, despite his deficient personal hygiene, had made it to the Fortune 500 list—the man knew how to negotiate by zeroing in on his opponent's weakness. The Daly site was prime land at the corner of Sussex and Rideau, in the heart of downtown and across the street from the Chateau Laurier, five minutes' walk from the Moulin de Provence, my favorite coffee-and-bagel hangout, and about a fifteen-minute walk from my office.

I tried to convince myself that I was bigger than being bribed with mortar and bricks, but I wasn't very successful. It was difficult to stand on principle when I had every intention of continuing with the case. Someone was using my name out there, and I intended to find out who. Surely, when I found him, I could find a way to persuade him to return Garner's building.

But before that, I wanted to check on something. I picked up the phone and dialed Winston's number.

"Charlie, how are you?" I said to his assistant.

"Mr. Meter. He's not in."

"When is he going to be back?"

"He's taken a few days off. He'll be back after Christmas."

"I need to speak to him. It's urgent."

"If he calls me, I'll relay your message."

"Come on, Charlie, I'm not one of Winston's clients. You can tell me where he is."

"Good-bye, Mr. Meter."

The click in my ear was definite. So, Winston was incommunicado. In the ten years I'd known him, Peter Winston had never taken more than two days off, let alone cut himself off from his clients.

Neola's assertion that Winston's behavior was suspicious had nagged at my brain until I'd decided to confront him. My take was that he had noticed the telecarb and decided to keep his own counsel. That would be typical of him as a lawyer and as who he was as a person. On the other hand, if he'd known what Thrittene matter was, he wouldn't have needed to comment on it.

Now he was gone.

I could always chase him down using the telecarb, but there were a few drawbacks to this method. If Winston had really decided to take a break, and knew nothing about the telecarb, I'd look like an ass chasing him down. If he wasn't who he appeared to be, I could land somewhere I didn't want to go, place myself in danger. The telecarb protected me from killing myself, but not necessarily from a broken leg or a few punches in the gut. Either way, it could be awkward. I decided I'd wait until after Christmas. If he hadn't surfaced by then I'd use the telecarb.

There was a shimmer in the room, and Neola appeared. She sported the same querulous look as Garner.

"You ready?" she said.

"Yeah." I picked up my coat from the back of my chair. "Let's take a cab."

She appeared surprised by the mildness of my response. "Sure."

I followed her downstairs. She chatted about another snowstorm in Colorado and the fact she hadn't been able to get out for supplies.

"I guess I'll have to pick up some before I get back. You'll have to point out the best places to get bread and cheese."

"The ByWard Market's the best place." If she was going to ignore our previous tiff, so would I. "They sell everything you can think of."

"Oh, good, maybe I'll make myself a nice piece of fish tonight. Haven't had a decent meal in ages."

Neither had I, but I didn't mention it. My office was set up with a hot plate and I could heat up canned soup or make mac-and-cheese, but that was just about the extent of it. With a start, I realized I hadn't cooked an elaborate meal, the way I used to when Annie was alive, in more than two years. Uncomfortable with the thought, I focused on our mission.

"We'll stake out the house first," I announced. If she was surprised by it, she said nothing. "If it looks no one's home, we get inside."

"Can you pick a lock?"

I sneered at her. "Can Santa Claus squeeze down a chimney?"

I flagged a passing cab, and we scrambled into it. Even though it was barely two o'clock, the day was gray, so the light was already fading. Christmas lights twinkled on porches, around store windows, on the trees along Bronson. Whatever snow we'd had was either melted or vaporized. Sidewalks and streets, drab under all this cheer, made the whole tableau more depressing than festive.

"Are you going home to Minnesota for Christmas?" Even to my own ears, my voice was gruff.

"No, I'll probably spend it at my house."

"I've been invited for Christmas Eve dinner at a friend's house. I said I'd bring you if you wanted to come," I said, looking straight ahead.

From the corner of my eye, I saw her glance at me in surprise. "Ah, thanks, but—"

I looked at her. "Betty's the worst cook in the world, and she always makes tons. You'd be performing a community service if you helped eat some of it."

She smiled slightly. "A community service, huh?"

"Well, we don't want the children to become wards of the state because the parents killed each other over a turkey."

Neola chuckled. "All right, I'll do my civic duty. How many kids are there?"

"Three."

"Ages?"

"Why would I need to know that?"

"Presents."

I felt myself pale. "You mean shopping, don't you?"

"Yep."

"I'd rather face a horde of bounty hunters."

"That's what it'll feel like, the longer you wait. We'll go after we've scoped the house."

"Here we are."

The taxi driver had stopped in front of the cult house we'd left the day before—for us, that is. We got off and stood looking up at it. No one had bothered to decorate with garlands or lights. The house had a desolate air, as if it had been abandoned.

I climbed the few stairs to the front stoop and knocked.

"What the hell are you doing?"

"Best way to find out if anyone's in." I knocked again and waited a couple of minutes. "No one's home or they're antisocial. Let's go around the back."

"Now you're making more sense," Neola muttered.

I surveyed the area. The street was deserted, the blinds in the houses across the street falling straight. The fence gate sported a brand-new, shiny padlock.

"Looks like they want to keep people out," I said. "Come on." I wished myself on the other side of the fence.

The yard was deserted; only a few candy wrappers twirled in the wind. I could imagine the young novice I'd talked to chomping on a Snickers bar before slipping into his robe and joining whatever ceremony this Abura had concocted for them.

The lock was simple, almost too easy. I opened the door quietly and stepped inside. As soon as I did, the smell of death choked me.

CHAPTER TWELVE

I CAME FURTHER INSIDE, NEOLA CLOSE ON MY HEELS. THE HOUSE WAS VERY warm, the smell overpowering. She uttered a wordless exclamation and covered her mouth and nose with her sleeve.

The pungent, rancid stench of decomposing flesh, feces and urine drifted in the air and out the door. I heard a high droning sound coming from behind the closed door straight ahead. I opened it to reveal a set of stairs going down into the dark. The smell and the buzzing became stronger. Shit. There had to be a world of flies down there. I swallowed bile rising up and decided I wasn't looking forward to whatever I'd discover.

"Should we call the cops?" Neola whispered.

"Let's see what's here first. It could be just a dead dog. I'd hate to look like a schmuck."

"That would have to be a dog the size of a horse." Her voice was raspy. "Make it quick. This smell is going to make me retch."

The entrance gave into a tiny foyer that could barely hold both of us. To the left, three steps led up to the kitchen. I pointed upstairs.

"Why don't you investigate this floor and the next," I whispered. "I'll see what's down there."

She nodded then moved silently past me.

I turned on the light switch and crept down the lighted stairs. My telecarb gave me no signal of danger, but the smell grew stronger as I descended. I didn't have to go far. Halfway there, the open risers revealed a carpet of flies buzzing over a dozen bodies lying one on top of the other. In their robes, they looked like discarded puppets.

Some of them were so bloated they barely looked human. Through the movement of the flies, I recognized one of the faces. I wouldn't do fake interviews with this kid again.

Something yellow and slimy oozed from the pile of bodies to the drain a meter away. I didn't want to guess what that was, but the flies seemed to have a jolly time landing on it.

"Holy Mother of God," Neola said behind me.

I hadn't heard her coming down the stairs. I swallowed, unable to speak, and gestured to go up with my head. Without prompting, she turned and kept going straight through the door and outside. There, we both gulped air. Neola slumped onto the ground.

"I've seen dead before," she said, her voice raspy, "but not like this. Not like this."

"You didn't touch anything, did you?"

She shook her head. I sat down beside her, took out my cell and speed-dialed Terry's office number. My hand was shaking so much I could barely hold the phone.

"Parczek here."

"Terry." I took another breath.

"Jack? Twice in a day—that's quite a record when I don't hear from you for over two weeks at a time. What can I do you for?"

"I need you to come to 122 Cumberland. Bring a forensic team."

"What's it about?"

"You know those cults we discussed? I've just come upon a mass of bodies."

"I'm on my way. Call the city cops. Don't move."

Neola was shivering. I wrapped an arm around her shoulders. I dialed 911, gave my name, my position then reported multiple deaths. Whether they were murders or suicides would have to be determined.

"Who's Terry?"

"A friend of mine. He's with the RCMP. He'll be here soon."

"Why'd you call him before you called the cops?"

"Insurance." Already police sirens were getting closer. "We'd better get up."

Tires screeched, doors slammed. I heard something snap—probably the padlock—then two cops burst through the fence, chest protectors in place, guns at the ready.

"Police!" one of them yelled. "Don't move."

We both raised our hands above our heads.

"You're the one who reported the deaths?"

I nodded, hands still in the air. "Jack Meter. This is Neola Durwin."

"Where are the bodies?"

"Inside the house, in the basement."

The other cop moved inside to check it out. One minute later he came back, looking green around the gills.

"There are at least a dozen dead down there. Kids, for fuck's sake. All dead. We need forensics."

"These people belonged to a cult," I said. "You'll need the feds."

"How do you know they were cultists?"

"I was investigating them. I'm a private investigator."

"ID." He signaled we could lower our hands.

I dug carefully in my jacket pocket and flipped open my permit.

"Who's your client?"

"Don't have one," I lied. "I was looking for an apartment when I met this kid and he talked to me about a cult. It sounded fishy. I decided to investigate."

"You work often without a client?

I shrugged. "I can afford it."

He turned to Neola. "And you are?"

"His partner," she said.

"My date," I said at the same time. We looked at each other.

"Which is it?"

"Both," we said together.

"I bet you don't have too many repeat dates," the cop said to me.

By then there were more sounds of cars arriving, doors slamming, voices raised. Terry appeared in the courtyard, glanced toward me then went into the house. A few seconds later, handkerchief over his mouth and nose, he came back out and strode over to where we stood with the cop.

He flashed his badge. "It's okay, officer, this man is clean. You were first on the scene?"

"Yes, sir," the uniform said. "Thompson went inside to verify the claim. Forensics is on its way."

Terry nodded. "We'll take it from here. The chief is coming over—brief her when she arrives, will you?"

The uniform nodded and left us to stand by the door.

"Jesus Murphy, Jack, I almost tossed my lunch *and* my dinner in there." He turned to Neola.

Most times, Terry looked like a nineteen-sixties reject, with his checkered pants and wide ties, and most people took him for harmless. They noticed the mismatched socks but forgot to pay attention to his eyes. He had them well fixed on her.

"You'd be the one on the same case as Jack then," he said in a country bumpkin tone.

Neola nodded soberly. I had a feeling she wouldn't make the mistake of underestimating Terry.

"Neola Durwin."

"You're not from around here."

"Minnesota. Currently living in Colorado."

"And your case brought you here, meshed with Jack's."

She threw me a glance. "In a matter of speaking."

"Is this a case of the less I know the better I'll be?" Terry asked me.

"I can tell you for certain you don't want to know what I'm working on. You wouldn't be able to use it to explain this."

"But you think there's a connection."

"My gut tells me yes. I have no proof."

"How'd you get involved, anyway?"

I told him about the kid I'd met right after he had mentioned the increase in cult activities.

"He said something that fit with my investigation so I decided to look into the house where they had their ceremonies. Unfortunately, I was detained somewhere else and couldn't make it until now."

"Those would be the two weeks when you disappeared, even though you thought this kid might be in danger. Why didn't you talk to me about this before?"

"As far as I was concerned, I was only gone for a day."

He frowned at me for a moment then shook his head.

"You're right. I don't want to know. I hope, Ms. Durwin, that your papers are up-to-date."

Neola smiled slightly. "Of course."

Terry turned when he saw the chief of police enter the yard.

"Don't leave town," he said.

"Terry." He stopped. "Could you let me know who owns the house?"

"This house and its contents have just become out-of-bounds. Stay out of it, Jack."

"You know I can't do that."

Terry signaled the chief to wait and came back to me. A telltale muscle spasm close to his ear told me how angry he was.

"You listen to me and listen good." He poked me in the chest. "I'm going to be up to my ass in alligators, and I don't need hotshots messing things up. Last time, if I remember correctly, an innocent woman died because you decided to take matters into your own hands. I'm telling you again—stay out of it."

"That was low."

"Yeah, well, live with it. I got work to do. Give your statement then go home."

* * *

A uniform gray sky began to dump wet flakes. They melted on the sidewalk at my feet, flew into my eyes and splattered against my jacket as the wind tunneled along the street. Without consulting each other, we opted to walk back to my office.

Neola brooded, which was fine, because I wasn't feeling chatty myself. I couldn't help seeing that kid sitting on a cushion in the middle of his empty apartment, a glazed look of wonder in his eyes when he spoke of the True Savior. Damn it, I didn't even know his name.

The half-hour walk didn't help my mood. When I opened the front door, I was wet, cold and pissed off. Neola climbed the stairs ahead of me. She was on the landing and I was halfway up when my telecarb began to tingle in warning.

For one endless second, I froze, and saw Annie blown up and bleeding in my arms. Then, more from instinct than thought, I charged up the stairs, tackled Neola and wished myself elsewhere. Between the moment I touched her and we left, I felt a pull, as if we were being sucked into the neck of a bottle. My telecarb tingled, heated, went cold.

When I opened my eyes, I was wrapped around Neola, and we were still on the landing in front of my office. That wasn't good.

"What the hell got into you?"

She pushed at me. I didn't let go but tried to use my telecarb. It was dead.

"Damn. Now I don't even have an office."

"What are you talking about?"

"Didn't you feel it?"

"Your hand on my butt? Yeah, I did. You don't want to lose fingers, Jack."

I shook my head. "My telecarb's dead."

That got her attention. "You're saying the house just got cut out of Earth."

"Yeah. And it happened just after we went inside. Someone must've been watching the house. Then zappo."

"Better be careful, Jack, your paranoia's showing." Neola clambered down the stairs. I followed her. When she opened the door, a swirl of dense fog greeted us. As soon as it touched our skin, red welts appeared. Breathing became immediately difficult, burning and choking at the same time.

Neola slammed the door closed.

"Okay," she said between coughs. "Your paranoia was right."

I suddenly remembered Charlie. I opened the door to Winston's office, but Charlie didn't glare at me across her desk. The place was dark, her desk clean. I closed the door with a sigh of relief. It was already more difficult to breathe.

"You can go," I said to Neola. "Use Mariental's OP." The tops of my hands were blistering. They burned as if I'd dipped them in acid.

"I'm not leaving you here." She shook hers; they must have stung as much as mine. "Shit. This thing isn't like your telecarb. It can only parse one being at a time. For both of us to get out of here, I'd have to find a portal to get us back, which means we'd have to go out in that crap. We'd probably be puddles before we got ten steps away from here." She bit her lower lip, winced when it started bleeding. "We're in trouble."

"That's an understatement."

"Any ideas?"

"Maybe." My lungs were burning, making the climb back up the stairs difficult. I was panting by the time I unlocked the door to my office. The air seemed more breathable in there.

Neola grabbed a towel from the bathroom and stuffed it into the crack between the carpet and the door. "It's not much, but it should hold us for a while."

"I have some anesthetic spray in the medicine cabinet."

She went back for it, sprayed her hands then mine. The fire toned down to a sting.

"Are you sure you can find a portal with that thing?" I said, pointing at her chest.

"Pretty sure."

"Not good enough. You have to be certain, and you have to make it fast."

"You want us to go out there. Are you nuts?"

"The fog seemed to affect mainly our skin and lungs."

"We didn't stay in it long enough to know that."

"Our coats weren't affected."

"So far."

"Granted. The way I see it, we have two choices. Either we stay here until we choke to death or we try to find a way out of here. There seems to be some oxygen; otherwise, we would be dead by now. We'll bundle up with towels and whatever we can find here." I dug in my pocket for my wraparound shades. "These should protect your eyes."

"What about you?"

I grimaced. "I'll manage."

"The portal could be miles from here. There's a good chance we won't make it."

"I'll try to use the telecarb at regular intervals. Maybe it's just in this spot that it doesn't work."

Something I couldn't read fleeted through her eyes. She plucked the shades from my hand.

"There's no moment to die like now." She grabbed my face with both her hands then kissed me soundly on the mouth. "That's for luck."

As she pushed away, I grabbed her waist and kissed her back with more enthusiasm than finesse.

"And that's for me," I said, grinning.

* * *

The fog was worse than I'd thought. We'd covered our hands and heads as best we could, but it managed to sneak into folds and cracks and burn the skin. Only a few minutes after we were out, my eyelids had puffed out and I could barely see; even with a thick wad of cloth over my mouth acting as filter, I could feel the capillaries in my lungs bursting. This was like smoking a million cigarettes at the same time. Fine time for my telecarb to call it quits.

I coughed, tasted blood. If Neola didn't find a portal soon, we'd be toast.

She staggered, and I steadied her by grabbing her elbow. She nodded to indicate she was okay, continued straight on. I'd tried to use the telecarb twice already, without result.

If there was anything in this universe, I couldn't see it. I couldn't even see my feet, let alone what I was stepping on. It reminded me of Thrittene, although a much nastier version.

Neola stopped. "I think I have something," she croaked through her filter.

I felt an intense burning on my thigh. I looked down. The fog had eaten through my pant leg. "Hurry. Our clothes won't hold up much longer."

"I can't," she said. "Jack, I can't open it."

"Concentrate."

She swore. "It's not a question of concentration, it's a question of knowledge. I don't understand the equations, don't know which to choose."

"Pick one, any one."

"What if I make it worse?"

"Nothing can be worse than this," I said, as a hole widened on the leather of my jacket.

The portal opened, and we stepped through into another fog world. It swam and whorled and formed into shapes. Bounty hunter shapes.

"Maybe I was wrong," I said, before I passed out.

CHAPTER THIRTEEN

When I came to, I couldn't open my eyes. I raised a hand and touched my eyelids. They made a squishy sound, and my fingers came away wet and sticky. The pain was incredible, as if someone had carved out my eyes.

I started feeling other places that hurt even more—my thighs, the back of one hand, my face. Every time I took a breath, I could feel the air go down my windpipe into my lungs like acid. Every intake burnt more, and I could imagine the spongy tissue turning to a brown gooey mess, melting, pitting the bones as it oozed through my ribs.

I was in bad shape. If I didn't get medical attention soon, Jack Meter would depart his very short life. I tried to speak, but all that came out was a weak grunt.

"I don't care if you die," someone whispered in my ear. "I get my money regardless."

"Who...?" I tried to swallow and started again. "Who...you?"

"Ah, he speaks. My name is Bakel. You understand me."

I nodded.

"Translator," I croaked. I didn't even try explaining that the Thrittene had modified part of my brain so that it could interpret any kind of grunt, snort or squeal. If I did, I'd have to explain, too, that I acted as a broadcaster so that it translated for anyone within ten meters from me, and I didn't have the energy. My lips had cracked and were bleeding. I swallowed something sticky when a blister on my tongue burst.

"Good, that's good," Bakel said. "I wouldn't want you to

misunderstand me. You need medical attention. So does your companion."

Neola. "She...innocent."

"Now, how would I know that? You entered here together. Maybe you're stealing together."

"Know where to go. For cure." Breathing was becoming more painful, and I couldn't recognize my own voice. For a panicked moment, I thought maybe we were back on the poisoned world. Then I remembered Bakel had been in a different universe.

"I thought you might. Pictures of you have been distributed. Handy, don't you think?"

Yes, I thought, very handy. "I...not stealing."

"No, I figured you weren't. But we'll talk about that later, if you survive. Right now, I'm more concerned about profit. You're worth a chunk of lekks. If I don't deliver you, I lose, and I'll have a bunch of colleagues upset at me."

My ears buzzed as pain lanced through me. I suspected I wasn't getting enough oxygen into my lungs.

"Just wait," I panted. "Won't be an issue."

"The problem is I'm curious. Curious enough to let you live for a while. There's one of those little houses like the one that was blown up not far from here. I could get you there."

"Her. Get her there, too."

"You're breaking my heart. If I let you go, Jack Meter, will you come back?"

I wished I could see him. On the other hand, maybe he didn't have a face and looking at him would be moot.

"Yes," I said. *If I don't die first.*

I must have passed out again, because something wet and cold brought me out of darkness. I still couldn't see, could barely breathe.

"Neola," I said with the last of my strength. "Need to touch her."

Someone took my hand and put it in hers. I felt the tingle of my telecarb just before everything turned black.

* * *

I floated in the white of Thrittene, and for the first time, I found comfort in that. Their voices—sounds I was beginning to understand—flowed around me like an aria and soothed my pain. Trebor, in a stern tone, had scolded me for damaging my body in a place where my telecarb couldn't protect me. He'd also told me the extent of my injuries—fifty percent of my lung tissue had dissolved, my vocal chords were damaged, both my eyes had melted, the eyelids had fused together, and I had five holes the size of apples in my thighs, down to the bone.

Neola hadn't fared much better, except for her eyes. The shades I'd given her had melted on her skin, sealing her eyes from the noxious fumes and giving her enough time to find the portal. I imagined what it would be like to have plastic fusing with your skin. She hadn't said a thing, just continued on. I was suddenly very angry and had to remind myself that going out to find a portal had been my idea.

Recovery was excruciatingly painful. Some of the acid fumes had entered our bloodstream. Trebor and Leinad needed to purge our systems and, to do so, needed constant feedback from us. I felt every blood vessel, every nerve ending, every ligament rebuild—very slowly. All that prevented me from screaming my head off were the Thrittene voices that tried to absorb my pain. Neola didn't have that, and more than once I heard her moan and sob.

Then, some interminable time later, I fell into blissful sleep. When I woke, I was my old self again, except for one detail. As I rubbed my face to wash the sleep away, I noticed they hadn't regrown my beard. It must've melted as well. I didn't hold it against them—they had other priorities. I wondered what I looked like without hair on my face. I'd had that beard for as long as I was old enough to grow one.

I got up from the table where I lay, feeling hungry. On a side shelf, I found my clothes, neatly folded. Trebor had even added a brand-new leather jacket. I hoped the clothes were real and not some form of Thrittene matter. Otherwise, I'd end up on Earth in my birthday suit.

Trebor surged out of the floor, followed by Leinad.

"Neola?" I asked before they could say anything.

"She is sleeping. We tried to remove the memory of the pain she had to go through, but some will remain. She may be fragile for a time."

"I'd like to see her."

"Of course."

A white platform rose from the floor; Neola lay on it. Some sort of sheet—white, of course—covered her up to her neck. I approached. Her features were as before, without a hint of scarring. I took her hand. She opened her eyes, looked vaguely around, focused on me.

"Hey," I said.

"Jack?" Her hand cupped my cheek. "You look younger."

"How are you?"

Her eyes glazed over, as if she were taking stock. "Okay. Hungry."

I smiled. "Me, too."

She sat up, holding the sheet to her breasts, but she kept her hand in mine. She looked around.

"My clothes?"

"Apologies," Trebor said. "We could not anticipate when you would wake up. They should be available to you momentarily."

She nodded at him then at Leinad, who hovered behind me.

"Thank you. I'm in your debt."

Rose tinged the white surrounding us, and sounds became somewhat discordant.

"You've embarrassed them," I explained when she looked at me.

"It's probably because they're used to your rudeness."

"True." I turned toward the two Thrittene. "Thanks, old buddy. Couldn't have survived without you."

"We helped out of friendship, Jack Meter," Trebor said, "even though you doubt it."

I shook my head. "Can't help it, Treb."

"Will you tell us what brought you here in such a state?"

It was the least I could do. Despite their often goofy attitude and sometimes crooked morals, the Thrittene had a good brain—although where it was I had no idea—and might be able to offer us some insights.

While Neola dressed, I told them what I knew so far. They exclaimed about the bounty hunters, lamented the death of the cult followers and mourned the disappearance of Nasus—even though they still couldn't remember her. The air filled with a dirge worthy of the worst bagpipe student. I had to snap them out of it, or we would've lost our hearing.

"We will have to think on this, Jack Meter," Leinad said. "What will you do now?"

"Have a meal, get Neola home."

I'd deliberately misread his question. For perhaps the first time since I'd known him, Trebor didn't protest or demand to know more. Maybe he'd been as disturbed by Neola's cries of pain as I had, or he knew me enough to know that I'd do all in my power to return Nasus to them—if she still lived, that is, which I doubted. Maybe that was the real reason for him not pushing it. He didn't want to know they'd lost another chunk of themselves.

At any rate, he only nodded. "Be well, Jack Meter. You, too, Neola Durwin."

I took her hand and wished myself to her home. In those surroundings, away from the unrelenting white of Thrittene, I saw she was as pale as the snow outside. She had the fragile quality of a thin sheet of ice.

"Sit down. I'll see what I can dig up for a meal."

"I have nothing in the fridge, remember? I was supposed to go grocery shopping."

"You must have a few cans for emergencies."

"Yes, but—"

"Just sit down, let the master work. I'll light a fire first."

Once I got logs going in the fireplace, I investigated her pantry. With a can of salmon, one of green beans, and one of artichokes, some instant rice and a bit of mayo, I managed to make a halfway decent salad. When I came back into the living room with two plates, Neola was drinking from a crystal tumbler.

"Scotch," she said. "Want one?"

"Nectar of the gods. I'll get mine."

"Give me a refill while you're at it."

She kept only the top of the line, so I poured myself a Lagavulin, splashed some Oban in her glass and added a few drops of water to each. When I came back with her drink, she looked up at me, her eyes swimming.

"I don't want to repeat that experience ever again."

I sat down beside her, set the glass on the table, wrapped an arm around her shoulders and pulled her toward me.

"I know."

She sniffled, straightened, picked up her glass and downed the contents.

"I want the bastard who made us go through that. I want him bad, Jack. When I find him, I'll bust his balls."

"So much for fragile," I muttered.

"What?"

When I shrugged, she picked up her plate and dug in. I wasn't sure she tasted anything.

"Someone wanted to kill us both," she said in between bites. "That means we were close."

"Yeah, but close to what?"

"It has to tie in to the cult. I didn't have time to tell you what I found on the second floor of that house." She set her fork on the side of her plate. "A cigar stub."

My gut tightened. "You're thinking of Winston."

"It was his brand."

"He's not the only one who smokes cigars."

"He's the one who has an office in the same house as yours."

I shook my head. "Regardless, I can't see Winston killing those kids. I've known him for ten years, Neola. Maybe you're right and he's more than he lets on, but he's not a mass murderer."

"I'm not saying he is. I'm just pointing out the coincidence."

I was suddenly very angry at her. I picked up the remote and zapped the TV on.

"I wonder what day it is."

Less than twenty-four hours had passed since we'd almost got melted. I wasn't going to try to figure out the time factor. I snapped the TV off.

"Winston's secretary said he's away until after Christmas," I said when I felt I had calmed down enough. "If he's still gone by then, I'll chase him down."

I picked up my plate. We ate in silence. When she was finished, I suggested she get some rest.

"I'm fine. I want to go with you."

"I'm not going anywhere," I lied.

She sighed. "Jack, those bounty hunters let us go. What kind of deal did you make with them?"

"I didn't have much to bargain with."

"You promised to go back there."

"There's nothing you can do."

"You don't know that. They set us down in a way station. I know how to use them."

"To go where?"

"Back here. It'll give us a mode of transport. The OP was fried. We barely made it back."

"Hmmm. I'll come back for you when I know what they want."

She crossed her arms under her breasts. "How would you like it if the roles were reversed?"

They had been, and I hadn't liked it much. I got up, put my jacket back on.

"Let's go."

We were inside the way station in a blink. Our hands had melded, but we were getting used to it by now and just waited until my cells realigned before she pulled away. I opened the door; it was as foggy as before.

"You're a man of your word, Jack Meter." I recognized Bakel's voice.

A misshapen body came out of the fog. It came to just about my waist, with long quills covering it entirely, reminding me of a porcupine. At the end of hairy arms were stubby hands with opposable thumbs. Round black eyes peered through a mass of hair. In place of a mouth was a bright yellow beak.

"Species-wise," Bakel said, "we're far from a match." He looked from me to Neola and back. "You're improved from last time we saw you."

"We?"

Bakel gestured. The small group I'd seen running after us when Mariental had dragged us from one universe to the other moved forward. The other four didn't look like Bakel at all.

"This is Gippy," Bakel said, pointing to a pink, round body with a snouty face. He was completely naked, his belly flopping down to hide his genitals.

"Sibut." The opposite of his companion, Sibut was asparagus-thin and wrapped in furs like a mummy, but appeared to be female from the impressive bumps I took for breasts. It was a wonder she could walk, let alone run. Yellow, slitted irises stood out in her copper-colored face.

Bakel pointed at the last two.

"Tshane." About Neola's height, they had the face of a frog and greenish skin, and their butts were fused together. When one of them bowed toward us, the other leaned back and kicked his legs in the air. They flipped around, repeated the process. I wondered if they twisted like a top when they ran or if they went head-over-heels.

"Quite a collection," I said.

"Pity we couldn't enroll one of your species. We could've reached you in a much shorter time," Bakel said.

"Time is relative." I crossed my arms and leaned on the doorjamb. "You want to tell me why you spared us instead of taking us in for the bounty?"

"Discrepancies. I hate being taken for a fool."

I was starting to like him.

"You don't believe I'm the one you're looking for?"

"Oh, you're the one, all right." He dug through his spines and came out with a small screen with my picture on it. "I was hired to take you, dead or alive, so the universe-bleeding would stop. Except it's been continuing while I had you in visual range."

"While you were chasing us."

"Exactly."

"As I said, time is relative. Screwy even. Maybe I could be in two places at the same time."

"In two universes, maybe. While I had you and your friends in visual range in this universe, spotters I have hired noticed you on another world two parsecs from here. As ubiquitous as you seem to be, time flows only one way in the same universe. It's a physical law."

"I didn't know hunters could use highbrow words like *ubiquitous*."

Sibut stirred. "We were not always such. Bakel is a physicist. Gippy and Tshane were procurators. I am a healer. We are the only ones left of our towns."

"As you see, we have a vested interest in revenge," Bakel said.

"Who hired you?"

"Ah, that is another problematic question. The one who hired us is the same one who helped you escape from us."

Maybe I couldn't be surprised anymore. All I could think was that Mariental had some explaining to do.

CHAPTER FOURTEEN

"THE BASTARD LIED," NEOLA SAID. I COULD HEAR HER TEETH GRIND. "The question is why."

Bakel nodded. "Mariental set up our device so we could open a portal to anywhere we wanted, except to your universe."

That explained why they hadn't dropped by Earth to nab me.

"He wants you to chase me but not catch me. How did you happen to be here when we met him?"

Sibut smiled. "We received an anonymous message that you would be here."

"Mariental?"

"We believe so," Tshane said, "although we have no proof. The device Bakel wears also serves as a communicator."

"Could anyone else know the frequency?"

Bakel's quills shivered. "It's possible, but whoever contacted me had to know that I had such a device. Mariental supposedly hired us in secret."

"He sends you a message then diverts our way station to land here. That USI must've been rigged." Neola planted her hands on her hips and faced Bakel. "We were nearly killed. A few seconds earlier, and there wouldn't have been any pieces for you to pick up. Remember—no body, no bounty."

"The missile was not ours," Bakel said. "Where would we find such weapons? How would we carry them?"

"So Mariental drops the bomb, knowing my telecarb will warn me of danger and get me out of there. He then accuses you of the deed.

That way, he can save us from you and convince us to follow him. The question again: why?"

"We have had no other communication with Mariental since then," Bakel said. "He will not answer our calls."

"Maybe he sees your job as finished."

"I don't think he anticipated us coming back here half-dead," Neola said.

Something Sibut had said earlier came back to me.

"You know that parts of your universe are disappearing?"

"Yes. We are not the only ones, surely?"

"So far, except for one other person I know of, I think you are. This is weird."

"Not to mention confusing," Neola said.

"We've been running after our own tails too long to make sense of anything. We need to put together what we know." I turned to Bakel. "I take it you're not in a hurry to turn me over to Mariental?"

"Not without further data." His beak clicked in a short staccato. "I am a scientist, after all."

"Let's go back to my place," Neola said, "since you don't have an office or an apartment anymore."

"You're funny. Can you use this way station?"

"I don't know. Give me a minute to find out."

Bakel watched her go then turned his beady eyes on me. "While you are trying to determine who the person responsible is, we will continue chasing you."

"And gather some information at the same time," Tshane said.

"We will need a way to communicate," Sibut said.

"If you can give me the frequency of your device, we can use this station as a comm at our end," Neola said as she stepped out. "I can get us home, Jack."

* * *

She wasn't joking. When I opened the door of the station, I stepped into a foot of snow—we'd landed in front of her house at the bottom of her driveway. Snow fell hard and fast. It stung where it landed, and

I realized my skin was still sensitive from the poisonous gases.

"Good thing you own a few acres of land," I said. "Otherwise your neighbors would wonder."

"Move, Meter, I'm freezing my butt here." She stepped around me and hurried to the house, plowing through the snow as if it were water. She shouldn't have mentioned her butt. My eyes followed her spine down to it, a nicely rounded package in the tight jeans. I shook myself like a wet dog and followed her.

I had to admire Neola. She'd gone through hell and still looked as composed as the first day I'd met her, only maybe angrier. She was focused on Mariental now, and had vowed to Bakel and his friends that we'd get to the bottom of it. She seemed to be convinced he was the one responsible for the universe disappearing, letting us flounder through misdirection and misinformation.

I wasn't so sure about her theory, but I'd kept my mouth shut. She needed to let off some steam before she would listen to reason. Someone was definitely yanking our chain and I didn't like it one bit, but my gut told me we hadn't finished uncovering the mystery.

We were thoroughly wet and freezing when we got inside. I lit a blaze in the fireplace while Neola took a shower and changed. I checked the date. We'd been gone five days. It was now the twentieth of December.

She came back, fully dressed, with a pair of jeans and a light blue denim shirt in her hand. "Here, try these. They should fit."

I picked up the clothes, raised an eyebrow. She shrugged, smirked.

"You're lucky I like guys your size."

The shower revived me. I took it hot, blanked out my mind and just enjoyed the bite of heat on my skin. The clothes Neola had given me fit perfectly; they were well used and comfortable, just the way I liked them.

I checked my face in the mirror. It sported a healthy stubble, which I rubbed happily. I felt more like myself already.

When I came out, Neola had unfortunately made coffee. I steeled myself and poured a cup.

"Okay," she said as she sat at the kitchen table, "let's recap."

"You first."

"The IGA sends me a message asking me to pay my boss a visit."

"Your boss the house."

"He's not..." She shook her head. "Never mind. Gweta—my boss—tells me several IGA agents have disappeared, that the universe is shrinking. He wants me to find out who's responsible and to retrieve our agents if possible. I start to set up alarms above planets and I'm about finished with this solar system when one of them is triggered. I pinpoint the source to your city. When I review the log, you appear as the visitor. Having heard of you, I figure you're involved and decide to pay you a visit."

"In the meantime," I said, "my client claims one of his buildings has disappeared. When I get on the site, my telecarb tingles, warning me of danger, although there's no building there and the people around are oblivious." Something tickled my memory. "Wait a minute. The woman at the restaurant. That's when my telecarb started tingling. I wonder if she's still there."

"You think she was involved?"

"I don't know. I'll have to follow it up. Anyway, I've barely started the investigation when you show up. You leave, I follow you."

She picked up the summary. "Another alarm is triggered and I follow it. But instead of landing on the spot where the disappearance occurred, I end up in the hands of Asela and her Kilosans. The problem is those two species don't belong together. My USI is burnt out, I'm taken prisoner."

I nodded. "When I try to follow you, my telecarb balks. After I go back to Thrittene to get it fixed, I arrive at my office to find out someone who means me harm is in it. When he's gone, I follow the USI signature and end up with Saurimo. I find out one of her own has been using the device. She kills him before I can ask him any questions."

"You think it was deliberate?"

"I can't say for sure, but I don't think so. Saurimo started a war against her sister because Asela didn't like her color. This doesn't speak for a rational mind."

"I've been wondering how I got there in the first place."

"Someone intercepted your transfer?"

"We have safeguards against that, but if we're talking about the AGES I'd say it's plausible. Mariental found a way to derail me by sending me to a hostile world and destroying my USI."

"I don't understand why they took you into custody and roughed you up like that. All Saurimo did was talk."

Neola shrugged. "Maybe one sister is more distrustful of other species."

That didn't really fit with Asela's reaction to me, either, but I didn't say anything more.

"You fall asleep in my office, and I begin the search for an apartment. The one I'm supposed to visit has already been taken by this young cultist who talks about the True Savior—someone named Ginir—who'll create a new land and take them there, with the help of Abura, the High Sage who leads this Ottawa chapter."

"After a useless stakeout, we use the coordinates in Karoi's pin to go back to Saurimo and instead end up in the fog world." She blinked slowly. "Mariental intercepted the way station this time."

She took a sip of coffee.

"Meanwhile, we have bounty hunters chasing me but hampered by the fact they can't get to Earth. They are aware that someone's stealing parts of the universe, whereas most others aren't."

"Do you think it's true?"

"What?"

"That you created another universe, and that someone is using the technique in reverse?"

I shook my head. "We'd have to believe that what we went through were parallel universes."

"Universes contained in—what did Mariental call it?—branes, floating along the eleventh dimension. Why did we buy it?"

"I wasn't too crazy about the idea, if you recall."

She smiled. "No, we left in a hurry. But what if it's true?"

"Come on, Neola, there has to be a better explanation than this."

"How do you account for the disappearing buildings, the mixes of races? When I was using the OP…it felt like I was crossing barriers of some sort. Then Mariental had that ISP in his way station, remember? That acts exactly like a Global Positioning System, but for alternate dimensions."

"It could be simply a nice con game." When she raised her eyebrows at my lame explanation, I made a decision I was hoping I wouldn't have to make. I grimaced. "There may be a way to find out if all this has a basis in reality. I'll have to use your phone."

It was barely one o'clock in the afternoon here, so I figured Claire would still be in her office. We'd talked only once since we'd last seen each other in Mueller's bunker. It hadn't been pleasant, but she'd been helpful anyway. Despite the fact she totally despised me, she was honest and compassionate to others. When I played it right, I could always arouse her professional curiosity and get her to give me the information I needed.

"Dr. Foucault here."

"Have you ever heard of the eleventh dimension?" I said without preamble. I knew she'd recognize my voice.

There was silence at the other end of the line, then: "It can't be that you grew a brain in that skull of yours, so you must have a good reason for asking."

"Well?"

"Yeah, I've heard of it."

"It exists?"

"According to M-theory, yes." She related a summary of the theory that jived closely to what Mariental had told us. The M stood for *membrane*. "What is this about?"

I hesitated to tell her then remembered she'd traveled to Thrittene and beyond.

"I've been jumping universes."

"What? Where are you now?"

I laughed. "Colorado. Did you think I could talk to you on the phone from the eleventh dimension?"

"You're as much a jerk as you ever were." She blew a sigh. "What's it like?"

I could hear a tinge of wistfulness in the last question.

"I couldn't tell whether I'd left our universe or not. The worlds I've been to are no more or no less weird than Thrittene or Entomon. My telecarb doesn't work in some of them. One world was full of poisonous gas."

"Too bad you didn't stay there."

"You nearly got your wish." I threw a glance at Neola, and an idea started to grow. "Listen, Claire, there's someone I'd like you to meet."

"I have no desire to see your face again."

"Have you ever heard of the IGA?"

"You're not talking about the grocery store."

"That's what I like about you, Claire. You're sharp. No, it's the Intergalactic Agency. A sort of detective agency for the universe."

Neola raised her eyebrows. I masked the phone transmitter with my hand.

"You just lost some agents, right? I bet IGA's recruiting." I brought the handset back to my ear. "I'm working a case with one of their agents. I bet they'd be interested if you offered your consulting services."

She didn't say anything. I had an idea what she was feeling. She'd be pissed off that I'd be the one to offer something that appealed to her scientific mind but irresistibly attracted to the idea.

"So?"

"I'll think about it."

"Good enough. I'll call you when we're in town."

"Who's your friend?" Neola said.

"I wouldn't exactly call her a friend. Annie knew her well." I sat back on the couch. "The brane theory exists. Nothing's been proven yet, as far as Claire's concerned, but it's gaining a following of quantum physicists."

"So Mariental could've strung us along or told us the truth." She drummed her fingers on the table. "What about this savior person? Where does he fit in this? Why did all those kids die?"

"Maybe the two aren't related."

"I hear a 'but'."

"My gut tells me they are."

She placed her hand over mine. "Winston was there, Jack. I know it."

I withdrew my hand, feeling an uneasiness unrelated to Winston's supposed disappearance. She was getting close to becoming the lady who protests too much. Maybe I was biased and didn't want to think of a friend as a killer. On the other hand, she seemed to bring it up at every opportunity, and I wondered why.

"I want to go back to that restaurant," I said instead, "sniff around if I can. I also want to find Mariental and ask him a couple of pointed questions. But first, I'll call Terry, find out if he knows any more about those cultists."

I got him on the phone.

"Jesus Murphy, Jack, where the frig are you? Do you know how many favors I've had to pull so you won't have a frigging warrant out on you?"

"I called you as soon as I could," I lied. "What's up, Terry?"

"I told you not to leave town."

"Have you been at my office, recently?"

"What office?"

"Exactly."

"I don't follow. You don't have an office."

"Where do I work from then?"

"Ah. . . Okay, where is your office?"

"Gone. That's why you don't remember it."

"I don't follow you."

"No, I'm sure. Do you have anything new on those cultists?"

"I want you to come down to RCMP Headquarters. Bring Ms. Durwin with you."

"It'll take us a while."

He was silent for a moment. "What the frig are you doing in Colorado?"

"Figured out the area code, did you?"

"Get your ass back here. Your prints were all over the damn house."

His words slammed into my chest.

"Impossible."

"Unless there's two of you, those are your prints."

Two of me. Shit.

"I didn't kill those kids."

"Of course, you didn't, you schmuck. But I need to prove it, don't I?"

"We'll be there as soon as we can."

I hung up, stared at Neola.

"There's two of me," I said.

"What?"

"The cultists' house? My prints are all over it. Parallel universes. Put it together."

"So the guy running around calling himself you *is* you."

"A much less pleasant me." I put on my coat, handed Neola hers. "Let's go," I said as I took her hand. "Terry's waiting for us."

"You go. I'll try to find Mariental."

"Right now, babe, you're my alibi. Terry needs your statement."

"Fine, but we go find him after that. I've got a score to settle with that bastard."

"Deal."

"And, Jack? You keep calling me babe, I might just tell Terry I met you two days ago."

CHAPTER FIFTEEN

WE MATERIALIZED IN TERRY'S OFFICE. HE WAS BUSY POKING AROUND ON HIS computer and didn't hear us. I cleared my throat. He jumped.

"Jesus wept, you scared the crap out of me. Where did you come from?"

"Colorado."

"You used that thing to get here? Are you out of your mind? You gotta be cleared from below."

"All you need is a statement from Neola, Terry. We've been together, day and night, for over a month—your time."

"What the hell does that mean?"

"As far as Jack and I are concerned," Neola said, "we've known each other only for a few days."

I grinned. "Time flies when you're in another universe."

Terry shook his head. "I don't know why I bother except that I don't like Aplin any more than you do."

That stopped me from grinning.

"Aplin's on the case?"

"He's investigating the cultists' deaths. He was delighted to find your fingerprints everywhere in the house."

"Who's Aplin?" Neola wanted to know.

I took off my coat and threw it on the back of a chair.

"Sergeant Nate Aplin, explosives expert, all-around asshole. He was convinced I killed Annie. Why is he involved, Terry?"

"There was enough C4 inside to blow up the house and the two beside it."

I threw a glance at Neola. She shook her head.

"Where did you find it?"

Terry grimaced. "Under the pile of bodies. If we'd been two hours later, we'd have been sifting through rubble to find pieces of DNA."

"Someone didn't want these bodies identified."

"Bingo. Aplin thinks that someone is you."

I ignored that. "Did you put names on those kids?"

"On some of them. Whoever killed them raised the temperature in the house so they would decompose faster. Some of them were in pretty bad shape."

He picked up a thick file folder from his IN basket and opened it. There was a stack of pictures, some with a sheet of paper clipped to them.

"Thirteen males were found dead of atropine poisoning. All between eighteen and twenty-two. None with a criminal record, which makes it difficult to identify them. The ones we've matched were from Missing Persons reports."

I walked around his desk and flipped through the pictures. I stopped at the one of the kid I'd done the mock interview with. There was a sheet attached to it.

"How about this one?"

Terry flipped the picture. "Name on the lease was Jason Broadjump. Parents live in Toronto. They filed an MP report on him a few months ago."

"He had heavy scarring on his arms," I said.

"Yeah. I thought the same thing—child abuse. Turns out that Jason was in a serious car accident. Five kids in the car, driver drinking. Jason's the only one who survived, barely. He broke nearly every bone in his body, was in the hospital then rehab for more than two years. During that time he underwent 'enlightenment.' His dad's word."

"He joined a cult."

"The Blue Sun Cult. Someone named Ginir is their True Savior."

"Yeah, it jives with what the kid told me. Someone named Abura was their High Sage. He's the one you're looking for."

Terry nodded, made a notation on the paper.

"Cult members are required to pay a tithe," Neola said, "or hand over some form of compensation for becoming a member. Do you know if Jason did?"

"Broadjump senior' said Jason had a trust fund. He signed the papers handing over all of it two weeks after he joined the cult. He disappeared from Toronto when he got tired of his folks trying to convince him to renege on the deal."

"How much money are we talking about?"

Terry looked at me over his shoulder then at Neola. "Estimate is over eight million."

"Holy shit," Neola murmured.

I went back around the desk and sat down. "And the other kids you've been able to identify?"

"Each handed over property and assets worth two million or more."

"To whom?"

Terry flushed, looked away. "It goes to a foundation. We haven't been able to trace the executives yet."

I had a bad feeling about this. Terry blushed only when he was hiding something embarrassing.

"What's the name of the foundation?"

"That's classified, Jack."

"Don't bullshit me, Terry."

He looked miserable. "The Annie Barnes Temporal Research Foundation."

Neola gasped. I swallowed, stopped breathing for a few seconds.

"Sonofabitch," I finally said. "Looks like I was right."

I glanced at Neola and saw in her eyes that what had just dawned on me had occurred to her—way before it did to me.

Parallel universes. An infinity of worlds moving along the timeline on the same dimension. In one of those universes, Annie might be alive and I might be dead. Or, in another one, she might be alive and living with Claire. Neola's husband might still be farming and she fretting about leaving Minnesota. An infinity of worlds for an infinity of possibilities.

Her chin rose a fraction, as if she defied me to go a round with her for not mentioning it to me as soon as she'd thought of it. The woman had guts—not many people faced me when I felt this dangerous. My heart beat hard against my ribcage; anger, frustration, anticipation and, most of all, confusion churned in my gut. I took a deep breath, pushed the feelings aside for the moment.

"Right about what?" Terry said.

I turned back to him. "I know this is going to be difficult to accept, but I'm convinced there's another me running around. Somewhere, I have a doppelganger who's intent on framing me for his actions by leaving his fingerprints, which are the same as mine, all over."

"Oh. Your ghost is leaving your fingerprints all over the place, trying to implicate you in mass murders." Terry couldn't contain his sneer. I suspected he didn't even try.

"Okay, more of an alter ego."

"Come on, Jack. Be serious." He stared into my face. The cracking of his knuckles was the only sound in the room. He cleared his throat, shook his head in surrender. "Have you seen this double of yours?"

"Not yet, but I intend to. He's far from subtle."

"You think he wants you to catch him?" Neola said.

"Maybe."

"I hate to say this," Terry said, "because it's against my better judgment, but I'll want to know everything you have, from the beginning of your case with Garner. That's when it all started, isn't it? It's either that or I'm going to have to call the Royal Ottawa."

I grinned. "I'm not crazy, Terry. No need to bring in the padded wagon."

"It wouldn't be for you, Jack."

I chuckled. Someone knocked on Terry's door, and it opened

before I could respond.

"Parczek, I need—" Aplin stopped in his tracks when he saw me sitting across Terry's desk. He sported his usual too-tight shirt and arrogant smirk. "Well, well, if it ain't my prime suspect. How'd you get in here without me knowing about it?"

"I have my ways. Miss me, Aplin?"

He moved into the office, slammed the door behind him. "Don't jerk me around, Meter. You're not in a position for it. You come with me quietly, and it'll go in your favor with the judge."

"What am I suspected of?"

"Thirteen murders," he said, eyes shining. "Does that ring a bell?"

"Sure, it does, since I'm the one who found the bodies. Look somewhere else, Aplin, I didn't kill those kids."

"That's for me to determine."

"Come on, Aplin," I said. "Do you really think I'd kill thirteen kids, fail to blow up the house, leave my prints everywhere then call the cops so they could arrest me?"

He threw a murderous glance at Terry. "You're twisted and arrogant enough to do just that."

Terry jumped in before I could sneak in another dig.

"Aplin, this is Ms. Neola Durwin. I was just about to take her statement. She's given Jack an alibi."

Neola inclined her head.

"Jack and I are working on the same case. We've been together," she smiled, placed a hand on mine, "night and day for a month."

Aplin's eyes narrowed. "Where are you from, Ms. Durwin?"

"Colorado. We've been using my house there as our home base. We came back here a week ago to check out this kid Jack had met when he was looking for an apartment—you're aware his apartment was destroyed?—and he realized this young man had joined a cult. Unfortunately, we arrived too late. As soon as we found the bodies, we called the police."

Nice twisting of the facts, I thought. Nothing better than to stick as close as possible to the truth when you were lying.

Aplin's breath was shaky. "That sounds reasonable, I'll say. How do you explain, then, that his prints were all over the damn house?"

"I know for a fact Jack didn't walk through the house. He went directly downstairs and found the bodies. He had no occasion to leave his prints anywhere or to commit these crimes."

Aplin ignored her. "When did you establish that foundation in Dr. Barnes's name?"

"I didn't. I just learned about it now."

"We'll see about that." He turned to Terry. "As a courtesy, I'll let you take their statements, but I want to read them as soon as you're through." He strode to the door. "You should also be aware, Parczek, that people are beginning to wonder why you're doing everything to protect a suspect. Some say you're emotionally involved and can't do your job properly." He opened the door. "I'm not finished with you, Meter," he said before he slammed it behind him.

"He's really got a hard-on for you, hasn't he," Neola said with a smirk.

I ignored her, and Terry's grin.

"We'll give you our statements, then we'll tell you the rest if you still want to know."

Terry took some forms out of his desk drawer.

"Listen, Terry," I said, "I'm a big boy. I can handle Aplin."

"Don't worry about me, Jack. Aplin and I understand each other. He's a good cop. It's too bad he's so anal about you." He handed us each a sheet. "Fill those in. I don't want you to disappear again, y' hear me? I want you to stay available."

"All I can promise is that we'll stay in town as much as we can."

"Where?"

What the heck, I thought. I wasn't doing anything with my money anyway. "The Chateau Laurier. I'll let you know which room as soon as I book one."

"If you can get one. It's close to Christmas, remember."

I swore under my breath. "I'll let you know."

Terry turned the telephone toward me.

"You're not leaving here until I know where you'll be staying. If you can't get a room there, try the Arc."

"A suite, Jack," Neola said. "We don't want to stumble over each other."

As luck would have it, the Chateau had one suite left. I booked it right away then settled back to go over our statements and the rest of the story so Terry could find a way to keep us out of Aplin's way for a little while.

Three hours later, my stomach lining nearly dissolved from countless cups of coffee, I wrapped up the story and my conclusions. Terry's eyes were glazed.

"Hello?" I called, when I'd stopped talking for half a minute and he still hadn't moved. "Anybody home?"

He shook himself, focused on me once again. "Your double is taunting you."

"I'd say that's more than likely. The fingerprints in the house are way too obvious. I don't think even Aplin would fall for something that obvious."

"He likes to keep his options open."

"Sure. And I'm interested in buying a bridge."

"You found something else in that house," Neola said to Terry.

Terry threw her a sharp glance. "How would you know that?"

"Just a wild guess."

"What else didn't you tell me, Neola?"

She raised her eyebrows at the tone of my voice. It usually made people blanch, but it didn't appear to faze her.

"I didn't think it was relevant at the time."

"Wait a minute," Terry said. "You went upstairs, didn't you?"

"Guilty. I didn't touch anything, I swear. You'll be able to prove that with the fingerprints you took."

"So, what else was there?" I demanded.

"What do you mean, what else?" Terry demanded.

"I mean apart from the bodies," I lied, thinking of the cigar stub she said she'd found. "Terry?"

"We found a leather jacket. Exactly the same as the one hooked on the chair behind you. It had a receipt in the pocket for the Moulin de Provence and your prints on it."

Despite myself, I was shocked. I tried to laugh it off.

"I hope it was for an espresso."

"It's not funny, Jack."

"What do you want me to say, Terry? It's overkill. So much so it's ludicrous. Why didn't he plant a big fluorescent arrow over the house with 'Jack Meter was here' on it?"

"He wants to slow you down, distract you," Neola suggested.

"Well, it's working."

"That guy, Mariental," Terry said, "he must know there's two of you."

I nodded. "If they're trying to use me as a straw man, they wouldn't have wanted me to discover I had a double running around. That's why he tried to detain me or convince me to give up the case and stay home."

I frowned. It didn't explain why he'd set the bounty hunters after me.

"Both of you are real, Jack," Neola said in a quiet voice.

"I can just see it," Terry said in a fake dramatic voice. "The two of you, side-by-side, and me having to choose which one of you is the bad guy."

"Please. This is enough of a farce as it is. You don't have to make it sound like a hackneyed B movie." I got up. "I'm wiped. I'm going to the hotel. I don't care what happens in the universe this afternoon; I'm taking some time off."

Neola got up, rolled her shoulders.

"Good idea." She grinned. "We'll use it to do some Christmas shopping."

Chapter Sixteen

I stood in front of Mrs. Tiggy Winkles, buffeted from all sides by hysterical shoppers.

"This is not my idea of fun," I said to Neola.

"You said you wanted to relax."

I stared at her. "And you thought shopping would do the trick?"

"You're the one who decided to take an afternoon off. I wanted to go after Mariental."

"Soaking in some opera, having a beer—that's what I call relaxing, not battling last-minute hordes of desperate consumers."

"Oh, stop grumbling. The faster we find presents, the faster it'll be over. How old are the kids?"

"Kids?"

"Terry's kids. You didn't find out, did you?"

"When did I have time?" I'd barely even seen Terry's kids. Even on football nights, they'd been in bed or playing in the basement. Since kids weren't my thing, I never gave them much of a thought.

"Terry must have talked about them, showed you pictures."

"Not that I recall. I know he had three the last time I was there. I think. Betty was talking about another one."

"Well, you're the great detective," she said, pointing to a public phone. "Find out."

I grimaced. I knew Terry was out of the office, so I'd have to speak with Betty. I liked her, but she liked to talk—a lot. She was a cop's wife and knew how to be discreet when she needed to, so safe topics like her kids would bring on the flood. I walked to the phone booth with as much enthusiasm as a kid about to eat Brussels sprouts.

Fifteen minutes later, my ear red from the receiver, I hung up on Betty's bubbly and halfhearted protests that I shouldn't bring her kids presents for Christmas in between her persistent invitations for dinner—with my "new friend," of course. Damn Terry's big mouth.

"Well?"

"They've got three—two girls, one boy, twelve, eight and ten respectively."

"You take the girls."

"Why?"

"Because boys are easy to buy for."

"You're a girl."

Neola planted her fists on her hips. "Took you that long to notice, huh?"

"I mean," I continued with a sigh, "you should know what girls like. You are one."

"And you're a man. You should know, too."

"I know what women like. That's different."

"No, it isn't. Just scale it down in price or size, and you've got it."

In the end, I took the easy way. Under Neola's despising look, I bought each of the girls a gift certificate for a CD. I would've bought them Cecilia Bartoli's interpretation of Gluck's little known works, but I doubted they went for opera. I couldn't resist, though, and bought the CD for myself, even if it would be a while before I could listen to it.

I grinned. "My shopping's done. How about you?"

"Oh, no, you don't. Since you're so goddamn clever, you can buy Terry's wife a Christmas gift while I find something for his son." She turned on her heel. "An hour, back here," she called over her shoulder.

She left me with my mouth open, a dying protest in my throat.

Someone bumped into me. "Excuse me," he mumbled. Automatically, I checked my wallet. It was still there but, even through the mind-numbing cacophony of noise, the overheated stores and the tinny holiday music, I noticed my telecarb tingled.

I turned, trying to remember anything about the guy. Shorter than me by a head, I thought, since his shoulder had knocked me mid-upper arm. Winter coat, dark blue, wool or cashmere—there hadn't been that swish I associated with parka material.

Slowly, methodically, I scanned the crowd. There. I began following him, pushing against the throng. I couldn't be certain the danger my telecarb had warned me about was directed specifically at me—there were a lot of crazies who cracked during the holidays. I had visions of bullets flying and people screaming. Not a good way to start festivities.

On the other hand, maybe the guy had it in only for me, which made it mighty coincidental he'd found me in the middle of Rideau Centre.

His fast gait led him toward the escalator and the food court, navy blue coat flapping around his ankles. It was too long, as if he'd borrowed it from a much taller man. He didn't look behind him once, but based on the way he suddenly slowed, as if to make sure I'd keep up with him, I had the feeling he knew I was following.

My telecarb wasn't happy with me. It kept tingling, warning me that what I was doing wasn't very smart. I was halfway down the escalator, and he had just reached the bottom, when he shoved his hand in his pocket. Simultaneously, he grabbed a young girl by the neck, whipped out a gun and pressed it to her temple.

"Move away," he yelled. "Just fucking move away!"

People around him screamed and scattered. He wheeled about to face me and backed up against a column as the escalator expelled me.

I raised my hands, palms forward, and stopped. The girl, maybe fifteen, whimpered.

"Easy, now. You don't need to hurt her. We can talk."

"She's my insurance. You move, she dies."

He didn't have the eyes of a desperate man. They were hard, cold, as if killing was something he did often and well.

"I have only a few seconds," he said, "before the cops are here. I came to deliver a message."

"You could've chosen a less dramatic way."

"Why? This is fun." He didn't smile. "Stay close to home, Jack Meter, and mind your own business."

"Looks like you're involved in my business."

He jammed the gun against the girl's temple. She began to cry. "Don't play dumb, or she fucking dies."

"Who sent you?"

"You don't need to know that. Just comply."

"And if I don't?"

This time, he smiled.

"You don't have that many friends. I'm sure you'd like to keep them."

He let go of the girl. Too late, I saw he had a USI hanging around his neck—one touch, and he was gone. I was fast enough to catch the girl as she fainted.

"That's always a stupid question to ask," I heard Neola say behind me. She was at the top of the escalator.

"How long have you been there?" I pushed some unfinished customer's meal off a table and laid the girl down on it.

"Just got here." She scampered down the stairs. "The cops are behind me. I vote we get out of here."

* * *

The suite at the Chateau Laurier was well appointed. I opened the mini-fridge, took out a bottle of Chivas and splashed some in a glass tumbler. I walked to the window and looked out. Ironically, it gave on the construction grounds of my future condo. As long as I brought Garner's building back, which, at this point, I had absolutely no idea how to do.

I'd spent a couple of hours with the cops and thought I deserved the drink. I'd decided I wouldn't disappear this time. There were witnesses, people close enough to hear and see what had happened. I played dumb, claiming I had no idea what the guy wanted. The fact that the girl was unharmed had played in my favor. She'd come to, already sobbing, claiming I'd saved her from a maniac. I was a hero.

"You're still angry with me," Neola said. I knew she wasn't talking about her suggestion we leave the unconscious girl alone but of the realization I'd had in Terry's office.

"Damn right."

Shopping had acted as a buffer, although if I told myself the truth, I was mainly pissed off at myself. All along it seemed I'd been a few minutes behind, never able to catch up. In part, it might've been because I wasn't used to having a partner—and one who I found attractive in more than one way. That, too, had hampered my clear thinking. I was torn between jumping her bones and feeling guilty about it because of Annie. Annie, who might be alive in one of these parallel universes.

"You could spend a lifetime looking for her," Neola said, as if she'd read my mind.

"Maybe I'd be lucky and find her right away."

"But she wouldn't be the same."

I gulped the rest of the drink, cracked open another mini-bottle.

"No. She wouldn't."

And that's what hurt even more, the fact that, even if I found her and we resumed a life together in another universe, she still wouldn't be the one I loved. After a while, the differences would become glaring. I wouldn't be able to help but compare. I'd lose her again. Twice was enough.

I poured more scotch.

"You're also vexed because I didn't tell you about the jacket."

"Vexed. That's a good word. You choose very carefully what you say to me, Neola."

"On some topics, yes. I swear to you I didn't make the connection between the jacket and a double until you started talking about doubles."

"You made the connection with the cigar. What happened to it, by the way?"

She hesitated. "I took it. I know Winston's your friend. I was about to mention the jacket when Terry called." For the first time since I'd met her, she looked uncertain. She rubbed her hands together in a twisting motion. "I can leave, if you want. We can split up, try to find things out separately. I'd appreciate it if you'd let me know if you find anything."

I poured a bit of bottled water in my scotch. "You seem to assume I won't give up the case."

She looked startled. "Of course. I thought..."

"You heard the guy. It's not worth putting my friends in harm's way while I chase shadows."

"Even if one of those shadows is your double?"

I shrugged. "It's only a meager theory. These parallel universes may be pure bullshit. A cosmic red herring."

"Okay then. I'll wrap the present I bought then I'll go. You can take it to Terry's son."

"I'll do that." I turned back to the window, hiding a grin. I bet to myself it would take her about five minutes to get back into the room. I lost. It took her two.

"You bastard, you're trying to get rid of me."

"Whatever gave you that idea?"

"I don't believe for one second you'll give up the case. That's not your style."

"A guy can change."

"Not you." She narrowed her eyes. "Wait a minute. You're not trying to get rid of me. You're trying to rile me."

I chuckled. "It worked, didn't it? You deserved it."

"That was low and childish."

"It felt great. Come on, let's go eat."

The phone rang. I groaned. I knew who that was.

"I take it that stunt in the Rideau Centre was you," Terry said. "I'm glad you didn't leave the scene of the crime this time."

"There wasn't much of a crime."

"There could've been. What did he want?"

"To warn me off the case."

"Did you know him?"

"No. He's a pro, though."

"Hiring a pro's expensive."

"Someone's just inherited millions."

"Yeah," Terry said. His voice was suddenly more cheerful. "You know, whoever said that money doesn't smell was wrong. It always leaves a trace."

"I'll leave you that lead." I paused. "You might want to send your family to your parents, very quiet-like."

"He'll go for my family?"

"Whomever I know."

Terry stayed silent at the other end of the line. Just as Neola had figured, he knew I wouldn't stay home knitting booties.

"There's no way Betty will want to leave the house. I'll take care of security."

"Could you also warn Claire? It'll go easier if it comes from you."

"Sure. I'll also tell the Super Bowl crowd, just in case. Call your sister."

"I will."

Lou, as usual, was cranky and not altogether happy to hear from me. She became downright hostile when I told her that she might want to visit warmer climes over Christmas. Ten minutes into the conversation, we were snarling at each other.

Neola grabbed the receiver. "Give me that," she hissed.

She took over, calmed Lou, explained everything in a reasonable tone.

"She'll go to Martinique," she said, hanging up. "She has friends staying on a small island near there for the holidays. That means her name won't appear in some hotel database."

"Thanks. I owe you one."

"More than one, pal. Your sister took a lot of convincing."

"She's stubborn as a mule."

"Must be in the genes." She stretched her neck, pulling her head toward each shoulder. "What do you say we eat in? I'm bushed."

"You go ahead. There's a restaurant I want to try out."

"What kind of food?"

"Run-of-the-mill. Nothing special."

She was looking down at my wrist. I realized I'd been rubbing my telecarb. I stopped.

"Ah, that restaurant," she said. "I'll join you."

It took nearly half an hour to get from Wellington Street to Richmond Road—all the shoppers had decided to go home at the same time. The taxi left us outside the restaurant, called the Richmond Grill. It looked like a normal family dining place, with nondescript-colored fabric on the seats of the booths installed near the two bay windows, which were framed by dusty drapes. A few dead flies decorated the windowsill, along with plastic potted ivy. A string of colored lights, flashing weakly on and off, ran around the frame of the door. Someone had painted a wreath on the glass. The ornaments looked like sick cherries.

"After you," I said to Neola.

She threw me a sardonic glance and opened the door. The same hostess as the first time I'd set foot there came to greet us. My telecarb tingled again. She didn't seem to recognize me.

"Do you have reservations, sir?"

I scanned the restaurant. It was nearly empty, and it was dinnertime. "No, but I guess that won't be a problem."

She flushed. "This way, please."

We followed her to the back of the room, where the tables were illuminated only with a candle in a red glass holder. It made me think of a funeral parlor, with the wall paneled in dark tongue-in-groove and a few dusty dried flower arrangements hanging at various intervals above the tables. The hostess dumped the menus on our table and promptly departed.

"You want to switch tables?" I said. "We may not be able to see our food."

Neola sniffed and sat down. "That might be a blessing."

We were no sooner settled than a broad, dark shape loomed over us.

"It's about time you got here, Jack. What held you up?"

CHAPTER SEVENTEEN

I LEANED BACK IN MY SEAT AND LOOKED UP. WINSTON STOOD THERE, AN UNLIT cigar clamped in his mouth, a grin on his face. My telecarb tingled more strongly.

"Pete," I said, trying to keep my voice neutral.

I threw a glance a Neola. The flame from the candle danced on her face. Her eyes were hard, her jaw set.

"Mind if I sit down?"

"Sure, go ahead. Neola, why don't you move to this side with me? Pete needs the space."

She frowned slightly, too quickly for him to see it. Wordlessly, she came around the table and sat by me. Winston thanked her and took her place.

"I thought you were on vacation," I said.

"I still am. Officially."

"Where is Charlotte, by the way?"

"Oh, I imagine she went home for the holidays. I told her she didn't need to keep the office open."

"That's good, because the office is probably a puddle of melted bricks, by now."

"Damn. They got to you, did they?"

"Who are 'they?'" Neola said.

"I'm not authorized to tell you."

"That sounds official, all right," I said. "What are you, apart from being a lawyer?"

"I'm an AGES administrator, assigned to Earth. Efforts are being coordinated. They yanked me out of the job so I could tell you to let us deal with this, Jack. You, too, Ms. Durwin." He placed what looked like a die on the table in front of her. "I have a communication cube from Gweta that relieves you from this investigation."

"You know me, Pete," I said. "It'll take more than that to make me lay off the case. I hadn't even heard of the AGES before I met Mariental."

"The agency is legitimate," Neola said, picking up the cube.

"Meaning I'm not?" Winston said. He shrugged. "I can show you a badge, but it'll mean squat. All I can say is this case is big. Too big for two people. We have the personnel; you'll just flounder. By the way, stay away from Mariental. We're dealing with him."

My telecarb hadn't stopped tingling. If anything, it was more intense, sending me little electric shocks. I decided it was time I listened to it if I didn't want to be forced to leave without Neola. I placed a hand on her arm.

"You know, I'm not real crazy about this place. Why don't we go somewhere else for a bite to eat then you can try to convince us to stay out of your way."

"Sorry, Jack, but I don't have the time. I need to get back."

"Come on, we haven't had a meal together in a long time."

Winston looked annoyed. "I've already eaten."

"You can watch us then. We need to talk about this."

"There's nothing to talk about. You lay off the case or we'll have to neutralize you. How would you like to spend Christmas on Alpha Taurus Four?"

"Pete, you know me better than that."

Winston grinned, but the smile didn't reach his eyes.

"I do. That's why I'll have to go to plan B." He slipped his hand into his inside breast pocket.

I pushed Neola off the seat, threw myself after her, yelling "Duck!" at the same time. The seat above me exploded. On all fours, Neola bolted behind a half wall that separated two sets of tables. I plunged after her.

"Go, go, go," I yelled. The top of the wall burst into splinters.

"Your telecarb," Neola whispered back.

"I tried. It's not working. We have to get outside." More of the wall flew apart. "Start running."

Still crouching, we started weaving around tables. I felt something hot slice across my back then sharp pain. I blocked it out and kept going. I raised my head and saw the hostess in front of us, feet planted solidly, hands holding a wicked-looking gun. I also saw we were close enough to the bay window.

"Aw, shit," I said.

In a split second, I made my decision. I grabbed Neola by the waist and threw myself at the window. I heard the crash of the glass at the same time as I wished us in our hotel room.

* * *

I woke up with a splitting headache. I was lying facedown on a bed; my back was also killing me. I wasn't sure where I was, but by the feel of the bedspread, I figured we'd made it back to the hotel.

I groaned and opened my eyes, pushed myself up on one elbow. There was now a whole city crew with jackhammers digging holes in my skull. I sat up and perched on the edge of the bed. Neola appeared in the door, holding a bunched towel.

"Here, I'll put this on your head. It'll help."

Gingerly, she applied the towel, which crackled from the ice wrapped inside. It pressed on a particularly painful bump on top of my head.

"Ouch."

"If I hadn't already known you had a hard head, I'd believe it now."

"How long have I been out?"

"About thirty minutes. You have a nasty gash on your back. And that knot on your head's pretty big. You might have a concussion. You want to go to the hospital?"

"I'll be fine." I got up and dizzily made my way to the three-way mirror in the bathroom. A ten-centimeter-long by two-centimeter-wide cut slashed upward beside my spine, the edges red and secreting plasma. Pain flared as if I'd been branded.

"I cleaned it as well as I could, but I don't have anything for burns. You should go to the emergency."

"I don't have the energy to make up a story about this. Besides, this sucker would have time to heal before I see someone in the ER. I'll call the concierge to get me some antibiotic cream. That'll do."

"I'll do it." She phoned from the bedroom, asking them to buy painkillers, too, for which I was profoundly grateful. "They say twenty minutes," she said as she depressed the switch. "I'll order us some food, too."

Slowly, I walked to the living room and sat on the ottoman. My shirt was on the couch. It looked in worse shape than I was.

"I'm going to have to buy another shirt," I said to her as she came back into the room.

She held up my leather jacket, which was intact on the outside. When she turned it around, the lining had split in two, in exactly the same spot as the gash I had on my back.

"It looks like that beam snuck right under your jacket. It's still wearable, with a bit of stitching." She checked her watch. "The stores are open late. I'll go and buy you a couple of shirts after we've eaten." She sat on the couch, our knees touching. Slowly, she raised her hands to my face, leaned forward and kissed me on the mouth. "You did good, Jack," she said with a slight smile. She lowered her hands.

"Are you hurt anywhere?"

"A few scratches. Our winter clothes protected us. When you broke the glass the telecarb brought us here."

"Those are wicked weapons. I hope they're not importing them into this universe."

"How did you know Winston was going to shoot us?"

"That wasn't Winston."

"What? He's the guy I met—" She stopped in mid-sentence to chuckle. "You're pushing this alter ego thing a bit too far, Jack."

"That wasn't Winston, I tell you."

"Okay. How do you know?"

"Winston wouldn't try to make me dead."

"Unless my theory about him holds."

"Here's something else then. My telecarb went into high alert as soon as that Winston got close. It made me suspicious. I was more certain of it when he told me that Charlie—who I never call Charlotte—had gone to see her family for Christmas. She doesn't have any family. She likes to work as late as possible on the twenty-fourth then volunteers her time at a shelter. The real Winston would've known that.

"The clincher, though, is when I called him Pete and he didn't say anything. Winston hates being called Pete. In fact, he even dislikes Peter. Everybody calls him Winston."

"I can see," she said in a dry tone, "based on this solid evidence, that this man definitely wasn't who he said he was."

"If you don't trust my reasoning at least trust my telecarb. It's programmed to protect me from harm."

"When it works." A knock sounded at the door. She rubbed her stomach. "I hope it's the food."

After checking through the peephole, she opened the door. It was our dinner, along with my medication. There's nothing like staying at a high-class hotel to get efficient service.

"You wanted Winston out of the restaurant," Neola said, twirling pasta.

"That place was making me nervous. The telecarb was going nuts, and I was afraid it would whip me out without you."

She smiled at me, doe-eyed. "But the telecarb doesn't work in the restaurant. You wouldn't have been able to leave anyway."

"I couldn't use it when I was in other universes, either." I cut a piece of steak and chewed. It gave me some time to think. "What if someone found a way to create a universe within a universe?"

"What for?"

I shrugged then winced when it pulled at the cut in my back.

"That's the rub." I chewed another piece. "Maybe it's a portal."

"The whole restaurant?"

I poured her some red wine. "Maybe not, but if there's a portal there, we might detect some kind of electromagnetic interference."

"Electromagnetic interference."

"Okay, I'm no scientist, but I know something's important enough in that restaurant for these guys to want to kill us." I forked mashed potatoes. They were seasoned with the perfect amount of garlic. "What do you say to a little B&E tonight?"

Neola picked up her glass and batted her eyelashes. "You're such a sweet talker."

*　　　*　　　*

The weather had turned warmer and a thin mist fell, making our surroundings glisten under the street lamps. Christmas lights lined Richmond Road. A couple of blocks down, a huge tree had been decked out in red and purple bulbs and a cutout of Santa in his sleigh blinked on the roof of a house. As was usual in Ottawa after midnight, the city looked deserted, as if all inhabitants vanished with the witching hour and only reappeared with the sunrise. The restaurant was dark. Someone had boarded up the bay window I'd flown through.

"I wonder if they called the cops," I said.

"I doubt it. I didn't hear anything on the news, at any rate."

"Let's try the back."

We took the long way around through the bank parking lot, into a narrow lane at the back of the buildings. The restaurant wasn't as deep as the bank, presumably to accommodate garbage containers. The recess in the wall provided us with cover from curious onlookers.

A feeble light on a post illuminated a back door made of metal, without a handle. "It opens from the inside only," I whispered.

"Damn," Neola said behind me.

I searched along the wall for a window, but all I could see was brick. The building had no second floor, and a flat roof.

"There," Neola said, pointing at the ground. She'd noticed a narrow window well dug into the pavement. I crouched down. The window, grimy with dust, wasn't barred. No wonder—you'd have to be a snake to get in that way. The well was less than twenty centimeters wide.

"Can you get it open?"

"Sure, but it's useless."

"No, it's not."

I heard the slide of a zipper and turned my head. "What are you doing?"

"Getting out of this parka. Otherwise, I won't fit through."

"You won't fit anyway."

She grinned. "Want to bet? Open the window, Jack."

I extended a leg into the well and kicked the glass in. The tinkle as it fell was loud in the quiet.

"Subtle."

"I want to make sure it's not wired or that someone's not there to greet you on the other side."

We waited for a minute. I couldn't see any movement inside, and no sound of sirens approaching broke the silence. With my gloved hand I felt for the latch and undid it.

"It's all yours."

Neola shed her parka on the ground in front of the window, which she pushed open with her feet then wriggled and bent backward so that she could slip into the space.

"What are you," I muttered before she disappeared completely, "hinged both ways?"

"Yoga. I'll meet you at the back door."

I picked up her coat and waited impatiently. Neither of us had mentioned the very real possibility that someone would be waiting for us in the restaurant and that she'd have to fight her way out by herself, since I couldn't use my telecarb to get in there. Come to think of it, it had been fairly useless up to now.

There was a scratching sound, and the door opened. I released a breath I hadn't realized I was holding.

"The stairs to the cellar are right beside this door," she said. "Handy."

"What took you so long then?"

She ignored my comment and grabbed her parka. She was shivering.

I closed the door and turned on the flashlight she'd bought along with my new shirts. We were in the kitchen. Pots and pans were tarnished and dull, a layer of dust covered the counters. There hadn't been any cooking done here in a long while.

"It's a good thing we didn't order a meal."

Neola shone her own light on the floor. It was also dusty. "No footprints."

"Yeah, unless they can float. Come on."

I tread lightly through the kitchen. My telecarb had started tingling the moment I'd stepped inside, but I ignored it.

Round windows had been cut out in the door leading to the dining room. I peeked through. Everything was dark and empty. I turned the light off and pushed the door open.

"There should be enough light from the street to see," I whispered.

No one had picked up the mess Winston had made while shooting at us. Pieces of wood crunched under our feet.

"There's nothing here," Neola said. "Maybe they closed it off."

"No, it's still live. My telecarb's signaling. We haven't checked out the bathrooms."

We followed the sign down a small hallway. The usual plaques indicating the men's and women's were stuck on the doors at the left. On the right, one door was marked "Staff Only."

"Let's try that one first," I said, pointing at the staff one.

Gingerly, I turned the handle and opened the door. It looked exactly like a bathroom, with the toilet, the sink and the trash can. There was an additional item, though—on the opposite wall, a glowing sliver of light, the width of my shoulders. I took Neola's hand.

"What do you say we take a trip?"

"Lead on, McDuff."

I stepped through, pulling her after me. There was a sense of disorientation; then we were there. It was a place we'd been before.

We stood right in front of Mariental's way station.

CHAPTER EIGHTEEN

I TURNED AROUND TO SEE THE PORTAL CLOSE UP ON US.

"We'll need to get inside the station when we want to get out of here," I said inanely, because I was totally confused. This was the last place I expected to end up.

"I told you Mariental is in on the whole thing."

"Looks like it." There was something not adding up, and I didn't know what it was. My skin itched. "We wanted to talk to him so let's see if he's in."

I banged on the door. No answer.

"We could wait here a long time."

"I can be patient when I want."

"Let me try the keypad. I watched him put in the code and I have an eidetic memory." She tapped on the keys, muttering all the time. After the third try, the door snicked open. She grinned at me, success making her eyes glow. "Open sesame," she said.

Too easy. Feeling even more uncomfortable about this whole situation, I entered the station. It smelled musty, as if it hadn't been used for days. I hit the light pad. A thin layer of dust covered the table and the screens on the wall. Lights on several panels blinked or were on, so the station appeared to be still functioning.

Neola made a beeline to the panel she'd called an IPS and started tapping keys again.

"I just want to know if this is still working," she said.

I sat down on one of the chairs and watched her.

It was time I started being smart about this case. Since the beginning, I'd been running around in ever-widening circles, moving nonstop, which gave me the illusion I was accomplishing something. I had a bunch of facts that didn't mesh, a series of players who popped in an out like shadow puppets, and here I was, back in a supposedly alternate universe. It was as if some invisible hand had pushed me into a direction I didn't want to go. I'd let myself be led by events, and it wasn't my style. Sure, I relied on guts and instincts, but eventually, the facts had to make sense. Here, they just didn't add up.

There was one major reason I hadn't been at my best: Neola.

I studied her as she fiddled with the equipment. She'd removed her parka. Her black jeans and black long-sleeved turtleneck showed off her body to advantage. I started salivating and realized I was getting off-track again. For the first time since I'd met her, the alarm bells I heard in my head weren't clanging guilt.

I wasn't usually that trusting when someone arrived on my doorstep with a story. Why had hers sounded so plausible? Had it been because she had the technology? She'd worn something slick and tight, stayed just long enough for me to pay attention. Had she counted on me following her?

Tonight she'd taken quite a long time to open the door to the restaurant. Was she only getting her bearings or did she take the time to reset the portal to bring us here, so I could be convinced of Mariental's guilt? I now found it quite coincidental the portal was still open when we arrived. That would've meant someone had gone through seconds before us. If that was the case, where were they?

I replayed the scene with "Winston" in the restaurant. Just before I plunged through the window, Neola had been face-to-face with the hostess. Why hadn't the woman fired at her? She'd had a clear line of sight, but she'd waited. For Neola to move aside, maybe?

I rubbed the palm of my hand on the jeans I wore, which Neola had given me. They were well-worn and fit perfectly.

As if they were mine.

I wondered if paranoia could be caught, like a virus. I was pulling at straws, putting facts together that were as baseless as the others I played with. The problem was, they felt right. Guts and instincts. Had to listen to them.

But Neola had almost died of acid poisoning along with me. Would she have risked her life that way? Maybe, for the right inducements. And she hadn't died. She had known the Thrittene could fix us.

Before I confronted her, however, I'd have to be sure of my facts. If she was involved in this, I didn't want her to disappear on me. One thing was sure, though. Even if she wasn't aware of it, our partnership had just dissolved, until further notice.

She was getting agitated.

"This thing doesn't work. He's taken a component out of it. We could be here forever, Jack. We don't have the luxury of waiting any longer. Let's go back to the hotel. We can talk to Terry, dig around, see what we can find out about the cult. It could lead us to Mariental through another route."

"You think Mariental is Ginir?"

"Makes sense, doesn't it?"

"Who's Abura then?"

She shrugged. "You'll get mad if I tell you."

We were back to Winston.

"You're right, let's not go there."

"I promise I'll keep an open mind, okay?" She took my hand, threw me a glance through lowered lashes. "Besides," she added with a smile, "you don't want to miss Christmas dinner at Terry's, do you?"

There she was again, trying to pull me in a different direction. Now that I was looking for it, I saw it perfectly. She was playing into my hands, though, because there were a few things I wanted to check out without her.

"You're right. We could be here a while. Let's go back to the hotel, see how much time we've lost then go from there."

The telecarb worked like a charm. It was still night outside. Neola turned on the TV—we'd lost twenty-four hours.

"I'm going to bed," I said. "My back is killing me."

"You want me to look at it?"

I shook my head. "I'll just crash. You can have a peek in the morning, okay?"

We said our goodnights, and I closed the door to my bedroom, locked it. I was tired, but I had no intention of sleeping. I had a small trip to make first.

I wished myself on Thrittene. As soon as I set foot on it, Trebor came out of the wall.

"Jack Meter, this is a surprise."

"I need to speak with Leinad."

Trebor split in two.

"Here I am, Jack Meter," Leinad said.

"I have a portal I'd like you to help me with."

The news delighted both of them.

"Where?"

"In a restaurant on Earth."

"Fascinating," Leinad said. "Who installed it there? What is it made of?"

"I have no idea. If I did, I wouldn't be here. I want to know where it leads."

"Generally, a portal can be programmed to lead anywhere."

"But what if it's used to go to one specific place most of the time?"

"You believe this portal might lead you to the one stealing pieces of universe? How did you find this portal?"

"It was opened when I found it."

"Leaving a portal open is very dangerous."

"That's why I think someone knew I'd find it almost immediately. The thing is, it didn't lead to the right place."

"Someone reprogrammed it." At my nod, Leinad frowned. "That complicates matters. We would need to monitor the portal and determine the authorization code as well as the coordinates while someone is coming in or going out."

"Can't you just look at past readings?"

"I doubt it. On any high-quality portal, the system deletes previous entries so it can't be used without authorization."

"Well, can you do it?"

"I surmise that you would not wish these beings to know we are obtaining this information."

"You catch on fast, Leinad."

"An exciting project," he said, changing from white to purplish-red. Sounds around us rose in volume and became more strident. Fortunately, with the modifications they'd done to my body, they didn't shatter my eardrums.

"I'm in a rush," I said.

Leinad returned to his calmer self.

"You always are, Jack Meter. You are fortunate that I have been experimenting with alternate matter, which means that I can build you what you need. You will have to place it near the portal. The unit will have a small dampening field that will prevent detection. It will not become active until someone comes through the portal."

"There's just one problem. I can't get in. My telecarb doesn't work in that place."

The room turned green, which I knew meant worry.

"Guys," I said, "you know I can take care of myself."

Trebor placed his hand over the telecarb. "You are injured."

"I'm fine."

Trebor shook his head. He forgot to have his eyes follow the rest of him, so they floated alone in mid-air for a split second before they re-attached to his body.

"I will never understand why your species enjoys taking risks injurious to their health."

"You didn't complain when I was trying to save your ass."

"Can you leave the premises, once you are there?" Leinad said.

"Yeah, no problem."

"We are stronger than your telecarb. We will send you there."

I didn't even bother asking them how they'd do it. Every time I did, I got the runaround about the smallness of my brain.

"I suggest we get on with it then."

Leinad disappeared into the floor. Trebor was still staring at me with the stern face of a scolding parent.

"Treb, buddy, I survived many years without a telecarb. I'll be fine."

The room sighed.

"How is Neola Durwin?"

"In fine shape." Something she'd said tugged at me. "You didn't repair her OP along with her, did you?"

"No," Trebor said. "These repairs were the most difficult we have attempted. I must tell you, Jack Meter—"

I tuned him out. At least Neola couldn't go anywhere. It had been clever of her to steal Mariental's device, since hers had been destroyed.

Trebor said something that brought me back sharply.

"Whoa, back up a bit. What did you just say?"

He looked nonplussed. "I said that the OP is a wonderful device, of much higher quality than we expected."

"No, after that."

"Well, for it to have resisted that combination of noxious gases is quite impressive."

"You mean the OP was intact?"

"Why, yes. That is the reason we did not have to repair it. It had even preserved Neola Durwin's skin around it."

Neola's wool jacket had melted almost immediately. Her cotton shirt had protected her better, but she'd suffered more burns than I. If she'd done that on purpose, she was one tough broad.

I had a more immediate problem than trying to figure her out, though. She could go anywhere she wanted, much more efficiently than I could. My telecarb couldn't sense the OP, and if I followed her, I risked getting stuck in an alternate universe without any means of coming back.

Damn.

If I'd had any doubts she wasn't on my side, her lie about the OP had just erased them.

Leinad reappeared, with something that looked like a white pencil in his hand.

"You must place this as close to the portal as possible."

I nodded and took the small stick. It was cool in my hand and felt almost insubstantial.

"Now, Jack Meter, we will send you where you wish to go. You may experience an unpleasant sensation due to the strength of the pulse."

Trebor and Leinad recombined into Trebor. He then placed a hand on my telecarb. I wished myself in the basement of the restaurant.

I lost myself and became Thrittene. I merged with the larger consciousness and understood all they were. My body lost its cohesiveness. My bones liquefied, my organs coalesced into white matter. Voices flowed through me like a current, and I understood unity and cohesion with blinding clarity. Time slowed. I floated.

Then, like Saint Elmo's fire, I was flashed across the universe into the restaurant. For a moment, an eternity, I connected the two planets.

My body snapped back into its own shape in a slingshot effect that threw me on the floor. My ears rang.

"Jesus, you guys will drive me back to drink." Unpleasant sensation, my ass. I'd been melted and fried, not to mention recombined. Every muscle of my body hurt. And, of course, now that I was in my body again, I'd lost all that incredible insight I'd acquired.

I listened for movement above, but it sounded quiet so I climbed the stairs—once I'd taken out my flashlight to see where I was going. In the kitchen, I shone my light on the other side of the center island. Sure enough, there were traces of a person with small feet having gone that way, twice. Neola had really snowed me. I would've been really pissed off at her if I wasn't too busy trying to stop beating myself to a pulp for being such a sap.

There was no one in the restaurant or the staff bathroom. I stuck the stick Leinad had given me under the sink, which was right beside the portal. It gave a little flash, which must have been the way it activated. When I looked under the sink, I couldn't see it anymore.

I'd hoped the portal would activate while I was there, but everything stayed quiet. I passed through the kitchen and out the door into the night. I'd check back with Trebor in a couple of days. Meanwhile, I had a few other things to find out, the first being what Bakel the bounty hunter had discovered.

I wished myself outside Neola's Colorado house. The way station stood where we'd left it. I entered, pressed a few buttons on the comm station.

"Greetings, Jack Meter," Bakel's voice said. "We need to meet as soon as possible. I will wait by the station for two days."

The time factor was iffy, but I decided to try anyway. I checked my time. There was no way I'd be able to be back before Neola woke up. I'd figure something out. I called up the coordinates for the fog world, the way I'd seen her do. When I stepped out, I was there.

"I was about to leave," Bakel said.

"I'm glad I caught you."

"Neola Durwin is not with you."

"I'm alone."

His eyes shuttered, his beak snapped. He took a step backward. The other bounty hunters appeared, weapons at the ready.

"I am in a quandary," Bakel said, "one which is impossible to resolve."

"Ah, you know there are two Jack Meters then."

"Yes, and I cannot know which one you are."

"Because Neola is not with me."

"There are rumors of a woman fitting Neola Durwin's description helping Jack Meter to steal pieces of universes."

"You can check the coordinates of the way station. They lead to Earth."

"Yes, but in which universe?"

"That's a problem."

"You see my point. You may be the one we were looking for. We will detain you only until another universe is affected. Then we'll know."

"All I can tell you is that I'm the good guy and I really don't have time to hang around."

"You are weaponless, and cannot return until we allow you inside this structure. I'd hate to kill you before I know the truth."

I had my trusty knife in my back pocket, but I wasn't going to tell him that.

"It would certainly cramp my style." I was close to the door of the station.

Before I could move a hair, a tall shape, followed by a squat one, came out of the mist. Mariental placed a hand on Mongo's head, who was growling at me, his fangs showing.

"I'm afraid Bakel is right, Mr. Meter. Killing you at this point would be a shame."

CHAPTER NINETEEN

"WE'LL RETURN TO MY HEADQUARTERS, SHALL WE?" MARIENTAL SAID, gesturing me inside the way station.

Bakel slipped a curved machete from a scabbard on Sibut's back.

"I'll be going with you."

I looked from Mongo's teeth to the blade and shrugged.

"If you insist."

Mariental blinked owlishly.

"Yes, I do have some explaining to do about your mission, don't I?"

Bakel clacked his beak and said nothing more. The three of us entered the station. Bakel closed the door and stood in front of me while Mongo positioned himself between the two of us, one eye turned toward me, the other toward Bakel. His lips rose in a sharp-toothed smirk.

Mariental fiddled with the controls. "Here we are," he said.

He slipped by us and opened the door; we were back in front of the Carlisle.

"After you," he said, with a grand gesture, made ridiculous by the tight hot-pink jumpsuit he wore. "We could've come out closer to the office," he said behind me as I exited, "but I wanted you to remember what you're dealing with."

Beings began to come out of their dwellings and follow us.

"These are real people, Jack, people who were stolen from their homes."

This time, I noticed clothes drying on lines, toys strewn in the dust, weavings or twigs hanging on the doors and mats at their foot.

"Some of them look like they've been here for a while," I said.

"We've been bringing in food and water. Given the number of species, that's been a challenge in itself."

"How long are you going to keep them here?"

"Until we find a way to send them back where they belong."

"They don't talk much."

"We've temporarily suppressed their memories and their personalities. Some of these species have been at war forever; most can't communicate with the others. We didn't want a bloodbath."

I didn't know if Mariental dealt straight with me. At this point, and with my doubts about Neola, I was ready to suspend judgment. The entire situation could end up being the biggest con that ever worked or it might unravel itself into something so simple it'd make a baby laugh.

When we reached our destination, he pushed the door open.

"This station is no longer secure, but we can use it for a while yet before we move our headquarters."

I followed him inside, flanked by Mongo and Bakel. Someone was already there. I recognized Winston even before he turned around.

"Jack," he said, his tone reserved.

"Fancy meeting you here," I said.

He came to me, pulled up my sleeve to reveal the telecarb.

"He's the one we want."

"For what, Pete, a little more recreational shooting?"

He grimaced. "Please, I'd rather you called me asshole than Pete."

"Maybe you are an asshole."

Winston grinned, plugged his cigar in his mouth.

"Here's one for you, Jack—Janine Easterly."

I pursed my lips and thought about the possibility that the other Winston knew about Janine. In a drunken moment of self-pity and reminiscence, I'd told him about my first love. I was four, she was six—I'd always had a thing for older women. It turned out that

Winston knew Janine. She'd copped ten years in the Kingston Pen for armed robbery, a sentence he'd had reduced to five. She was coming up for parole in a few months.

"Okay, maybe you are who you say you are. How about Charlie?"

"She's safe. I stashed her in a hotel, since she insisted on doing her good deeds at the shelter for Christmas. That woman's head is harder than a rock." He lighted his cigar. "Good to see you again, Jack."

"Looks like you've hidden a few things from me."

"Need to know and all that crap."

Bakel's beak snapped. "You can vouch for this man?"

"I can," Winston said. "The other Jack Meter doesn't have a telecarb, so they didn't select him from a completely parallel universe. It's also just like Jack to worry about someone who wants to break his balls. My secretary," he added when Bakel's quills rose. "They don't get along."

"Charlie has her own charm," I said. "Did you know there's another Winston floating around? He loves to be called Pete."

"That's damned insulting. What the hell is he doing?"

"Working with me, I gather. The other me."

"So's Neola Durwin."

It was still a shock to have my suspicions confirmed.

"Yeah, I got that."

"She's been double-crossing the IGA and the AGES for a while. We've been able to trace her activities for the past five years."

"You could've warned me."

"I tried," Mariental said, "when I wanted to keep you away from the case. It was mainly to separate you from Neola Durwin that I went after you. Unfortunately, she knew you well, and she guessed rightly how you would react."

"She knows me, all right, but she's misjudged a few things. First, she made a mistake by having my prints left all over the cult house. Maybe she thought I'd get nailed for the thirteen kids they killed, or she just wanted to keep me busy. If Aplin had been on the case by himself it would've worked, but she didn't know about Terry."

"Your Mountie friend," Winston said.

"Right. I piss him off regularly, but he knows I'm not a killer. Anyway, if I were to kill someone, I'd be smart enough not to leave my prints and my jacket at the scene of the crime. Because of that, I figured out there had to be another me running around."

I turned to Mariental.

"I was trying to tell you that," he said. "Obviously, it was too subtle."

"Yeah, give me hard facts anytime. Neola's second mistake was that she tried to make me believe that Winston was bent. That didn't compute."

"Why?" Bakel said. He'd set the machete on the table. I breathed more easily.

"It's hard to work in the same building with someone for ten years and not get to know something about him. I realize I know dick-all about some parts of Winston's life, but there's one thing I do know—he always fights for the victims. He's a softie."

"You make me sound like a sissy," Winston said in a garrulous voice.

"But a sissy who wouldn't condone killing for gain."

The others chuckled.

"The last thing that Neola miscalculated," I continued, "was to bring me here from the restaurant. Bakel had told us Mariental hired him to hunt me down. She'd counted on that to convince me he was part of the conspiracy."

"That would've made sense to me," Bakel said.

"That's it—it was too pat."

"You concluded she was leading you on because it made sense."

Winston chuckled. "I told you, Mariental, he's special, that one. Works on instinct, brains and guts."

"Stop," I said, "you'll make me blush."

"It's too much to assume that Neola doesn't know you're on to her now," Mariental said.

"I'd say she has an inkling. I was supposed to be gone only a couple of hours."

Mariental shook his head. "The time differential has been a problem all along and the reason we haven't worked in your universe. It seems to be on a different temporal line from most other universes."

"So, what next?"

"I guess it would be useless to ask you to let us do our jobs."

I simply raised an eyebrow. Winston puffed his cigar.

"Told you," he said to Mariental.

"Besides," I said, "I have a couple of leads I want to pursue in my own universe. They may direct me to Jack number two and Neola." I looked out a loophole. "How about the people here?"

"This place is a dump. Before a portion of a universe disappears, the inhabitants are sent to this one." Mariental's lip curved. "How would you like to end up here, with no understanding of what happened to you and no means of return? Believe me, if we had a way to return them to their homes, we would do it without hesitation."

"One thing's been bugging me, though. Their families or friends have no idea they're gone. How could that happen?"

"We also suppressed *their* memories. We didn't want total chaos on our hands, which is what would have happened if we had not intervened."

"But by keeping it quiet, you're playing into their hands."

"It's a risk we must take," Winston said. "We're hoping they'll become overconfident and make a mistake."

"How about Garner?" Then I understood. "You didn't wipe out his memories. You sent him to me instead."

"We're not certain if he's mixed up in this or not. We'd hoped that involving you would flush out your double's accomplices."

"And possibly kill two birdies with one building."

I was getting ticked off. Winston saw it.

"Sorry, Jack. I wasn't authorized at the time to bring you in."

"Not that he didn't argue the point," Mariental said.

"This is all well and good," Bakel said, "but what will happen now?"

"Is there a chance I could get an OP?" At Mariental's unbelieving stare, I grimaced. "Thought so. Here's what I suggest then. Since I can't move around in other universes, I'll stick to my own. If I can catch Neola, I'll keep her for you."

I decided not to tell them about Leinad's device to detect the portal end coordinates. I did tell them, though, about the Barnes Foundation and how Terry was trying to track down the trustees. I also told them about Neola's house. I planned on setting a few traps there myself.

"She loves that place, apparently. It looked permanent, so I suspect she won't be able to resist going back, even though she knows I can track her down there. She'll count on her ability to disappear fast."

I shoved my hands in my pockets. In one of them, I still had the curses Saurimo had given me. That gave me an idea.

Mariental gave me a one-way communicator that would relay messages to him if I needed to. The last I heard before I wished myself to Asela's tent was Bakel asking about the AGES. It looked like Mariental would gain another agent.

Asela stood in the tent opening, looking out at the field below. A lone Kilosan hissed and rose on his tail. Asela turned. I dangled the curses.

"I still have them, can still use them," I said. "I wish you no harm, just want to talk to you."

"When one threatens us, it is difficult to believe one wishes us no harm."

"You've got a point. Here." I snapped all three discs in two. Asela winced. "The curses are broken. I'm defenseless."

"One just destroyed powerful weapons."

"I told you, I'm not interested in your feud. I just want information."

"And why would we want to provide it when one is the companion of the one who brought us here?"

Bingo. I now understood why Neola had been roughed up.

"That's just it, see. She made me believe you were the bad guys, but I've learned a few things since then."

"One has foiled our attempt to get back to our world."

"It's Orapa, right?"

Asela inclined her head.

"I could try to get you there, but what would happen to them?" I pointed a thumb at the Kilosan watching our exchange. "They come from a world called Kilosa. I'm sure they'd like to go back, too."

"Couldn't one do that?"

"Too many of them. I'd need whatever equipment Neola used."

"Neola would be the female we had captured?"

"Yes. Did she bring you here before or after the Kilosans?"

"Before." She turned black, which I knew from before meant she'd been afraid. "We have no remembrance of being brought here. We found ourselves desperate, alone in this hostile world." She turned and looked out. The dying sun was setting fire to the clouds. In that light, she looked purple. "Then there was a strange, low sound we could barely hear, but it seemed the ground moved with it, changing gradually into a ground quake that made us fall down."

That sounded very similar to what I'd experienced when Mueller had activated Annie's clone.

"What happened then?"

"The sky splintered, and a large sphere floated down. Slowly, small fissures spread all over. The sphere's chroma changed constantly, and a multitude of screams filled the air. The fissures widened and through them flew a light as bright as the sun. Everything extinguished at the same time. Pieces of the sphere floated in the wind. The Kilosans were there. Soon after, Saurimo and her monsters arrived the same way."

Mariental had been right. They'd found a way to use the conjugator technology for their own purposes. What Asela had described was an almost exact rendition of Annie's clone's destruction. The conjugator had used a kind of mist to break up the various parts of universe that Mueller had put together. I wondered what they were using.

And who had developed the technology? The conjugator had been designed and built on Entomon, a planet Claire had stayed on for several months. She might be able to tell me if the inhabitants—Entomons? Entomonians?—could build a device powerful enough to literally move mountains.

"What will one do?" Asela said, breaking into my thoughts.

"I'll try to find the machine that brought you here. I may be able to reverse the process."

"One must make haste. Without us, Orapa will perish."

"Don't tell me you're the queen or something."

"No, but Saurimo and we are the largest Landlords in Orapa. Without our guidance, the land will wither, Orapans will die."

"Surely, you could delegate."

She shook her head. "There is a genetic symbiosis between Orapan land and the Landlords. Without the right chroma, which is developed at conception, the Orapans cannot communicate with the land." She closed her eyes. Her skin paled to sky blue. "Unfortunately, we had not thought an offspring would be necessary so quickly. Neither did Saurimo." She placed a long-fingered hand on my arm. "One must help us, or millions of Orapans will die and so will the land."

Gee, talk about pressure.

I patted her hand. "I'll be back."

I was kind of curious to see this Orapa, but so far my telecarb hadn't worked in any of the other universes I'd gone to. I decided I'd visit an old friend instead.

She was in her lab, typing madly on a keyboard with her eyes glued to the eyepieces of a microscope. I cleared my throat. She jumped, turned.

"Hello, darling," I said to Claire. "Long time no see."

CHAPTER TWENTY

SHE TURNED BACK TO HER MICROSCOPE. "I DON'T HAVE TIME FOR YOU."

"Anything I can help with?"

"You can help with disappearing."

"Come on, Claire, where's your Christmas spirit?" Then a thought struck me. "I haven't missed it, have I?"

That got her attention. She turned back to me with curious eyes.

"Where have you been?" You couldn't fault her for being slow on the uptake.

"Several other universes. The time differential is a killer."

"I thought you were putting me on last time."

"Nope. Brane theory is not a theory anymore."

Despite herself, she was interested. Her eyes shone then dulled.

"I have to finish this report. Go away."

"Fine, I'll keep it for your bedtime. It makes a nice story to sleep on."

"I don't want you in my apartment."

"Your choice, babe." I leaned on the counter beside her, stuffed my hands in the pockets of my jacket. "Would it help your mood if I told you I have woman trouble?"

"I have less interest in your love life than in the gross national product of Swaziland."

"I'm talking professional problems here."

She raised an eyebrow. "With that IGA agent you mentioned on the phone?"

"Yes." I grimaced. "It turns out she's not quite what she said she was."

"You got taken in." That made her smile broadly. "So this Intergalactic Agency doesn't exist?"

"You know, I forgot to ask."

"Ask whom?"

"Winston. You remember Peter Winston, the lawyer who I share my office building with? He's an AGES agent. That's the Agency for Governance of Entities and Systems."

Wariness flashed over her face. She slowly got up from her stool.

"Sure, Jack. Whatever." She backed away from me, very slowly, hands out as if to keep me back.

"Oh, come on, Claire, why would I make up something as crazy as that?"

"Because you're nuts?"

"I'm not nuts."

"You were before."

"That was different."

She crossed her arms below her breast. Her chin rose stubbornly. "I'll need some proof."

"That I'm sane? Jesus, woman, you're unbelievable." I dug out my cell, pressed the programmed key for Terry's. "Hi," I said, when he came on the line. "Everything's fine…Yeah. I got a favor to ask you. Could you tell Claire I'm in possession of all my faculties?"

I passed the phone to her. I could still hear him laughing.

"Terry?" She said hi, listened for a few seconds. A slight smile lifted one corner of her mouth. She passed the phone back to me. "Terry wants to speak to you."

"What was that all about?" he said to me.

"I'll tell you when I see you."

"Tomorrow night, right?"

Christ, was it Christmas Eve already? "Right. I'll be by myself, though. I'll explain." I disconnected. "You satisfied?" I said to Claire.

"Terry said you were a crazy sonofabitch but not certifiable."

"There. That's an endorsement if I never heard one."

"What do you want, then?"

"I'm suddenly out of a partner."

She snorted. "Stuck again, are you?"

"I hate to say it, but I need you."

"Now I know I'm going to hate it." Nevertheless, that spark of interest glimmered in her eyes. She checked the clock. "You have fifteen minutes."

It took me much longer than that, but once I'd started, Claire didn't interrupt. When I came to Asela's description of the universe transfer, she paled. Like me, she'd recognized the effects of the conjugator.

"Damn it, Jack," she said between clenched teeth. I knew she was thinking of Annie's clone and the decision she'd made, there at the end, to help me destroy it. It didn't matter that it hadn't really been Annie. She'd been devastated for a while. "How did they get hold of the technology? How can they operate it on that scale?"

"That's just it. Would the bugs from Entomon be able to build a machine like that?"

"They might." She shuddered. "God, I hated that place. Six-legged human-sized creatures scurrying about, that chitinous whispering constant in the air. Gave me the willies."

"How long would it take for them to make one—and why would they?"

"Time flows faster there, so they'd have plenty of time to do the research and implementation. As for why they would do it, they thrive on challenge. They can't resist a dare. That's almost their national pastime."

"So if someone came along and dared them, they'd be compelled to build it. I wonder why they'd hand it over. Maybe Neola and company stole it."

She threw her hands in the air.

"What difference does it make? They have it." Her eyes narrowed. "Oh, no. I'm not going back there."

"They know you already, you worked with them."

"They give me the creeps."

"You know, your talent and intelligence are wasted here." I must've sounded sincere, because she stopped pacing.

"No deal."

"You don't even know what I'm going to say."

"I don't care."

"Okay, fine. I'll find another way to go to Entomon. But before I leave, let me tell you about Asela's planet, Orapa. It has a—what did she call it?—a genetic symbiosis with its Landlords. The land can't exist without them. As a biochemist and a researcher, that's right up your alley."

She groaned. "You're a bastard."

I grinned—I had her. "I know."

"I'll go to Entomon on one condition. I get to meet Mariental."

* * *

Less than twenty-four hours later, I stood in front of Terry's house, the presents Neola and I had bought all wrapped by the hotel staff. When I'd gone back to the hotel, she was gone. I'd asked to change to a smaller suite, but the hotel was full. They'd promised to switch me as soon as one became available, puzzled that I'd want to downgrade. I didn't bother explaining that a potential mass murderer currently knew where I stayed.

Since I wanted nothing other than a chat with Neola—I'd gone by her empty house—I took the day off and chilled.

Claire and I had decided to wait until after Christmas for her to go to Entomon. First, we'd need the Thrittene's help, since they were the ones who knew how to get there. There was a matter of a time bubble, as Claire called it, to allow the switch from our time speed to theirs. Then we had a visit to Mariental scheduled afterwards. She'd take the entire Christmas holidays off, which would give her the time buffer she needed.

So I lounged around in my hotel room, watched *A Christmas Carol* on the tube and, oh, bliss! listened repeatedly to Cecilia Bartoli's divine voice on the CD player I'd discovered came with the suite. Gluck's little-known arias filled the room and allowed me to disengage my brain. Opera could always rewind me, center me, let my subconscious work out the problems I gnawed like bones without much success.

The door opened, and Terry stood in the entrance, wearing a dark-green suit with what seemed like a half-a-meter-wide red tie decorated with laughing reindeers.

"Hey, man," he said as he shook my hand, "glad you could come. Merry Christmas. Come on in."

"Nice tie."

He looked down, grimaced. "The kids gave it to me last year. I have to wear it at least once."

I bet he was responsible for the suit, though.

"Where's Betty?"

"Putting the finishing touches to dinner." He glanced behind him then leaned close to my ear. "If you smell something burnt, don't mention it, okay? The turkey's skin's a little crisp."

"My lips are sealed with duct tape."

He heaved a sigh of relief. "How 'bout a drink?"

"Sure, scotch if you have it," I said as I took off my leather jacket and pulled off my boots. In honor of the occasion, I'd put on a white shirt tucked into black jeans. I was preparing to follow Terry into the den when I saw three small faces peeking through the rungs in the stairwell. "Hi," I said.

"Hi," the oldest of the girls said. She had big blue eyes and caramel-colored hair that curled around her face.

"What's that on your arm?" the boy said. Without thinking, I'd rolled my sleeves above the telecarb. I flipped them back down.

"Did you bring us any presents?" the other girl piped in.

I chose to ignore the boy. "Of course, I did."

"Evie!" Betty said from the entrance to the kitchen. "That's not the way I raised you."

"It's okay," I said, going back for the bag I'd left with my boots. "Hi, Betty." She came out, and I kissed her on both cheeks.

"Something smells good in here."

Evie sent a mischievous smile to the two others, something their mother, who was busy blushing at the compliment, didn't see.

"Thanks, Jack. Merry Christmas."

I took out a box wrapped in silver foil with a huge red-and-silver bow. I'd decided on a bottle of Chanel No. 5 from the hotel boutique. I figured every woman enjoys perfume.

"Merry Christmas, Betty."

"Oh!" She blushed even deeper. "You really shouldn't have."

"My thanks for inviting me." I handed the bag with the other goodies to Evie. "Here you go, kids."

"Under the tree," Betty said, handing them hers, "until tomorrow morning."

Three groans, one "Oh, Mom" and an "Ours are smaller" from Evie, and they were gone.

"I've got to check on dinner. I imagine you two want to talk business for a while?"

"Half an hour?" I asked sheepishly.

"Sure, I can delay dinner until five-thirty."

I could never understand people's compulsion to eat dinner in the middle of the afternoon. However, when in Rome...

"Thanks, Betty."

Terry had already poured my scotch and himself a beer. He motioned with his head toward his office. When we were inside, he closed the door.

"I had to do some fast talking to prevent Betty from inviting Laura tonight," he said. "You owe me one."

"Thanks."

"So, how come you're solo?"

I gave him a rueful look. "I humiliated myself in front of Claire, I might as well continue with you."

"You talked to Claire?"

"It's all part of the mess."

I told him about Winston and Neola and their role in the case.

"I see." He sat down, extended his legs. His socks were also red, with gold stars embroidered on them. I was afraid to ask in case he said he'd picked them himself. When my glance went from his feet to his face, I saw he looked smug. "In for a pound, Jack."

That meant he was going to make me feel even more of a dumbass.

"What now?"

"I found at least one familiar name on the list of trustees for the Annie Barnes Temporal Research Foundation—Lambert Garner."

It took a few seconds to register.

"Sonofabitch." I gulped some scotch. "Are you sure?"

"No question. My people will pick him up, let him cool his heels inside tonight. That should make him amenable to questioning tomorrow morning."

"You're going in on Christmas?"

Terry grinned. "Ever heard of delegating? I passed it on to Tomkins."

I remembered Tomkins as the young corporal I'd saved from the explosion of Mueller's lab. His pal Baxter hadn't been so lucky.

"Don't worry," Terry said, as if he'd read my mind. "He's grown up since then."

"Are you sure he's the right Lambert Garner?"

"Meaning the trustee's another double? We'll see. I can't bring Tomkins in based on that angle, but he'll find the holes in Garner's story, if there are any. That kid's got a flair for interrogation."

A knock at the door, and Betty's head poking in put a stop to speculation.

The kids were already seated, fidgeting in their Sunday clothes. Terry sat at the head of the table, Betty at the other end. I sat beside the oldest, to Terry's left.

"This here is Eleanore," Terry said, pointing at her. She'd tied a red ribbon around her head, with the big bow on top. "Then there's Eric, the middle one, and Evelyn, the youngest."

Eric had Betty's brown eyes and Terry's square face. The little one was a younger replica of her sister, bow and all.

"I'm eight," Evelyn said.

"Who cares?" Eric said.

"I do. I'll have more presents 'cause I'm the youngest."

"Will not."

"Will too."

"Kids," Terry said. They subsided, but not before Evelyn stuck her tongue out at her brother.

Dinner continued in the same vein. The "Triple E," as I came to call them, bickered, poked through their food, whined and laughed hysterically for no apparent reason. I could tell both parents were looking forward to Santa dropping by and putting them out of their misery. Terry would throw me an amused glance occasionally. I became convinced the dinner was retribution for all the trouble I'd caused him these past months.

When I wasn't caught in the crossfire of childish babble, I tried to look like I enjoyed the food. Terry hadn't lied—Betty was a godawful cook. The burnt turkey tasted like cardboard and the mashed potatoes were lumpy, although I wasn't sure what the lumps were until I made out partly dissolved instant potato flakes that had glommed together. When Terry asked about them, Betty flushed and explained that she'd realized she wouldn't have enough, so she'd added the flakes to the real stuff. The gravy was a grayish color, with little flecks of burnt turkey skin sprinkled in it for good measure. I wasn't even able to pass on dessert, which consisted of an overly sweet mincemeat pie in rock-hard pastry.

Betty was offering me a second piece of pie, and I was trying to find a non-offensive way of refusing, when the phone rang.

"That's probably Laura," she said. "I told her you'd be here tonight, Jack, so I'm sure she wants to wish you Merry Christmas."

Yeah, I thought, and wrangle an invitation to dinner at a posh restaurant for New Year's Eve. Laura liked the fine things in life. That was probably why she wasn't eating with us.

Betty came back, her face somber.

"It's the office, Terry."

"Shit," he said, snapping his napkin on the table and getting up.

"You said a bad word, Daddy," Evie said.

"Sorry, sweetie. I'll be back."

Betty heaved a sigh and sat down. "He'll probably miss midnight mass now."

Terry came back into the dining room looking grim. He went around the table and kissed foreheads, amid groans of realization that he had to leave.

"I don't know when I'll be back, Betty. Don't wait up for me." He looked at me. "You might as well come along."

I hastily thanked Betty, said goodbye to the kids and followed him. We put on our boots and coats in silence, slipped into the cold air.

"What's up?" I said.

He opened the door of his metallic-blue Trans Am. "They found Garner. He was in his house."

"Was."

"He's dead. Someone slashed his throat from ear to goddamn ear."

CHAPTER TWENTY-ONE

Garner's house was a cantilevered box of steel and glass balanced on a larger box, surrounded by at least three acres of walled property. The wrought iron gate opened on a cobblestone lane, currently occupied by half a dozen blue-and-whites. They weren't flashing their lights, probably in deference to the neighborhood, which included the Governor General's residence. A couple of uniforms guarded the front door, their breath a white plume in the cold air, their eyes miserable at the duty they'd copped on such a night.

Terry showed his badge and muttered a "He's with me," flashing a thumb behind him.

A glass chandelier that plunged down for at least two meters reflected endlessly in a floor-to-ceiling mirrored hall larger than my old apartment. The bare, gleaming black marble floor also shot back the light, adding to the cold coming from the open outside door. The hall led to a series of rooms I could barely make out in the shadows.

Another cop directed Terry to the second floor. We took the wire-suspended stairs, our feet ringing on the brushed stainless steel treads. We followed the sound of low voices to a room in the back. Terry nodded to a tired-looking man in plain clothes who leaned against the wall. Tomkins stood beside him, a bit pale but seemingly holding his own.

"Powell," Terry said, extending his hand.

Powell pushed away from the wall and shook it.

"Merry fucking Christmas, Parczek." He turned toward me, shook my hand, too. "I should've known you'd be involved in this, Meter."

"You know me," I said, "can't stay away from excitement."

Powell grunted. As city cops came, the head of the forensics division was one of the rare ones who didn't walk around with a stick up his butt. I figured, when you dealt with gore on a regular basis you tended to see things in perspective.

"What's your interest in Garner?" Powell asked Terry.

"Remember the cult killings a couple of weeks ago? We hoped Garner might have some information related to them. We were bringing him in for questioning."

"Too late now."

"Yeah. When did you get called?"

"About an hour ago. Tomkins placed the call."

"When I got here to serve the warrant," Tomkins said, "the gates were open and so was the front door. I didn't like the look of it, so I radioed for a blue-and-white and waited until they came to enter the premises. When we found Mr. Garner, I called Detective Powell. Then I called you."

Terry nodded.

"Can we take a peek?" I asked.

"Why the fuck would you want to?" Powell said. "It's pretty messy."

I couldn't tell him I wanted to make sure it was the real Garner he'd found. I shrugged.

"He was my client. I might be able to see something your boys won't pick up on."

Powell stared at me for a moment then nodded.

"Stay on the threshold. I don't want you to contaminate the scene."

Terry and I stood in the entrance to the room where Garner had been killed. Butchered was more like it. He was sprawled halfway on a sofa, as if he'd fallen backward. The killer had severed his head almost completely; it lolled to the side, eyes and mouth wide with surprise. Blood had spurted over the pewter-colored fabric of the cushions, the glass coffee table, the gray carpet. It was dark, almost black, and its metallic scent mixed with the stench of death.

I forced myself not to think about the meal I'd just finished and concentrated on the body. His robe and pajama bottoms were drenched in blood. Where it hadn't fallen, the robe had a grayish cast, as if it had been white at one time. The bottoms of the pajama legs were fraying and so were the sleeves peeking out of the robe. Both of his slippers had holes at the big toe. His greasy hair was plastered over his skull, and he still had the scraggly stubble over his face.

"So?" Terry muttered.

"There can't be two slobs like him," I muttered back. "I'd say he's the real Garner."

"He knew his killer," Powell said from behind me. "Preliminary analysis indicates the neck was severed from the front, probably with a broad, heavy blade."

"And a well-sharpened one, too."

"I'd say. It happened fast—there are no defensive wounds. You see anything unusual?"

I surveyed the area. Several people were busy going over the scene, which was some sort of informal living room.

"He liked the streamlined look, at any rate," I said.

Apart from the blood, the place was pristine, also filled with steel and glass. One wall had a sleek, state-of-the-art entertainment center recessed into it. There were no ornamentations, pictures on the wall, nor any of the knickknacks people gather after living in the same house for fifteen years.

Which was why the intricately ornate Chinese vase near the floor-to-ceiling window didn't fit at all. I watched as one of Powell's people picked it up, dusted it, peered inside then put it back in its place. Why would Garner have a vase like that? Just a whim, maybe, something he'd decided he liked, even though it didn't fit in his décor?

Only...my skin was itching. I backed away from the door.

"What's the case you were working for Garner?" Powell said.

"He wanted me to look into one of his properties he's having problems with."

"Title search and such?"

"Not quite. There's been some trouble with it."

Terry threw me a glance. "Garner came up as one of the trustees in a bogus foundation that took in the money from those cult kids who were poisoned. You know Jack found them."

"You get around. Any link between your investigation and Jack's case?"

"Not sure. Jack was at our house for Christmas Eve dinner when I got the call about Garner. I asked him to come along."

Powell nodded. He began to talk technicalities with Terry, forensic stuff like splatter patterns and blood-settling time, which I wasn't too keen to listen to. I waited for a while, and when they were engrossed I slowly moved away, wandered down the hall, back toward the stairs.

The entertainment room took the entire space at the back of the house. The short hall had four other doors. Behind the first one was a full bathroom with a connecting door that led me to another bedroom, from the size of it probably the guest room. Again the streamlined style, this time in bleached wood, likely Scandinavian. White carpets, white drapes. I went out the bedroom door and stepped across the hall into the next room.

The smell hit me first: dirty socks and BO. I was sure I'd found Garner's bedroom. He'd chosen the spot well. With the curtains left open and the light off, I had a full view of the Ottawa River and the twinkling of multicolored lights on the other side. I walked in farther, mesmerized, and promptly stubbed my toe on something. I swore, hit the lights.

I'd hit a leather suitcase. I picked a pen from my pocket and lifted the lid. Thrown pell-mell into it were a couple of shirts, a pair of pants and a .38-mm revolver. I let the lid drop and surveyed the room.

Even though there was not a thread out of place, it had a more lived-in look. The chair beside the window still bore the imprint of Garner's butt, and there were scuffmarks on the rug, a few flakes of dandruff on the dresser. The counter in the bathroom held grooming products, doubtless more for decoration than actual use. More Scandinavian style for the furniture, chrome and mirrors in the bath.

Beside the chair was a bookcase with dog-eared books, probably bought from a secondhand shop; most had a library "discard" stamp on top. Garner hadn't struck me as a reader. I scanned the titles: *Cults and Their Attractions, The Psychology of Cults, How I Got Out of a Cult and Survived.* Not one novel in the lot.

An eighteen-inch flat-screen television faced the bed. On a shelf below I found a row of videotapes on cults. I figured I'd found Abura.

Mariental's hunch had become fact—Garner was involved, but how?

This place looked like his favorite room, one in which, judging by the smell, he spent a lot of time. If an object had caught his fancy, wouldn't he have put it where he could see it most often? There was no sign of a Chinese pot.

I left the room and headed downstairs. The hall gave onto a grandiose but cold living room. More chandeliers hung from the ceiling. Antique Persian carpets covered white marble. Black leather furniture competed with glass-topped tables. I didn't stay and look around—it was pretty obvious no one had set foot in that room for a long time.

Next was a games room with a pool table covered over with a dustsheet, a dining room with a table that could seat twenty people easily and an industrial kitchen with brushed steel appliances, granite counters and halogen lighting. I opened the fridge. It was nearly empty, except for a hunk of yellow cheese, a dozen bottles of imported beer and some eggs. The freezer was chock-full of frozen dinners. The dishwasher and garbage can showed evidence that Garner had eaten dinner before he was killed.

At the end of the kitchen was a closed-in sunroom. I tried the patio doors; they were locked. I unlocked them and stepped outside. Down three steps to the pool area, a kidney-shaped hole surrounded with rocks and shrubs to make it look like a pond. It was half-empty, covered with a tarp. I raised my head and saw people moving about on the second floor. The entertainment room overlooked the pool.

"What are you doing?" Tomkins came out of the patio door.

"Just looking around."

"Don't touch anything."

I raised both hands, showing that I still wore my gloves.

"That's quite a house," I said.

"He didn't seem to do much living in it."

I had to give the kid credit. He had a good sense of observation. It occurred to me that my hope of getting a good deal on a condo had flown south.

"He liked buildings," I said.

"We're going to help the city cops with the door-to-door. Sergeant Parczek says to go back to your hotel. He'll call you tomorrow."

Door-to-door. I suddenly remembered Winston mentioning he lived across from Garner. I also remembered Winston collected chinoiserie. Was the Chinese vase in Garner's entertainment room a message? Would they be arrogant enough to hole up in Winston's house while Winston was away?

It was perfect, though. The fake Winston could come and go, and no one would question my presence there. I had a bad feeling about the whole thing.

"Where's Terry now?"

"He was going to take the other side of the street."

"Shit. Come on." I ran through the house and out the door, down the lane. As I got to the gates, I saw Terry climb the porch stairs then raise his hand to ring the bell.

"Terry!" I yelled.

No time. As if in slow motion, I saw him press the doorbell. I wished myself a few feet from him. As soon as my feet hit the ground, even though I wasn't fully together, I tackled him mid-body.

At the same time, the world blew up. All my bones jarred when I landed on the ground. Something whistled past my head, and I ducked.

I could hear nothing else except the quickly approaching sound of feet from across the street.

"Terry," I said to my friend, who was lying on his back, eyes closed. I extracted myself from him and felt for a pulse. It was strong, if a bit fast.

"You know," he said, his voice rough, "I'm getting really tired of being nearly blown up when you're around."

"Everyone all right?" Powell said.

"I think my leg's broken," Terry said. "Maybe a dislocated shoulder, too. This guy fell on me."

I got up, caught Tompkins's eye. Barely, so that he would be the only one to see it, I shook my head. His mouth thinned, but he said nothing.

"How about you, Meter?" Powell said.

"I'm fine." I turned toward the house. "Looks like it's only the door that was damaged.

"Now, why in hell would someone jury-rig that door to explode?"

"I think Garner's killer must've been staying in this house. They knew it was empty."

"How did they know that?"

I shrugged. "The house belongs to a friend of mine who's away at the moment. Garner knew that. Winston's the one who introduced me to Garner before he left."

"How convenient."

"Isn't it."

"It still doesn't explain the explosives."

I glanced at Terry, who was still lying on the ground. Someone had covered him with a blanket.

"They wanted to implicate Jack," he said. "Keep him busy."

"How would explosives implicate you?"

"It's a long story, Powell," Terry interrupted before I could answer, "and parts of it are classified." He winced. Sirens were quickly approaching.

"Let's just say that the RCMP's explosives expert doesn't like me," I added.

"I see," Powell said, although he obviously didn't.

The ambulance screeched to a halt and two medics spewed out of it. In a few seconds, they examined Terry and moved him to a stretcher. I took advantage of the confusion to slip away to the back of Winston's house.

The yard was terraced, with a deck and patio doors; his home was a lot more modest in size than Garner's but had old money written all over it. Sandstone and ivy—now dormant—covered the walls, and sculpted white trim ran along the gabled roof and the dormer windows. He'd said to me once that his house was listed as a historic building, in which some Prime Minister had lived at the beginning of Confederation.

I tried the door—locked. I wished myself inside the house, but my telecarb refused to work, which confirmed to me they were using it as another portal.

Steps rustled behind me. I froze, waited in the dark. Tomkins stopped beside me.

"Last time, you did the same thing, didn't you? Except you saved my life, too." He raked his hand through his hair. "I saw it. I saw you disappear, no—melt away. Then in the blink of an eye, you were close enough to save the sergeant. How do you do it?"

"If Terry were here, he'd give you the same answer as last time."

"It's just the two of us."

I sighed. "Forget what you saw, okay? Just imagine I'm a really fast runner."

Tomkins threw me a stubborn glance. At that moment, he looked about eighteen.

"I'm going inside with you," he said.

"Who says I want to get inside?"

"You can always wait for Aplin, see if he'll let you in."

"The door's locked."

Tomkins' teeth flashed in the dark. "Then we'll have to do it the official way. It's called probable cause."

Chapter Twenty-Two

I WASN'T HAPPY TO HAVE TOMKINS TAGGING ALONG, ESPECIALLY WITH WHAT I thought I'd find inside, but I had no choice. I wanted to slip in before the boys began to roam all over the house. Right now they were busy with Terry and they were waiting for the bomb squad, but it still didn't give me much time. I'd have to deal with Tomkins when the time came.

"Go ahead," he said.

"I told you, the door's locked."

His teeth flashed in the dim light. "I'll go check around the house, make sure no one's coming."

Okay, maybe he looked like a kid, but he wasn't naive. I dug out my tools from the inside pocket of my jacket and had the door opened in three seconds—I'd have to tell Winston to change his locks. Breaking in had been way too easy.

Tomkins came back as the patio door glided open soundlessly.

"I'll go first," he said and took out his gun.

"I'm not crazy about guns," I said.

"Standard procedure." He threw me a glance. "You can stay here until I clear it."

"Yeah, right." I detained him by pulling on his shoulder. Terry would kill me if something happened to this kid, especially since we had no business going in, in the first place. "Since it was my idea," I said. "I'm going first." When he shook his head, I added, "Face it, kid, you have no more jurisdiction here right now than I do. Want to keep your career? If we get caught, you can at least say you followed me in to arrest me."

He stared at me for a second then nodded and moved aside.

As soon as I entered, my telecarb began to tingle. We were in the kitchen; French doors across the room ostensibly led to the rest of the house. On our left, a plain door was half-opened. Tomkins tapped my arm and handed me a penlight. I turned it on, pulled the door toward me. The thin stream of light showed stairs leading to the basement as well as a very narrow flight going up.

"This must've been, like, the servants' way," Tomkins said, his voice low.

I turned off the light. "Let's do this floor first."

We went through the French doors. Even though the front door was now a pile of matchsticks, the inside hall door was intact and the drapes had been pulled tight—none of the outside light seeped into the house, so the boys outside couldn't see ours either.

I flashed my light around. On the right was a formal living room. On a table was the twin of the vase in Garner's house. Another table showed a circle without dust.

"Now we know where the vase came from," I said.

"Vase?"

"There was a vase just like this one in the room where Garner bought it."

On the left, past the stairs going to the second floor, was the formal dining room. The remnants of several meals had been left on the antique table.

"They've been here for a while," I said.

"Not much at cleaning up after themselves."

"Let's go upstairs. We don't have much time left."

The upstairs, divided into three bedrooms and two bathrooms, was empty. They'd left the drapes open up there, so there was enough light to see. My telecarb was still tingling, but more feebly here than downstairs.

A picture frame on one of the nightstands caught my eye. I walked to it, picked it up, angled it toward the window. It was a picture of

Annie, looking just as she was before her death. She stood on the beach, arms extended, head back in her typical posture of joy, laughing. In one hand, at the tip of her fingers, she was holding a leather jacket, as if she were whirling around with it. I swallowed hard.

Annie and I had never been to the beach. It wasn't a picture I'd taken.

I set it back down hard enough that the glass cracked. Bastards. They knew I'd eventually end up here and they'd left the picture, hoping to emotionally weaken me. And if I didn't get to it before the cops, it would hang over my head like a goddamn Sword of Damocles.

Whose idea had it been? I'd bet on Neola—she'd seen enough of my feelings for Annie to play cat-and-mouse with them.

"There's nothing on this floor," Tomkins said, coming back into the room. "Hey, are you okay?"

I took a deep breath. "Yeah, I'm fine. Let's check the basement."

Before I followed him down, I quickly opened the back of the frame, slipped the photo out, stuffed it in my pocket. I dug up the end of my shirt and wiped the fingertips off the frame. I rushed downstairs ahead of Tomkins, now convinced the portal must be in the basement.

"Why don't you stay here?"

"No way. I'll cover your back."

"Did Terry put you up to this?"

"No. I owe you."

"This is going above and beyond, kid."

I was halfway down the basement stairs when I heard a slithering, clinking sound. The basement was quite cold—I could feel the difference of temperature on my face.

"There's something alive down there," Tomkins whispered in my ear.

"Rats, maybe," I said in the same tone. "Here goes."

I felt my way down the rest of the stairs, crouched, turned on the penlight and swept it around. In one corner, a Kilosan dozed. That was why they'd kept the basement cold. Like any lizard, the Kilosan was a cold-blooded creature, unable to function in low temperatures.

"Holy shit, what the hell is that?"

"Don't shoot, for God's sake. Turn on the basement light, will you?"

Tomkins obeyed. I looked around; there were no windows to reveal our presence to the guys outside. I approached the Kilosan slowly. He was chained to the wall, with restraints at his neck and forelegs. He opened his eyes, tried to raise himself but seemed too weak to be able to do so.

I took out my tools again and unlocked his restraints. "We have to get him out of here."

"Are you crazy? That's a big fucking lizard. We'll let the Humane Society take care of him."

I tried to lift the beast by myself but he must've weighed over a hundred kilos. I looked up at Tomkins, who stared at me as if I'd gone purple-and-green.

"I don't have time to explain, kid. This isn't an ordinary lizard, and he doesn't belong here. I need your help to get him out of here."

"Where are we going to take him? The place is surrounded by cops."

"Just outside. I'll take it from there."

"We'd be tampering with evidence."

"He's not evidence, he's sentient."

"Aren't these dragons an endangered species, or something?"

"Not these. Not yet, at any rate." I shook my head. "You said you owed me one. I'm calling in my marker."

He shifted from one foot to the other then came down the stairs.

"I'll take the tail."

Climbing the stairs with a giant semi-conscious reptile was as easy as pushing Jell-O uphill. By the time we arrived in the kitchen, we were sweating.

"Come on," I panted, "put some effort into it."

Tomkins told me to do something creative with my own anatomy and frog-marched after me through the patio door, the Kilosan between us.

Aplin's voice suddenly resounded.

"Where the hell is Meter?"

"Oops. See you around, kid. Go be a cop."

I took hold of one of the Kilosan's claws and wished myself in Alesa's tent.

* * *

The Richmond Grill was still boarded up and dark—not too surprising since it was early Christmas morning. Neola and her gang had obviously abandoned the portal at Winston's house. They probably had dropped the one in the restaurant, too, but I wanted to make sure and retrieve Leinad's gizmo.

I looked left and right. Not much going on at four o'clock in the morning. I wished myself into the restaurant. After a second, I realized I was still freezing my butt on the sidewalk. I pulled up my sleeve. The telecarb's colors swirled in the same way it always had. Either the portal was still active, or the transportation part of my device was defective.

I crossed the bank parking lot into the back alley, all the while hugging the crowbar I'd swiped from some construction truck parked on the street. I needed it to break open the door, since my waistline didn't compare to Neola's. I slipped the tip between the door and the wall at waist level and pushed. The door groaned but didn't budge. I pushed again. The lock held.

On the third try, I heard a snap and the door whipped open, projecting me onto the wall. The crowbar clanged on the asphalt like a church bell.

I waited for a few seconds. No one came running, so I went in through the kitchen to the staff washroom. My telecarb tingled all the way down. I groped around under the sink until I found the cylinder Leinad had given me. I plucked it off and slipped it in my pocket. In the silence, I heard a car door close, quiet-like. That piqued my attention. From the corner of my eye, I saw a tiny red light on the wall across the washroom, and it was flashing.

Shit, I'd triggered an alarm when I broke into the restaurant.

"Freeze!"

I raised my arms above my head and turned around very slowly. The uniform was young enough not to need to shave and he was pointing a big gun at me. That worried me.

"I'm not armed," I said.

"On your knees, asshole."

Obviously, he wasn't happy working during the holidays. I complied. He marched around behind me then holstered his gun and cuffed me.

"Up," he said. He patted me for weapons, found my knife in my back pocket. "We'll let you explain yourself at the station."

He recited my rights at the same time as he was pushing me into the back of a blue-and-white. He drove fast toward downtown and the police station.

The rookie had made a mistake, though: he hadn't asked me my name. I didn't have a record, the place was dark, and even with his training, he'd probably be hard-pressed to recognize me if he met me in daylight. I mentally said "Adios" and wished myself on Thrittene.

Nothing happened.

I silently cursed Leinad black-and-blue. Obviously, the telecarb was malfunctioning. Unless...

I thought about the stick I had in my pocket. Maybe it worked as a dampening device for the telecarb, the same way the portal did. It wasn't Thrittene matter, so maybe it wasn't compatible with the telecarb.

The cop brought me into an interrogation room after I handed over everything in my pockets against a receipt. Fortunately, Leinad's gizmo must've looked like a high-tech pen. The uniform listed it and slipped it in a brown envelope along with my knife and wallet. My gut tightened when he added Annie's picture to the collection.

I'd waited in the room for about five minutes when a man in

plainclothes came in and sat down across from me. He looked down at a piece of paper in his hand then stared at me.

"I'm Detective Simmons," he said, his voice rough as if he'd smoked too much in the past hour. "This interview is recorded. Your name is Jack Meter?"

"It is."

"And you're a private investigator."

"That's right."

"Tell me, are PIs working on a different set of laws than the rest of the population?"

"Not that I know of."

"So, by breaking into the Richmond Grill, you admit you broke the law."

I smiled slightly. "The door was already opened. I went in to investigate. That's what I do."

"There was a mere two minutes between the time the alarm sounded and the arrival of one of our cars."

I shrugged. "Maybe whoever broke the door realized he'd triggered the alarm and didn't go in."

"But you did."

"I did."

He turned the paper he held around and showed me what was on it.

"See this? It's an APB with your name on it. You've just added to your case, pal."

I raised an eyebrow. "Aplin worked fast."

"The Special Crimes Unit and the RCMP are looking for you in connection with a murder and an attempted. You're also a suspect in the mass murder of thirteen young men who were part of a cult. You want to talk about it?"

"Nope."

There was a knock at the door, and Powell entered with Aplin. Both looked tired and rumpled. Simmons got up and nodded to them. I almost asked him to stay.

"Well, well," Aplin said as he jiggled change in his pocket, "it's nice to see you where you belong, Meter."

He pulled out a chair, sat down. His belly was nearly bursting his shirt buttons and a few tufts of hair poked through where the tip of his tie stopped.

"Why did you leave the scene, Jack?" Powell said. "It doesn't look good."

"Tomkins said he thought you went into the house," Aplin said, "but when he followed you, he couldn't find you. Where'd you hide?"

Now I owed Tomkins one. I didn't know if he'd reserved judgment on what he saw, or if he'd done it out of respect for my friendship with Terry, but he'd bought me some time. All without implicating himself. Smart kid.

"Nowhere."

"We found your prints all over Winston's house," Aplin said. "And guess what? They're all over Garner's house, too."

"It doesn't mean I killed Garner."

Aplin snorted. "Give me a fucking break, Meter. You're dirty and I'm putting you away."

I looked at Powell. "I wasn't near Garner's house when he was killed and you know it."

Instead of agreeing, he said, "Where were you between four-thirty and seven last night?"

"At four-thirty I was already in a Blue Line cab going toward Orleans. I took the cab in front of the Chateau Laurier at quarter after four. Traffic was heavy on the Queensway and I didn't want to be late for Christmas dinner. I arrived at Terry Parczek's house around quarter to five. Tomkins called him, at—what?—around seven-thirty? I was still there. We were still eating. Ask Terry."

"He's been sedated for the night."

"Ask Betty, his wife, then. You can also check with the doorman of the hotel and the cab driver."

Aplin was pale, probably from rage at my having an alibi.

"Believe me, we will," he said.

"As for my prints in Winston's house." I tried a sheepish grin. "It's true I went in. I'd forgotten my gloves," I lied, "and I wanted to look around for myself before you guys took over. I was stupid. Maybe it was the shock of Terry almost dying. Or severe indigestion from Betty's turkey," I added as an afterthought.

Powell coughed, his hand in front of his mouth, trying to hide a broad grin. Obviously, he'd been a victim of Betty's cooking, too.

"That's a load of bullshit," Aplin snarled.

"There's still the matter of the Richmond Grill," Powell said.

"The back door was open. I investigated."

Powell stared at me for a moment then nodded.

"I'll have a uniform drive you home." He grinned. "And stay with you in your room until we've verified your alibi."

I grinned back. "Fair enough. Thanks."

He led a griping Aplin out. Ten minutes later, I was signing for my possessions then sitting in a blue-and-white again. The young cop who'd arrested me at the Richmond Grill was driving.

"So," I said, "what'd you do, piss off the mayor to get the Christmas Eve graveyard shift?"

He looked at me in the mirror. "I'm the one with the least seniority, plus I've got no family here. Hard to argue with that."

"Well, at least you'll be able to rag on your buds a bit. You're going to spend Christmas in a suite at the Chateau Laurier."

That seemed to brighten him a bit.

There was little traffic on the roads, so we got there in five minutes. I installed him in the suite with the menu—on me—and the remote then said I was going to bed.

I hid the stick in Neola's old bedroom and went into mine. I wished myself on Thrittene and there I was. I heaved a sigh of relief as Trebor and Leinad appeared.

"Hey, guys," I said, "I couldn't bring back your gizmo. It doesn't work with my telecarb."

Leinad was all the colors of the rainbow, and screeches flowed in the air. He attempted a grin but in his excitement split his head in two.

"Oh, no need, Jack Meter. We were monitoring the portal. We extracted the coordinates when someone used it. We know exactly where the universe you seek is."

"Great."

"But even better, Jack Meter," Trebor said. "We can get you there."

CHAPTER TWENTY-THREE

"AND WHERE IS 'THERE?'"

Leinad made the approximation of a human shrug.

"Some distance along the eleventh dimension. Of course, I am using the word *distance* so that you may understand. You cannot really apply a dimension on another dimension. All I can say is that it is both infinitely long and very thin."

I was afraid to ask. "How thin?"

"At its thickest part, a trillionth of a millimeter."

"Yeah, right. How can a whole universe fit on that?"

Clucking sounds resounded from the walls.

"You are not paying attention," Trebor said. "The eleventh dimension exists only one trillionth of a millimeter from every point in your three-dimensional Earth, as well as in any other part of our universe. It is closer to your skin than even the telecarb, yet you cannot sense it. The universe you asked us to find can regularly intersect with others without destroying them. Whoever developed the technology to do so is nothing short of brilliant."

I still didn't get it, but it wasn't that important as long as they'd found the damn thing.

"So, how do I get to that universe?"

"We have been working on reconfiguring part of your telecarb based on the device Neola Durwin wore."

"You copied the OP?"

Leinad turned a shade of purple. "We needed to understand the Osmotic Parser in order to repair her. It was attached to her body."

I snickered. "Yeah, and I've got a block of ice you can sell up north."

Static came out of the walls. "Why would we wish to sell ice?"

"Never mind. Instead of tinkering with my telecarb again, why didn't you just build another OP?"

"It would have been useless for you."

Not the smallness of my brain again. "Neola had no difficulty using it. If she can, I can."

Trebor smiled. I saw mischief twinkle in his eyes, even though they weren't real.

"No doubt of it, Jack Meter."

"The coordinates are extremely complex," Leinad said, "but they could be entered in memory so you would not have to remember them yourself. The problem is that this is a universe within a universe."

"I thought that was impossible."

"Theoretically, it is. As soon as such a universe is created, it would give rise to its own space as it grew and disengage from the birth universe."

"So what's the deal?"

"There is a special type of membrane around this universe, one similar to the field that held Annie Barnes's clone together."

The Thrittene turned green, and I started to sink.

"Whoa, keep it together, guys," I shouted over the moans.

The sinking stopped mid-knee. The noise abated.

"You've got to stop being led by your emotions. It's dangerous for my health."

"Our pardon, Jack Meter."

"I take it you've now accepted that one part of you is missing."

"And being used in slavery," Trebor said in a mournful voice that was echoed thousands of times by our surroundings. "We have always believed you, Jack Meter, even though we could not feel the extraction or subsequent absence of the manifestation of us. We now have the proof, however, that what you said is correct. The us you call

Nasus is being used to contain that universe. If it continues to grow, I am afraid she will not be the only one who will disappear."

That concept I could understand. If a small strip of Thrittene matter could glue different chunks of the universe into a whole then an entire Thrittene would hold an entire small universe together but she'd end up stretched too thin at some point.

"It is because one of ours is containing this universe that we can get you through," Leinad said. "By our enhancing the parameters of your telecarb, you will be able to get there."

I sensed a but. "More importantly, will I be able to come back?"

They both looked away.

"Uh-huh. This is a one-time shot."

"You will need to find an alternate way to return to our universe. One of their portals, perhaps." Trebor raised his hands, palms up, in a gesture of helplessness. They spent entirely too much time with humans. "You must understand, Jack Meter, that this technology almost defied our scientific knowledge. We cannot do more."

"My goal isn't only to get there but to find out how to dismantle that universe."

"And return our matter to us."

I thought of the first time I'd met Nasus, a bedroom voice wrapped in hourglass curves with a brain like a Venus flytrap.

"I happen to kinda like that matter," I said, "so, yeah, that's the plan. To do that, though, I've got to find out where they keep their equipment."

"That we cannot help you with."

"That's why I'm the PI and you're not." I rubbed my hands together. "Okay, guys, let's get going. Once we're finished here, I've got cops I need to lose."

* * *

A knock at the door woke me up. I was disoriented for a moment, expecting my sagging couch and the smell of cigar. Then I remembered I was at the Chateau, luxuriating in a king-size bed.

The door burst open, and a silhouette stood in the entrance.

"Detective Powell would like to speak to you," Jablonski, the young cop guarding me said, his voice sounding relieved.

I squinted from the light flooding from the room behind him. I felt groggy and sluggish.

"What time is it?"

"Near six-thirty."

"In the morning? Shit, you guys ever sleep?" I'd been dead to the world for less than two hours. I dragged myself out of bed. "Coffee," I moaned. "Otherwise, I can't guarantee you'll live."

He quirked a smile. "Remember who you're talking to."

He left the door open and went back into the living room. I prayed he'd take pity on me and order some coffee. I shoved my arms into the robe the hotel provided then followed him, yawning.

"Jesus, you look as bad as I feel," Powell growled. His eyes sported bags over his bags, and his three-day growth of beard inched toward the five-day mark. "Your conscience couldn't let you sleep, Meter?"

"Slept fine, thank you." Just not nearly long enough. "I always look like this before I get my dose of poison."

"I heard it was scotch at one time."

"That was then."

"Coffee coming right up," the young cop said.

"If you were a girl, I'd kiss you."

Powell shook his head with a rueful smile.

"Go home," he said to the cop then waited for the kid to leave.

"You could've waited until he had breakfast."

Powell pointed at the tray on the coffee table. It was laden with dirty dishes.

"Judging from the remains, you'll have a hell of a food bill. I think the kid's still growing."

There was a knock at the door and a key inserted in the lock. A uniformed waiter pushing a cart came in. I quickly signed the bill, added a fat tip—it was Christmas, after all—and poured myself a cup of coffee.

"Want one?" I said to Powell.

"Sure. Can't be worse than the slop I've been ingesting."

Coffee went down hot and black. I took a moment to savor it, waiting for the caffeine to kick in, then noticed croissants on the tray. Not as good as a bagel, but since I was starving, I silently thanked my young cop for his foresight. I stuffed half of one in my mouth, gestured for Powell to go ahead.

We ate in silence. After a second cup, I was more awake, even though I felt punchy.

"You know," I finally said, "being a PI and everything, I've come to the conclusion that, since you've dismissed the cop and we're sharing a meal, I'm off the hook."

He nodded while he swallowed a last bite of croissant. "I just came from the General. Parczek confirmed your alibi. You were at his place while Garner was getting his throat slashed. Terry also said the Richmond Grill is part of an ongoing investigation you're involved in." He pursed his lips, finished his coffee. "Never heard of the RCMP using civilians before."

"Think of me as a consultant."

"I'm not crazy about your methods, Mr. Consultant. It's a good thing we can't find the owner of that restaurant, otherwise he could be pressing charges against you. As it is, we'll fine you for damage of property and that'll be that. For now."

I had a sudden inspiration. "Check with Garner's secretary. I bet he owned that restaurant."

"That doesn't help your case."

"Maybe not, but why would I lead you in that direction then?"

He thought for a few seconds then nodded.

"All right, I'll do that." He picked up his hat and walked to the door. "Us poor schmucks have to work for a living, so I'll leave you to the rest of your breakfast."

As soon as Powell left, I took a quick shower and gulped down more coffee. Powell had said they'd stashed Terry at the General, so I headed out there. I owed him again for keeping me out of Aplin's grasp.

I found Betty and the kids in the waiting room near the elevators. Evie and Eric sat on the floor, mauling paper with crayons. Eleanore sat on one of the plastic chairs, her arm tight through her mother's. When Betty saw me, she got up, eyes awash in tears.

"What happened, Betty? Is Terry okay?"

"He's fine. As fine as he could be, considering." She placed her hands on my shoulders, stood on tiptoe and kissed me softly on the mouth. She smelled of gardenia and lemon tea.

"What was that for?" I smiled.

She glanced over her shoulder at the kids, who all looked at me with serious eyes.

"For saving Terry's life," she whispered.

"I didn't do much." She was looking at me with such adoration I started to get uncomfortable. "Listen, can I see him?"

"The doctor's with him right now." She gave me a weak smile. "Terry's been grumbling since they brought him in last night. He makes the nurses miserable, repeats that he wants to go home. I think they'll get rid of him this morning, just so the other patients can have a rest."

I chuckled. "The teddy bear has a roar."

"Mrs. Parczek?" An intern stood at the edge of the waiting room. He looked more fed up than tired. "Your husband can go home."

The kids cheered.

The intern raised a hand. "On the condition that he stays in bed, with his leg elevated. I'll give you some instructions."

I took Betty's hand. "I'll be only a couple minutes, okay?"

She sighed. "Sure. He's in room 407. Don't take too long, though. The kids are hungry."

I squeezed her hand and went into Terry's room. He lay on the bed closest to the window, his entire leg in a cast suspended from a frame with a set of ropes and pulleys. They'd put his left arm in a sling and taped it to his body. His skin was pale; his right eye had begun to turn purple and it was almost swollen shut.

"You've looked better," I said.

He turned his head. "So have you."

"Long night. Thanks for getting Powell off my back."

"Hey, no problem." He hesitated then: "Jack—"

"Listen," I interrupted quickly before he got mushy. "I'm going to leave town for a few days."

He frowned, looking relieved and worried at the same time.

"That'll burn Aplin's ass. I'll be out of commission for a while, won't be able to run interference for you. Do you think you can handle yourself?"

I laughed. "I'll keep you posted as much as I can. Take care of that leg."

I checked the time; it was a little before noon, so Claire should be at home. The taxi took the Queensway. Her apartment building fronted the river, near the Nepean Sailing Club, and soon the driver got off at Carling. Traffic was heavy, the drivers impatient. I remembered it was Boxing Day, all these people rushing out to exchange socks and blenders they had no use for.

The afternoon had turned beautiful, the sky pale blue with a few stringy clouds. The sun warmed me through the glass and made me drowsy. I wondered idly what kind of weather they had in my other self's universe.

Had that Jack Meter killed Garner? I hoped not. I refused to think that I'd grown up that different in another universe.

I asked the driver to wait until I found out if Claire was at home. Although I'd never been to her place, I knew she lived on the fourteenth floor. Sure enough, I found the initials C. F. beside buzzer 1405. I pressed the button and held it for several seconds then waited. No answer. I repeated the process. Still nothing.

I felt let down. She was usually so predictable that I'd been sure she'd be there. She rarely let a day pass without going to work, but on weekend and holidays, she never went in before one o'clock.

The driver honked, and I gestured to wait a minute. I tried the buzzer again but when I still got no answer I went back out and jumped in the cab. As it was turning around, I noticed Claire's Jeep in the parking lot. Odd.

I stopped the driver, paid him and got out again.

Claire had a relationship with her car. She'd even named it. She took it everywhere, the way someone else would a dog or a child. Maybe she'd broken the habit and had left in a cab or a friend had picked her up, but somehow I doubted it. She was too much of a tightass. Then again, maybe she was in her apartment and didn't want to be bothered.

I had to check anyway. If she was there, the most I'd get would be a dressing down. I was used to those from her.

There was no one around. I walked behind her Jeep then wished myself into her apartment. I landed in her living room.

It suited her personality. It was done in vivid colors, as fiery as her temper—rust on the wall, white leather on the couch, red and green pillows and matching rug over hardwood.

"Claire?" I called.

There was no response. I checked the main door—no sign of break-in. I wandered through the rest of the apartment: kitchen, dining room, bathroom, office. Every corner was pristine. It made me think of Garner's house. I wondered what prompted people to keep their house as tidy as a monk's cell. I preferred the lived-in look of a couple of empty pizza boxes and dirty coffee cups.

The picture was different in the bedroom. The bed was unmade, the sheets half pulled off the mattress, the duvet crumpled. Cotton pajamas had been dumped on the floor in a heap in front of the open closet. Her lingerie drawer was half-opened. Her watch was still on her night table. It was such a contrast to the rest of the apartment, I knew something had happened to her.

Then I saw it. On the bedside table farther away from me, a small pin rested in a glass dish. I picked it up.

If I didn't know where Claire was, I knew who had her. Clever Neola had left Karoi's USI for me to find. That meant they were on to us and had somehow discovered Claire was a threat to them. Because of her experience in building the conjugator, in all probability she could operate their equipment. So they'd kidnapped her.

Neola obviously liked to brag and wanted me as well as Claire. Claire's image flashed in front of my eyes, her skin waxy pale, her copper hair knotted, her throat slashed and bleeding. My heart thumped hard, and I couldn't swallow.

I pushed the image away, mentally slamming a door against it. I couldn't afford to think that way. But if Claire was dead, I swore the guilty would pay.

The game had just gotten more serious. When I found Claire, I'd find the others. And I would find her.

Chapter Twenty-Four

I SAT ON THE COUCH OF MY SUITE, EXHAUSTION NUMBING MY BRAIN. A TRIP TO visit Saurimo had yielded nothing more positive than the knowledge she and her sister had declared a truce. I'd gone there on the off-chance Neola had dumped Claire with her. After all, the pin had belonged to Karoi, one of her subjects, even if he was a traitor. Neola might've seen that as a kind of irony.

I arrived on the same spot before Saurimo's tent. Down in the valley, soldiers had erected tents on both sides of the river. They weren't fighting. When I turned to the tent, none of Saurimo's turtles greeted me, so I went inside. I found her having a drink with Asela.

They both rose when they saw me.

"Has one come to send us home?" Saurimo said.

"Not yet, but I'm getting close." I described Claire and asked them if they'd seen her. Neither of them had.

"We are sorry for one's friend," Saurimo said. "We hope one will find her." She sat down again. "As one can see, we and our sister have declared an armistice. We are readying for the time we will go home. Do not disappoint, Jack Meter."

It was a bad sign when Saurimo used one's name. That meant she was thinking of acting on her threats. I assured her I was making every effort then wished myself back to my suite.

I had a couple more options, I thought, as I got up and walked to the window and opened the drapes. I looked out, time-confused again. I'd left Claire's apartment a little after one. Now night had fallen, and tens of thousands of blue, red and white lights spiffed up the trees along the Rideau Canal. A countdown clock on the wall of the Conference Center across the street showed less than thirty-six hours before 2003 kicked in. Tomorrow was New Year's Eve. I'd lost four days.

I tried not to think about Claire. Every day I didn't find her increased the probability she was dead.

I turned my back to the window and forced myself to think. I could use Leinad's gizmo and get to their universe. If Claire wasn't there, though, and I couldn't find a portal that brought me back here—or someplace where my telecarb worked—I'd be stranded. I couldn't even ask for an OP from Mariental—Leinad had said it wouldn't work in that universe.

On the other hand, considering Neola's arrogance, maybe she'd stashed Claire in her house in Colorado. I'd planned to go back there, anyway, to see what she'd done with the way station. If they didn't have her at the house, I might find a hint as to where they'd taken her.

I couldn't figure out how they'd linked Claire to me. Only a select few knew about the business with Mueller and that she had collaborated in the development of the conjugator. No one knew we were planning to send her back to Entomon—I hadn't even told the Thrittene yet. Maybe they'd taken her on spec.

Or maybe a bug from Entomon had mentioned her name, and Neola realized I could use her to find out more about their equipment, even destroy it. If that was the case, their timing had been damn near perfect.

I decided to go back to Claire's apartment. Maybe she'd left me a clue I'd missed. As soon as I got there, I made a beeline for her bedroom and stood in the entrance, studying the mess she'd left behind.

They'd given her time to dress, considering the pajamas on the floor. Did that mean someone might see her and find it odd she was wearing nightclothes?

Then it hit me. I remembered Neola had said the OP couldn't

transport two people. If they wanted her, they'd have to take her the ordinary way—through the door.

I strode to the hall closet, opened the door. Her winter coat and boots were gone.

Shit. Neola had played me like a harmonica. Again. By leaving Karoi's pin, she'd counted on me going to see Saurimo and wasting time. Meanwhile, they could make their way to wherever they wanted to keep her. If it was Colorado, they'd probably used a private jet. I had to go to the airport, check it out.

Something rippled across my skin, beginning from my telecarb and up my arm. At the same moment, Neola appeared right in front of me. She saw me at the same time, her eyes widening in surprise. By the time I'd stepped forward, she had a gun trained on me.

"Don't you have one of those laser things?" I said. "Guns are messy."

"Yes, but they work almost anywhere." She frowned. "What are you doing here?"

"Looking for you, sweetheart."

"Funny, Jack." She gestured with the gun. "Why don't you sit on that dining room chair? That'll make me feel better."

Since she was the one with the deadly weapon, I did what she said.

"Where's Claire, Neola?"

"Don't worry about her, Jack. We're taking care of her. Did you think you could use her to outmaneuver us? I know you better than anyone. I can anticipate all your moves."

"You mean the other Jack can."

She chuckled. "There's that, too. It was good of you to visit Saurimo. That gave us enough time to take care of things at this end."

There was little consolation in knowing I'd been right. She stepped behind my chair.

"I hate to hit and run," she mumbled, "but..."

A sharp pain exploded at the back of my head. Everything went black.

*   *   *

I came to with a groan. My mouth felt like sandpaper, and I had a bump the size of an egg on the back of my head. Fortunately, my skull was a hard one, otherwise Neola would've cracked it. As it was, I wasn't feeling too steady on my feet.

I staggered to the kitchen and poured a large glass of water, which I drank thirstily. I wondered why Neola hadn't killed me, but then through the fuzz it came to me—she knew the telecarb would whisk me away if she shot me. At least this way, she knew where I was. That she hadn't even tied me up was a sign of her arrogance, maybe even her way to vex me.

All the lights blazed in the apartment, which she'd turned upside-down. She'd been searching for something, but I had no idea what it could be.

If Neola could anticipate all my movements, I might as well oblige her, I thought. Unlike her OP, my telecarb could take two people anywhere. All I had to do was find Claire. First stop, Colorado.

I wished myself in the glass tower. No one had turned on a lamp there, but the reflection of the moon on snow was enough for me to see by. I listened for a minute. I figured if they were in the house, they were all sleeping. Slowly, making sure the stairs didn't creak, I crept down to the lower level.

Someone had stayed here recently—the smell of bacon and toast lingered in the air, an empty brandy glass sat on the ottoman, one of Neola's sweaters hung on the arm of a chair. The kitchen was empty, a couple of dishes draining on the counter under a fluorescent light. The plates were dry, but there was still a bit of water on the drainboard.

Neola had showered recently. A towel, still damp, smelled of her soap. No one in her office, or in her bedroom, although there was more evidence she'd been around not so long ago.

I'd left the guest room for last. I tried the door. It was locked, but the key wasn't in the lock. I knocked.

"Claire, are you in there?"

There was no answer, but I heard rustling inside. I took out my tools and poked at the lock. It was a simple one, and I had it opened in a second. I opened the door. The room was dark.

"Claire?"

I heard the rustling again then saw some movement from the corner of my eye. I had just enough time to raise my arm when a heavy object hit me full force on the shoulder. The strike propelled me forward. I twisted around to face whoever was trying to knock me down, tripped on the carpet and fell back onto the bed. Claire rushed forward, a heavy brass urn raised above her head.

"Claire, for Christ's sake, stop!"

She was just about to hit me with the vase when I pulled my sleeve and showed her the telecarb.

"Look, it's me, the real Jack."

She lowered her weapon but kept it in her hands. "It could be a fake."

"Well, it's not. I'll whip you out of here, that should convince you."

She backed up a step. "You're not laying a hand on me until I'm sure of who you are."

My shoulder ached. "Did you have to hit me so hard?" I said, rubbing it. "No wonder Mueller ended up in the cabinet when you hit him with a shelf. You pack quite a punch."

She relaxed a fraction.

"It's about time you got here," she said, throwing me the urn.

I caught it, examined it. "You dented it."

"I was rather hoping to break your head."

"I already tried that," Neola said from the door. She hit the lights in the bedroom. She had her gun in her hand.

"Neola," I said. "Nice to see you again."

"I'm sorry to say the pleasure isn't mutual," she said. "You should've stayed away, Jack."

I shifted position.

"Ah-ah, stay away from her. Otherwise, I'll have to shoot her."

"I'd rather not go through that again, if you don't mind," Claire said.

Neola frowned then shrugged. She gestured with her gun to Claire.

"You first. In the living room. Then you, Jack. You sit on opposite sides of the couch."

* * *

She sat facing us. "Your timing isn't good, Jack, I'm sorry to say. We're close to finishing what we started. We intend to do it without your interference."

"I'm hard to get rid of."

"All I have to do is shoot you in a couple of places. It should take some time for the Thrittene to fix you up. Just enough time for us."

"Whatever did you see in her?" Claire said, a sneer on her face. "You're such a jerk, Jack."

"I'm not taking flack from you, Claire. You've caused me trouble enough."

"Trouble? I'll show what trouble is." She crossed her arms under her breasts and glared.

"I thought the two of you were friends," Neola said.

"I hate his guts," Claire said between her teeth.

Good, I thought, Claire was mad. She was always at her most brilliant then.

"Oh, come on, sweetheart, you're just saying that to hurt my feelings. You love it when I'm around. It adds excitement to your life."

Claire growled. I laughed. Someone's feet appeared on the stairs from the tower. I stopped laughing.

"Uncanny, isn't it?" he said to me when he'd reached the main floor. He walked to where Neola sat, placed a hand on her shoulder. She covered it with her free one.

It was definitely spooky. I was looking at myself as if I were looking in a mirror. The clothes were different—under a coffee-colored bomber jacket, he wore black jeans and a black turtleneck with black half-boots while I wore my ratty black leather jacket over a white T-shirt and stone-washed jeans with high-tops. Everything else was the same, though, from our height to the length of our beards.

"You've been making a mess of things, using my name," I said. "I resent that."

"It's my name, too."

"You don't live up to it."

"White knights in armor tend to have short lives. I'd rather look out for myself."

"Why did you kill Garner?"

A shadow fleeted across his face, but before he could answer, Neola squeezed his hand.

"I'm the one who killed him. Using a knife was a bit gruesome, but that's what I had on hand. The little rat was getting a bit too greedy for my taste."

"So, Garner was in on your scheme from the beginning."

"No. We rented the Richmond Grill from him. Unfortunately, when we tested the portal, the Carlisle beside it got shifted. He was in the restaurant one day when we were going off-world and followed us in. He didn't care about what we were doing. All he wanted was compensation."

"Why didn't you kill him then?"

Neola shrugged. "We thought he'd be useful. He kept you busy, gave me a chance to contact you."

"You wanted the AGES to concentrate on me."

"It worked for a while."

"What is it, exactly, you're trying to do?"

"Haven't you figured it out, Jack?" Claire said. "They're getting rich."

"Ah, yes," my other self said, "you're clever in both worlds, Claire. Garner knew what he was doing, you know. There's a fortune to be made in real estate."

It was all suddenly clear.

"You're creating a universe and selling portions of it."

"Perfect, isn't it? You take a bit here, a bit there, merge it together and voilà—you have a new world ready to be inhabited. There are many races in many universes who are awfully crowded and want a new place to live."

"Although in some cases, people need to be convinced to give up their worldly goods in order to move elsewhere."

"You're referring to the cult," Neola said. "I had nothing to do with those kids' deaths except to give the job of Abura to Garner. Once the kids signed over their assets he didn't see the use for them, got them to drink some juice. He planted the bomb, too, expected it would go off and eliminate the evidence. You screwed up things for him."

"What percentage were you taking?"

She shrugged. "It was our operation, after all."

"So you killed him."

"Initiative is all well and good, but recklessness is unforgivable."

"You tried to deflect the investigation by wiping out his prints and planting mine instead."

"Gotta use what you have," the other Jack said. "I had to leave a perfectly good leather jacket behind."

"You can afford plenty of others," Neola said, patting his hand.

He smiled. "That I can."

"I didn't know about the bomb, but it was perfect." She grinned. "I like Sergeant Aplin." She stopped smiling. "So, Jack, maybe you can persuade Claire to tell us what she's done with the anti-conjugating device."

Clever Claire, indeed. She'd bought herself some time by inventing the existence of a device that could counter their equipment.

"And lose my chance to stop you?" I said. "I don't think so."

"Fine, then," Neola said, raising her gun.

"Not again," Claire said. "Jack Meter, it's always the same thing when you're around. They threaten you, they know you can't be killed then they point the stupid gun at me, you tell them go ahead, kill her I don't care, and we're back to square one."

"What the hell are you talking about?" I shouted. "You died only once. Big deal."

"Big deal?" she squealed. "Why, you rotten, shag-faced, no-dick asshole," she said, "I'll feed your heart to my bugs." She launched herself across the couch. From the corner of my eye, I saw Neola tilt the gun toward her. I reached for Claire's hand, wished myself at the hotel. The gun went off.

We landed on the floor, Claire on top of me.

"Are you hurt?" I said.

She pushed off me. "No, but that was close."

"Well done." I got up, took her hand. "Let's get out of here. Neola knows this place." I thought quickly, discarded a few options then had it. We landed in Terry's basement. Evie screamed.

"Evie," I said, "it's me. Don't be scared."

She stared at me, blinked several times then rushed up the stairs. "Mooooooom!"

"I see you have a positive effect on children," Claire said, her tone sardonic.

"Must be the shag face. Let's go say hi to Betty and Terry."

I followed her upstairs. One thing about her kidnapping—she wouldn't need any more convincing to go to Entomon. The lady had a mean streak when it came to getting revenge.

CHAPTER TWENTY-FIVE

EVIE HAD GONE UPSTAIRS AND COME BACK WITH BETTY, WHO WAS FAR FROM happy we'd scared her daughter. She gave me a tongue-lashing I'll remember for a long time, sniffed then told us she'd fix us a snack.

"You'd better go with her," I said to Claire, "and let her know you're a vegetarian. Otherwise, she's bound to make you a salami sandwich."

"How about you, aren't you coming up?"

"In a moment."

She scowled. "You're not going to disappear on me, are you?"

"No. I just want a minute to sort things out."

"I know what you mean." She climbed a couple of steps, turned. "You know, I didn't like your other self any better, but at least, in this world, you're your own man."

I listened to the tap of her feet on the stairs then to her voice as she spoke with Betty.

As usual, in her own disagreeable way, Claire had zeroed in on the reason I wanted some time alone.

I was miffed.

I recognized the pettiness of it, but it rankled that my alter ego was such a wuss. An unprincipled wuss, at that. I could play hardball when I needed to, but if Annie had told me she'd slashed a guy's throat because he messed up her plans, I'd have done more than wince. And there Neola was, patting his hand as if he were a dog that had just performed a trick, and he took it. What had occurred in his world to make him so different from me?

To make matters worse, Neola had played her cat-and-mouse game with both of us, and it had worked. I had to ask myself if I didn't have more in common with that wuss than I thought, which I found profoundly disturbing.

On top of which, I had another concern. Knowing how fluid the Thrittene's ethics were, they could've helped Neola reach Entomon. I'd never asked them if they knew her before she arrived, half-dead, with me on their world. She'd had her USI to get to Thrittene, but she'd needed a time bubble to get to Entomon, at least according to Claire. I couldn't see how else she could've made her way there, which meant my white friends had probably stuck their melting fingers into the pie again. I'd have to have a conversation with them when Claire and I went to visit. Which would have to be soon, because I was getting real tired of running after my own tail.

The patter of tiny feet on the stairs jolted me out of my brooding. The triple-Es appeared, Eric in front, as if to protect his two sisters. They smiled hesitantly.

"Mom says to come up for your snack. Daddy wants to wring your neck, too."

"That's what he said, huh?"

Eric nodded. "That's 'cause you're an insiderate jerk. What does insiderate mean?"

"I think you mean inconsiderate."

"Mom says we're supposed to thank you," Evie said from behind Eleanore.

"You're welcome," I said, not moving from my supine position on the couch. "What for?"

"The presents," Eric said.

When I only nodded, Evie shuffled forward. "Is it okay if I give my cerfiticate—"

"Certificate, you dummy," Eric interrupted.

"Takes one to know one," Evie said, instantly distracted from her goal. "You're a booger-brain, anyway."

"Ah…kids," I said, before this generated into war, "how about staying on track?"

"Uh?"

"Who'd you want to give your gift certificate to, Evie?"

She pouted. "To him." She pointed at Eric.

"I thought you didn't like him."

"I don't." She stuck her tongue at him.

"She wants my Spiderman costume," Eric said.

"It's gonna be a Spider *woman* costume."

"There's no Spiderwoman, you double-dummy."

"Is too."

"Is not."

I sat up. "Whoa, time out. You guys can do what you want, okay?"

They both smiled, suddenly looking like angels. I knew better.

"Gee, thanks, Mr. Meter."

They both turned and scrambled back up the stairs. Eleanore rolled her eyes.

"They're such babies," she said, looking disgusted. "I'm gonna buy a Lil Bow Wow CD."

I had a feeling she wasn't talking about recorded barking dogs.

"Good for you."

Her eyes sparkled. "Mom didn't want to buy me one, but she said I can now with my certificate. So, thanks."

"You're welcome." I had a sudden idea. "Ellie, if you had something really special you didn't want anyone to touch or play with, where would you hide it?"

The question seemed to intrigue her. "Is it big?"

Good question. "I don't know."

She shrugged. "Doesn't really matter, I guess. I'd make it look like something else, maybe. You know, like those books I saw at the craft fair. You open them and there's a big hole in the pages, so you can hide your jewelry or your gun. I bet you have one."

"I don't have a gun," I said absently. Her idea had merit. "But what if your mom and your sister and brother knew all your hiding places?"

"I'd find a more clever one." She frowned. "Or I'd take it to Rhea."

"Who's Rhea?"

"My best friend. She lives two houses down from us. Hiding something there's not as good, because I'd have to go to her place when she's at home to get it and if she's not there then I'd have to wait, but no one would know she has it, right?"

"Unless Rhea told."

"Then she wouldn't be my best friend anymore."

"Ellie," Betty called down. "Supper."

"I'm coming, Mom." She smiled shyly. "Did I help?"

I smiled. "You sure did. Thanks, beautiful."

She giggled and ran up the stairs. I followed her up.

"Oh, good," Betty said, sounding harried. "You can take dinner to Terry while I feed the kids. I put a sandwich on the tray for you as well."

"I'm sorry I scared the kids, Betty."

"Oh, I'm over it now. Once they got over their surprise, they were excited. You seem to be a hit in our house."

"Where's Claire?"

"In the shower. She said she might not have another occasion for a while."

I squeezed her shoulder and kissed her cheek before I took Terry's tray, showing her my appreciation for her not asking questions she knew she wouldn't get answers to.

"Can you believe it?" Terry exploded as soon as I went into the guest bedroom where Betty had set him up. "She won't let me smoke. I'm lying here, going frigging nuts from boredom, and she won't let me smoke. Says secondhand smoke's not good for the kids."

"You won't get any pity from me," I said. "That thing around my wrist forced me to quit."

"Yeah, but you didn't have the withdrawal symptoms."

"I still feel like lighting up once in a while." I thought longingly of my Gitanes.

"Thanks," he said acidly, "I really needed to know that." He lifted the cover over his plate and stared mournfully at the dried-out leftover turkey and the lumpy mashed potatoes. "I'd kill for an all-dressed burger with fries."

"Too much cholesterol."

"Who are you, my family doctor?"

I laughed, sat down on the chair beside his bed to watch him eat. I lifted the bread from my sandwich and peered at the mystery meat under a piece of limp lettuce. I dropped the bread and set the plate aside.

"Give me an update, will you?" he mumbled.

I narrated to him what I'd learned so far. He didn't interrupt, only frowned when it came to the reason for Garner's murder.

"That's one mean woman," he said. "Do you know why she turned?"

I shrugged. "Maybe she saw too much. Or maybe she always had it in her."

"That's a frigging complicated scheme."

"Can you get Tomkins to dig deeper on the Foundation? She must have plans for that money. I suspect both her and the other Jack are trustees."

"She means to keep the money for herself."

Terry might look like a badly dressed teddy bear, but it never could be said he hadn't a mind like a sharp blade.

"If you were her, would you share?"

"If she stays on Earth in this universe," Claire said from the door, "one of you will be redundant."

I was surrounded by geniuses.

"I wondered when you'd catch that. And then maybe she won't need any man whatsoever. It's dangerous keeping someone around who's been a witness to all your dirty deeds. But I think we'll get married first."

"I see," Claire said. "She eliminates you, gets the other Jack to stand in for you then gets rid of him when she doesn't need him anymore. She's greedy, isn't she?"

"She wants your money?" Terry said.

"She wants everything."

"Come on, Jack, that's just speculation at this point." He set his plate on top of my sandwich. "And maybe a lot of offended pride."

I sighed. "Maybe. It might've been just a game that got out of hand and she's too damn proud to say she fucked up."

Claire sat down at the foot of Terry's bed, glanced at me with sober eyes.

"You saw her face when she said she'd killed Garner. She enjoyed slashing his throat."

"Speaking of Garner," I said, "I think their equipment is at his house."

Terry shook his head. "Both the city cops and our guys went through the house with a fine-tooth comb. They didn't find anything."

"Maybe it looks like something else."

"Like what?"

"No idea. First thing is to find out how big this equipment is. That's where Claire comes in."

"Neola had the means to travel to Thrittene. Do you think they helped her?"

"That's one thing I'll be sure to ask Trebor when we get there," I said.

Claire took a deep breath, nodded once. "We might as well get started. I'm not looking forward to this visit."

* * *

"How lovely to see you again, Claire Foucault," Trebor said. "We were not expecting your visit."

"Claire needs to get to Entomon," I said before she could answer. "Can you send her?"

Leinad split from Trebor, like a tree axed right in the middle. "We can," he said. "Is this pertaining to your case, Jack Meter?"

"Yeah."

I gestured for Claire to go with Leinad. She threw me a speculative glance then nodded.

"Listen, Trebor," I continued after she left, "when I first talked to you about this case, you said you knew about the Intergalactic Agency, right?"

He nodded. "They have operated across the universe for dozens of your years. We have never had cause to use them, of course."

"Did you know that Neola was an IGA agent?"

"Of course. That is how she introduced herself. Her credentials were in order."

"And that was before we came here together?"

"Yes, maybe—let me see, your timeframe can be so confusing—two weeks after you solved the Mueller case. I am surprised she did not mention it."

"Did she go to Entomon?"

Trebor turned a pale shade of blue. "We sent her, yes. Was it wrong?"

Shit. "What did she give you?"

Trebor shook his head. "Give us? Nothing. The IGA is entitled to demand our help at any time. She said she needed to make the trip as part of an investigation into the reasons why Mueller was able to create the clone. She said she had been in contact with you. Was that not so?"

The lady had done her homework. I wondered where she'd got all her information.

"Did she come back with something?"

"She did not come back here. She was sent back somewhere else. The Entomons have the technology to do so."

That stopped me. "So, she could go back and forth several times, once you built the bubble for her."

"As long as the Entomons were willing to keep the portal open."

A new piece fit into the puzzle. "They're the ones who built your Transworld Portals?"

"Yes, of course. Although they needed our help to synchronize the time factor. It was an easy enough adjustment."

I paced up and down the white room, for once appreciating its lack of features. There was nothing else to do there but think.

"Okay, let's see." The walls seemed to absorb my words as soon as they came out of my mouth. "Let's say that when I used the conjugator I created another universe, triggering an alert at the AGES, who got involved in closing it off, but not quickly enough. Neola found out how it worked, so she goes out and finds another me in a parallel universe and gets him to run around creating havoc, implicating me in murder in this universe.

"In the meantime, she keeps me busy, leading me on a false trail while the other me is using the equipment the Entomons built for them, including the portals, to put a universe together by stealing pieces of other universes."

I stopped in front of Trebor, who was trying to frown but wasn't very successful. He'd turned a dingy gray, indicating he was worried.

"Anyone who can do that is powerful. Are you certain you should pursue this, especially when your telecarb works only sporadically?"

"Hey, there's another me running around ruining my reputation."

"Not for long," Claire said as she came through the wall.

I'd never tried that stunt and I didn't plan to in the near future.

"The Entomons have signed a contract with Neola Durwin." Her lip curled when she said the name. "They gave me the gist of it."

"How much is she paying them?"

"Not one penny, or whatever they use there for money. That's the worse part. They're doing it for the scientific challenge. What scientist wouldn't jump at the chance of creating a universe?"

"So, they don't know Neola and the other me are getting rich on the project."

"They don't care. What they care about, though, is that once Neola has finished her little project, no one else gets at that technology."

"I get whiffs of the Manhattan Project."

Her eyes became hard. "Exactly. They'll have exclusivity over that technology. Then—" She stopped, swallowed. "In six months—their time—they'll reverse the process and attempt to destroy the universe Neola and her buddies created. With everyone in it."

She stepped in front of me. It was the first time I'd ever seen her bone-deep terrified.

"Understand this, Jack. This is untested technology. There's a chance—a minor one, they've calculated—that we could lose parts of our own universe in the process. They've built contingencies to protect themselves, but to hell with the rest of us. If they try this dismantling with other universes, chances increase exponentially that they'll eventually create another Big Bang."

She rubbed the bridge of her nose with index and thumb. "We have to find the equipment, bring back the beings that were displaced and shut the entire operation down before they do. Otherwise, I can't guarantee we'll survive this."

"How long does that give us, Earth time?"

She raised her head, looked me straight in the eyes.

"Forty-eight hours."

CHAPTER TWENTY-SIX

AFTER I GOT THE THRITTENE TO SETTLE DOWN AND KNOCK OFF THE DIRGES, we got down to planning, as much as it was possible to do so.

"How big is their equipment?" I said to Claire.

"Surprisingly small." Despite the grimness of the situation, her eyes shone with excitement. "About the size of a briefcase."

I whistled. "It must pack quite a punch."

"Let me see if I can explain it so you can understand it," she said with a smirk. "It zeroes in on a portion of matter, a bit like a telescope, then cuts it up and folds it. Instead of using a bacteriostatic agent that inhibits the function of the whole, it manipulates several dimensions at the same time so that the matter they've excised becomes infinitesimally small. Then they reverse the process at the other end."

"What's holding the universe together?"

Claire threw a glance at Trebor and cleared her throat. "Ah, I couldn't say."

"No need to try to spare us, Claire Foucault," Trebor said. "We are now aware that part of us is being violated for use as a universe membrane. The Entomons have betrayed us." The last said with a thousand echoes.

"Hey, don't take it that way," I said, after the noise had died down. Because of their tinkering, I could bear it, but I could tell it took a toll on Claire. Her auburn hair accentuated the pallor of her skin and the bruises under her eyes. She rubbed her temples as if she had a headache.

"They're bugs, Trebor," I continued. "Bugs have no feelings."

Besides, I almost added, he should relate to the Entomons' behavior. The Thrittene themselves had shown a more than flexible sense of ethics when it suited their own purpose, but I didn't think it would help matters if I pointed it out.

"Is the equipment moveable?"

"Yes, but not portable. Every time it's moved, it needs to be recalibrated and that takes time. We don't have that luxury. I'd have to operate it where I found it."

"The Entomons showed you how it works?"

She looked at me down her nose. "Of course not. As you pointed out, they're bugs. They're brilliant when it comes to research but quite stupid in other areas of their lives. I used their lab to fix a couple of machines that had broken down. Simple repairs, like we used to do in grad school with the cheap equipment we had to work with and maintain. While I was in the lab, I snooped."

I grinned. "We'll make an investigator out of you yet, Claire."

"Bite your tongue, Jack Meter. I am not, and never will, do anything for you, especially not become your partner."

"Except when the universe is near collapse. That's grand of you, Claire."

"There are people in this universe who are more important than you, you conceited jerk."

Trebor cleared his throat, which had the effect of a gong resonating through the room. This time, we both winced.

"This bickering is unproductive and childish. You have said that time is short. Your priority is to find this equipment, not try to out-insult each other."

I shook my head. "I hate it when you're right. Okay, let's cool off, here. I have an idea where we might find this super-conjugator, so I'll start there."

"Super-conjugator," Claire said with a grimace. "I suppose it's as good a name as any. You're still stuck on Garner's house, are you? Terry said they'd already searched it."

"Yeah, but they didn't have a chat with a canny twelve-year-old." At her blank look, I added, "Ellie gave me an idea where to look."

Her eyebrows shot up in derision.

"Look," I said, "all you have to do is operate the damn thing when I find it. And I'm telling you it's at Garner's house."

She threw me a pitying glance. "Of course."

I hesitated then risked asking the question again. I leaned over and murmured for her ears only.

"You will be able to destroy the SC once we're finished with it, won't you?"

A muscle in her jaw twitched and her hands became fists. She'd understood me right away. Last time we'd worked together, she almost hadn't come through at the crunch. It had been hard for her, and I wanted to make sure she could hold up her end this time.

"You're a real bastard, aren't you?" she said between clenched teeth.

I stared into her eyes. "I have to know."

"What if the AGES want the technology?"

"My point exactly."

She took a deep breath, let it out very slowly. "I'll do what I have to do."

As a promise went, it wasn't very satisfying, but I knew I had to accept it. I nodded once.

"Someone should warn Mariental and Winston," I said in a louder voice.

We turned toward Trebor.

He shook his head violently. "Another telecarb is out of the question. We will not scatter more of our matter at this time."

I fished the broken USI from my pocket and threw it to him.

"How about this?"

Instead of catching it, he absorbed it where it landed, just below his neck.

"Ah, yes, we can certainly repair this device then program it with the coordinates we have gathered from your telecarb, Jack Meter."

"Still keeping an eye on me, are you?"

Trebor almost smiled. "Your last sorties have been quite exciting. We despaired of your using your telecarb again. Fortunately, although it lost its transport capabilities in other universes, it has retained its homing signal."

"Living by proxy is pathetic, you know."

"We have learned much."

"I bet. Claire, you go to Mariental while I try to find the SC. Once you've explained the situation, meet me back at Garner's house. Trebor can program that in as well."

Arms crossed under her breasts, she shook her head.

"No way. Either I learn how to use it myself or I'm not budging from here."

I nodded. "Show her how it works, Trebor. She's got the brains for it."

Claire blinked in surprise at the compliment.

"Thanks, Jack," she said. Then her lips thinned, and she had an annoyed look in her eyes.

"Don't worry, I won't make it a habit." With that and a grin, I wished myself in Garner's bedroom.

* * *

I'd chosen his bedroom instead of another room in the house just in case Neola and her buddies were there, which I thought might be likely since they had little time left to cut, paste and sell. I figured the likelihood of anyone staying in that room for any length of time was fairly slim.

Choosing Garner's house hadn't been based solely on gut feeling. If Neola had ever kept the SC in her house, she would've moved it early on, just in case I caught on to her. Winston's house was out—she couldn't guarantee I wouldn't confront him there and, when I saw he wasn't there, snoop around to confirm or deny her suspicions.

Garner's house was an ideal choice. I'd never been there and wasn't likely to go. Every time I'd talked to him, he'd made sure to come to my office.

The smell wasn't much better than a couple of days ago when the resident owner had involuntarily vacated the premises. Black powder covered every flat surface—the OPD boys had been busy lifting fingerprints. They'd taken the sheets off the bed. I shuddered to imagine what kind of fluid they were looking for.

I took a cursory look around but didn't bother searching. I just couldn't see Neola coming in here at all hours of the day and night to use the SC—Garner would've certainly thrown a hissy fit over that. Plus, he had bought it in the entertainment room. Either he'd surprised Neola in there or they'd had an argument. Either scenario didn't help him, but my hunch told me that's where I'd find the equipment.

Failing that, I'd try the kitchen. Maybe they'd disguised the SC as a microwave.

Dawn crept in through the opened curtains and bathed the room in vivid orange. It would rain by nightfall, I thought pointlessly.

I cracked open the door. Light splayed from the entertainment room along the dark corridor. Neola's arrogance showed again. The cops still considered Garner's house a crime scene and cruisers would regularly patrol the area. Knowing Aplin and the bug up his butt he had about my being involved in Garner's death he'd probably asked for a regular rounds of the house just in case I came back, just as I was doing. Yet there these guys were, all lights blazing, as if they didn't have a care in the world.

Which meant a quick escape route. I hesitated, wondering how many of them were in there now.

That moment of caution saved me. All of a sudden, a Winston-shape obscured the doorframe. I heard his characteristic rumble but couldn't understand what he said to someone behind him, all the while walking toward me. I pushed the door closed but didn't latch it, in case the click caught his attention. He passed by; then a lighter set of footsteps followed. They clanged downstairs. I was about to open the door again when I heard Neola.

"Hey, bring me back a sandwich, will you? And a glass of wine."

"No problem," my voice answered back.

Working on the assumption Neola wouldn't want too many partners, there was now only one person left in the room. Unfortunately, she was fond of her gun. For once, though, maybe I could use my double to my advantage.

What I saw when I entered the room almost made me croon. Not only had I been right, but I wouldn't have to spend precious time looking for the equipment. The flat screen of the TV swiveled on hinges—the OPD boys had missed that—and behind it on a shelf sat a black contraption that looked very similar to a laptop. Neola sat facing it and fiddled with some kind of knob.

"If you're looking for your cigarettes," she said without turning, "they're on the table over there." I approached her without speaking. "I'm having a bit of a problem configuring those last coordinates," she continued. "Why don't you come over here and give me a hand. Pete can bring you a sandwich, too."

I stopped behind her. She glanced over her shoulder then did a double-take. "Hey, you're not—"

Before she could turn around, I slapped a hand over her mouth and wrapped an arm around her midriff. She wriggled like an eel, but I managed to keep hold of her and back away from the SC at the same time.

She fell limp in my arms, and I relaxed slightly. Big mistake.

"Ow!" She'd slammed her heel on the top of my foot, at the same time rammed her elbow in my gut. My foot howled with pain; I couldn't breathe. I dropped her in reaction. She pushed me away. I expected her to turn and finish what she'd started. Instead, she ran away, around the sofa to the other end of the room. Too late, I spotted her gun on a glass table near the window.

She grasped it and whipped around to face me. I stopped dead in my tracks.

She grabbed her gun with both hands, took a stance. At the same time, I heard someone run up behind me.

"This time, Jack, I'm putting you out of commission." She all but snarled it.

I wished myself out of the room.

Neola fired. Twice.

I felt something pass through what should've been my right shoulder. I fell on my knees and watched my body reassemble itself. Something warm trickled down my arm. Blood dripped through my cuff onto the back of my hand to the tips of my fingers. Neola's legs appeared in front of me. I hadn't left the room, probably because of the super-conjugator.

"What's the matter, Jack, having problems with your telecarb? That's too bad. You're staining the carpet, but I imagine a little more blood won't make a difference. Since this wound isn't life-threatening, I'll remedy that." She raised the gun to my temple.

People with guns always get too cocky. I'd already anticipated her move. With my good arm, I slapped her gun aside. She grunted, unbalanced. Still on my knees, I rammed the heel of my right hand under her chin. Her teeth snapped together, her head flew back. Her eyes glazed then she crumpled to the floor.

I got up, favoring my right arm, which was throbbing by now.

"That's for Nasus," I said, without any remorse at having decked a woman.

From the corner of my eye, I saw movement in the doorway. When I turned, my alter ego stood there, leaning on the doorjamb, a .38 Magnum pointed at me.

"There'd be a kind of irony if I were to blow your brains out," he said, half-smiling.

"You'd be shooting yourself."

"Exactly." He pursed his lips. "Neola explained about your telecarb, that it'll whisk you off to Thrittene if your life is threatened. She was pretty sure even those magicians couldn't pick up all your splattered brains and put them back together."

"You're right, I'm not immortal, but those guys are amazing. Swallowing a bullet hurts, anyway, so I'd like to avoid it." I paused, stared him straight in the eyes. "But you won't shoot me. You're not a killer."

His face darkened. "Don't make the mistake of thinking I'm you."

"Believe me, I won't. I'd never associate myself with the likes of Neola."

He grinned. "You did for a while."

"Yeah, but eventually I saw through her. How come you didn't?"

He said nothing to that. He moved inside the room, gestured with his gun at the two feet pointing upward.

"Check on Pete, will you?"

Winston number two was sprawled in the corridor. I stepped over Neola, bent over Winston. A large red stain had spread over his chest. I searched for a pulse, found none. Now I knew who had come up behind me. Neola must've shot him when I changed into Thrittene matter.

"He's dead."

"Shit." He said nothing for a moment. "So long, my friend," he finally whispered.

Neola moaned. His gun still aimed at my head, he walked over to her, crouched and patted her lightly on the face.

"Come on, sweetie, wake up."

As soon as she opened bleary eyes, he got up and waited. Slowly, she rose on all fours then pushed herself up, using the other Jack for support. When she saw me, her face tightened.

"You sonofabitch, you nearly broke my jaw." She picked up her gun. "You'll pay for that."

"Wait," Jack said to her. He motioned me toward the TV. "You're going to pack up the equipment for us."

"Listen—"

"Shut up," he said, his voice hard. "You want to stay in one piece, you keep your lips zipped. I'm not interested in anything you have to say. A friend's dead because of you. Right now, I'm exercising restraint."

I glared at him for a moment then shrugged.

The SC was very similar to a laptop. All I had to do was fold a couple of antennae-like devices then snap the screen on top of the command panel. It was surprisingly light.

"Put it on the floor and back away."

My shoulder was killing me, the bullet wound still dripping on the floor. Neola grinned, walked to me and pushed the butt of her gun under my chin.

"Now it's time to say goodbye, Jack."

"Neola," the other Jack said, "we don't have time for this."

Her eyes hardened. She turned sideways. Before she could say anything, I felt a chill from my telecarb, and Claire appeared behind the sofa. Neola reacted immediately, aiming at her.

"Claire, down!"

She threw herself on the floor. I dove after her. Jack and Neola fired in our direction. A bullet plonked into the stuffing right above my head.

"Come on," I heard Jack say, then running, two pairs of feet, away from us.

I cautiously peered over the back of the sofa. No one was in sight.

"Great going," I said, jumping over the couch and running after my double.

A door at the end of the corridor stood open and a round doorway to another world showed through. I watched my double step through, followed by Neola. I rushed to follow them, but as I watched, the portal closed with a sucking sound.

"Damn," I said. "We've lost them."

CHAPTER TWENTY-SEVEN

LET ME SEE THAT," CLAIRE SAID, AS SHE PULLED AT THE SLEEVE OF MY JACKET. I fended her off. "I'm fine."

"Yeah, that's why you're bleeding all over the floor." She poked my injured arm.

I swore, took my coat off. "And you say I'm a bastard."

"Oh, I do so enjoy hurting you." She dragged me back to the entertainment room, stopping in her tracks at the sight of Winston on the floor. "Is that our Winston?"

"No, the other one. Neola killed him while aiming at me. Guns are dangerous for your health."

She threw me a derisive glance, pushed me to the sofa and sat me on the side that wasn't stained with Garner's blood, gone a rusty brown against the white.

"Wait here," she said.

I leaned back, frustrated. I'd run out of places where I could look for Neola and Jack. She'd had the presence of mind to pick up the super-conjugator before they'd escaped.

Claire came back with bandages and a brown bottle.

"Garner didn't have much. Hopefully, that'll be enough." She pulled up the sleeve of my T-shirt. I clamped my teeth against the pain.

"Just a graze at the top of the arm. You were lucky—she could've shattered your shoulder joint." My wound had stopped bleeding, but it ached like the damned. She applied the stuff in the bottle and made me yelp.

"Jesus, woman, what's in there, acid?"

"Just iodine. Wimp." She stuck a large pad of gauze over the gash, which she fixed with tape.

I pulled my bloody sleeve down. "Any ideas?"

"They're out of portals." She stood and looked down at me. I obviously looked confused. "The Entomons built three portals for them. There was one at the restaurant, one at Winston's house and this one. They don't have any more."

"Neola never set up one at her house in Colorado?"

"No. I suppose she knew she'd take you there eventually and didn't want to take the risk."

"So, there are only three places where they could come back to finish the job."

"I have a feeling it *is* finished. They can't take the risk to continue."

"Neola is nothing but arrogant."

"Yes, but she's far from stupid. Do you know where that portal leads?"

I hit my forehead with my palm then winced at the pain.

"Talk about stupid." I took out the stick Leinad had made to detect the portal coordinates and set it on my telecarb. The two merged for a minute.

"What is that?"

"Leinad wanted to reconfigure my telecarb so I could get into Neola's created universe, but I convinced him it was a lot of tinkering for a one-time shot. He amplified this gizmo instead. It records portal activities and will enhance my telecarb's capability to get there." I looked up. "That's where they've gone, all right."

"Then we go check it out."

"No."

"No?"

"There's no 'we' here, sweetheart. I'm going by myself."

"You dragged me into this thing. I'm seeing it through to the end."

I got up and faced her, toe-to-toe.

"Listen, you twit, where I'm going has a good chance of being pulverized in a few hours. You're not coming."

"Don't you dare turn all macho on me, Jack Meter. I'm fully aware of what's going on."

"Freeze!"

We both jumped and turned toward the hallway. A city cop held a gun pointed at us. Behind him, Aplin's grinning face appeared.

"Aw, shit," I said, as I raised my hands above my shoulders.

* * *

They'd separated Claire and me as soon as we were on the landing, Claire being led away first. All I had time to say to her was to call her lawyer.

"I don't have a lawyer, you schmuck," she yelled as she went down the stairs.

"That's real good advice," Aplin said to me. "You should follow it. Who's your lawyer, Meter?"

I looked down at Winston the second. Another cop was calling an ambulance, while at the same time shaking his head at Aplin, signaling that he couldn't find life signs. I figured it would be futile to explain that this wasn't the real Winston.

I pointed at the corpse. "He's right there, Aplin."

"Well, that's just too bad, because you're in dire need of one and this one's not gonna be able to help you."

"I'll figure something out."

"If I have anything to do with it, you won't. Take him away," he said to the two cops waiting for me.

When they took me outside, I realized I'd been wrong in my weather forecast. Instead of rain, snow fell hard and tight, promising the first big storm of the year. I lifted my eyes to the sky, letting the flakes melt on my face. I wondered what kind of weather Neola and Jack had where they'd landed.

* * *

"Okay, let's take it from the top," Aplin said.

I glanced at the clock. I'd been in a cubicle at the police station for the past ten hours. I could feel time running through my fingers. My skin itched, and had been doing so for the past hour.

I'd stuck to my story, which was pretty skimpy, making Aplin angrier by the minute. Even though he was a prick and had a fixation about putting me in jail, he was far from stupid. He knew there was more to the tale than what I was saying.

"I told you—how many times, now?—I wanted to see for myself if I could find something in Garner's house you guys missed."

"And you brought Ms. Foucault with you."

"That's right."

"Why?"

I shrugged.

"Why did you kill Peter Winston?"

"I didn't."

"Where's the gun?"

"With the killer, I suspect."

"What was behind the television?"

"It was opened like that when I got there."

"Did Winston shoot you?"

"No."

"Who did?"

"Neola Durwin."

"And you say she also shot Winston."

"She must have. I didn't see it."

Aplin dug into an envelope and came out with the universe-hopping device the Thrittene had made for me. And therein lay the crux of the matter, I thought. I'd have vanished a long time ago if it hadn't been for Aplin holding on to that device. That, and wondering what was happening with Claire. She had a brilliant mind, but I couldn't guarantee she was smart enough to get out of this mess by herself.

"You carry some interesting stuff on you," Aplin said, as he slid the stick in between two fingers.

Because it was made of Thrittene matter, it had the same infinity of swirling colors as my telecarb, which he'd scrutinized with interest.

"Just something I picked up at a curio shop."

"Sure, sure. Like what you have around your arm. I wonder what it's made of. Some NASA stuff, maybe?"

"I have no idea." I ignored the sarcasm.

Aplin put the stick back into the personal items envelope. "Tell me what you were doing at Garner's again."

I nearly groaned. "Listen, Aplin, I've been cooperating. I've been here for hours and you still haven't charged me with anything. How about you get on with it or you let me go?"

His face turned red. I hoped he wouldn't have a coronary right there—I'd probably be blamed for that as well.

Someone knocked at the door, and a cop stuck his head through.

"Telephone, Sergeant Aplin. It's Mr. Meter's lawyer."

Aplin glanced at me then got up.

"Watch him," he said to the cop, who nodded and stationed himself inside against the door.

My lawyer? I had no idea who that could be, especially since I hadn't called anyone. I didn't think Claire would've called one for me, since she'd probably love the idea of me rotting in jail forever. She also knew we were short on time.

Twenty minutes had passed when the door opened and Winston appeared on the threshold.

"Hello, Jack," he said, cigar planted in the corner of his mouth. "Sorry I'm late. Claire called me."

It seemed I owed Claire an apology. I got up, picked up the envelope Aplin had left on the table.

"So glad to see you're not dead."

"Yeah, me, too. Let's go."

Aplin was nowhere around. He must've shit a brick load when he saw Winston standing up. I would've loved to have seen it.

Outside, the wind had picked up. There was already twenty-five centimeters on the ground, and it didn't look like it would be letting up soon.

"Where's Claire?" I said.

"At my house." He walked me a bit away from the station, which soon disappeared in the gloom and snow. "Let's get there now."

He took my arm and fingered something under his coat. I blinked, and we were in his living room. Claire sat in an armchair, sipping tea.

"I didn't think you had it in you, Claire," I said.

"If that's an apology, save it."

I shook my head.

"I'm going with you," she continued. "I'm the only one who can operate the super-conjugator."

"Claire, I told you, it's a one-way ticket."

"I can evacuate as many beings as possible before they collapse the universe. I want to save Nasus."

"You'd have to collapse the universe yourself to do that."

"I know how to do it." Her voice was far from assured.

"Winston, talk reason to her."

"She's right, Jack."

I closed my eyes, tried to hold on to my temper. I wasn't sure I understood why I didn't want Claire to take that kind of risk.

Or maybe I did. She was the only connection to Annie I had left, and I didn't want to lose it.

With that admission, I calmed down. Claire was a big pain in the butt, but she had innate compassion and courage, reminding me why Annie had liked her so much.

"All right. Let's go."

I held out my hand. She looked at it with distaste then put hers in it. I activated the stick and off we went.

* * *

We arrived at the bottom of a hill. It was daylight, but the sun was weak and the air thin. High up, at the end of a twisting lane, sat a log house, its huge bay windows looking over the valley below. Neola seemed to have a preference for heights and glass.

I looked around with curiosity. There was no indication the planet we were on had been patched together. Thick grasses covered the ground, mixed with yellow and purple flowers. A few low-lying trees crouched on the edge of the hill.

"They did a good job," Claire said.

"I never asked. How big do you think this universe is?"

"Not big. They didn't have that much time, and the complexity is immense. Remember, it was supposed to be an experiment. I'd say they put only a few planets together. I'll know better when I look at the conjugator."

"My telecarb is useless here."

"So's the USI."

"Then let's hoof it." We started climbing.

"They may be gone already."

"Always the optimist. If they decided to pack up and go, they're up there now, finalizing the deals, having moneys transferred. If not, and they're trying to get out, Winston has the portals watched. If they come out there, he'll have them."

"Now who's the optimist?"

I didn't say anything to that, saving my energy for the climb.

We arrived at the top out of breath. About three kilometers in the distance, a small village showed some activity. Farms dotted the valley, and I could make out cattle, although I wasn't sure they were of the cow variety since presumably Neola could've sold to any kind of species.

I motioned to Claire that we should go around the back. We ducked below the windows and made our way to the backyard. When I tried it, I found the door unlocked. I turned the knob and slowly pushed the door open to reveal the kitchen.

Angry voices, words indistinct, came through the doorway on the other side of the room. I motioned Claire to stay where she was. She shook her head. I tiptoed through the kitchen with her behind me.

"What else should I have done?" Neola said. Her voice came from the left.

"You could've tried something else. Like persuasion. Except it's not your strength, is it?"

"What's wrong, Jack, getting squeamish all of a sudden? We had a deal and I took care of my end. I have my own methods, and you'll have to accept that."

"Well, your methods suck."

"I need that equipment."

"I'm sure you do."

Disgust and frustration tinged Jack's voice. It was enough for me to take a risk. I stepped through the door.

"She won't kill you now because she has plans for you," I said. "But she will eventually."

Both of them stared at me in surprise.

"God, you're like a bad penny," Neola said, as she recovered first.

My double grinned. "I'm impressed."

Neola reached behind her and pulled out the gun she'd stashed in the belt of her jeans.

"Your telecarb won't help you here. You've reached the end of the line, Jack. Isn't this fun?"

Chapter Twenty-Eight

My other half reached out and pushed down Neola's gun arm. "There's no point in killing him. We'll just leave him here. He won't be able to go back anyway, and we're finished with this universe."

Neola thought for a minute then smiled. "That works, too."

"What made you so mean, Neola?" I said, relieved I had a few more minutes to live.

"You don't know what it is to be poor. I told you I hated the goddamn farm. Working like a slave to make ends meet, always worried about the weather or a plague of locusts, skimping and scraping just to be able to afford a miserable weekend in town. When Michael was killed, I saw it as the perfect way to get out of there."

She chuckled, but there was no humor in the sound. "Except I got sent to all the godforsaken corners of the galaxy, and for what? For a pittance."

"That house in Colorado wasn't built with pennies," I said.

She shrugged. "There's always a way to make people grateful. They wanted to reward me. Should I have stopped them? I never had altruistic motives. All I've ever wanted was enough money to be able to live in the manner to which I wanted to get accustomed. Well, I wasn't going to get that from the IGA, was I? The beings we dealt with were even more pitiful than those Minnesota farm boys. And you. Look at you. You have so much money you don't know what to do with it, and you live in that pigsty you call an office. That's pathetic."

"I would've preferred some sociopathic reason for all this," I said, motioning around me. "Greed is so...ordinary."

"Spoken by someone who's never had to worry about money."

I didn't choose to contradict her by saying that we'd lived hand-to-mouth until my ever-absent father had had an attack of conscience on his deathbed.

"At least I didn't steal it."

"The people who paid for a chunk of this universe got what they paid for," my double said.

"That's what you think," I said, turning to him. "Where's the conjugator?"

He raised an eyebrow. "In a safe place."

My heart speeded up. So, Neola didn't have it. He'd either stashed it around here, or he'd taken a small detour somewhere.

"From the discussion I interrupted, I'd say dear Neola wants it."

Jack threw a glance at her. "She does."

"What a bummer, eh, Neola? If you don't get that conjugator back, those bugs won't be very happy. A deal's a deal, after all."

She raised the gun again, a vicious look on her face. "Shut up, Jack."

"Go ahead, shoot. It'll only speed things up."

Jack stepped up to her, grabbed the gun and twisted. She snarled and let go.

"Give me back the gun," she said between clenched teeth.

"Not before you explain what he means."

"He means nothing. Don't you see, sweetie?" she said, her tone changing from harsh to honeyed. "He wants to split us up. It's a typical ploy. Divide and conquer."

"There's more to it than that."

"Why don't you tell him about your deal with the Entomons, Neola?" I said. "Come to think of it, why haven't you already? Maybe you knew he wouldn't go for genocide. Or maybe you intended to leave him here."

Fury flashed across her face.

"Ah, that's it, isn't it. How were you going to get your hands on my money then?"

"Explain the genocide thing," Jack demanded, turning to me. "Then you can follow up with the idea of her leaving me here."

"Neola challenged the Entomons to build a device that could create a universe within another universe. She made a bargain with them—I try it out, you let me sell the chunks of universe to overcrowded worlds for immigration."

"Nothing new there."

"Ah, but there's a catch. Claire," I called out, "why don't you tell my double what you found out?"

Claire stepped into the room. Jack raised an eyebrow and leaned against the fireplace mantel, the gun loose in his hand. Neola stayed where she was, trying to look relaxed, but her fisted hands showed she was getting nervous.

Claire stood beside me.

"The Entomons are a highly advanced, intelligent race," she said in an even voice, as if she were lecturing colleagues on the latest finding in entomology. "They not only believe knowledge is power, they live it. I think it's safe to say that they aim to be the most powerful race in the galaxy.

"What Neola offered them is a possibility of gaining more knowledge. They had built a small conjugator at my request and the results fascinated them. What they didn't know was that, by using the device, Jack created a universe. When Neola approached them with the idea of creating one on purpose, they were fascinated."

My double raised his hand. "I thought the conjugator thing had happened only three months ago. They couldn't have developed a device like that in such a short time." He glanced at Neola. "You told me it took them years to build the device."

"Time flows differently there," Claire said. "It fluctuates. Think of a stream. In spring, it rushes with the thaw, in late summer it's almost dry. Neola arrived in spring. Time flew much faster there than on Earth."

"So they *had* years for their research."

"Exactly. The thing is, the Entomons want to close the circle. They know it's possible to create a universe..."

"So, now they want to know if they can destroy it," Jack concluded. "Is this true, Neola?"

She shrugged. "So what if it's true? Those people were dying on their worlds anyway. No one will miss them."

"I can see why you didn't tell me that part."

"I had no choice, don't you see? That was the deal. They want all the technology back."

"So they can keep it for themselves."

"Like the secret of nuclear power," I said.

"You have to give me the conjugator, Jack," Neola said as she stepped toward him, eyes pleading.

"I don't think so."

"Neither of us will be safe if I don't. You don't want to have bugs chase you down for the rest of your life, do you?"

"Very unappealing, I grant you."

"Then we have to do this."

"It's 'we,' now, is it?"

"It's always been 'we.' You must know that." She was looking at him with doe eyes, wet with contrition. I always found women at their most dangerous when they cried—or as least faked it.

She stepped in front of him. I was about to call out for him to watch out when she grabbed the gun and backed away, laughing.

"Men are such suckers. Sorry, Jack, dear, but there's a lot riding on this. I'll be going, if you don't mind. I have an idea where you put the conjugator anyway."

"Really."

"Annie's apartment."

Bull's-eye. And for both of us. I heard my own gasp and saw my double twitch.

She grinned. "You're much too sentimental. Too bad you won't have time to correct that flaw. How about giving me your key."

"How about you come and get it."

"Okay." She fired. Jack's body recoiled and hit the mantle. He looked down in surprise as blood poured out of his belly and stained his shirt. Slowly, he slid down into a sitting position, holding the wound.

She turned toward us, frowned. "Where's Claire?"

Startled, I realized Claire had disappeared. "I have no idea. Maybe she's gone after the conjugator."

"She can't leave here without the key."

"The Thrittene have modified her USI," I lied. Where the hell was she?

"Well, goodbye, Jack." She walked closer to me and raised her gun. I closed my eyes.

I heard a *thunk*, a grunt, the gun going off. I waited for the pain to come.

"You can look now," Claire said, her voice dry.

When I opened my eyes, Neola was on the floor, out cold. Claire held a thick book in both her hands.

"You knocked her down with a dictionary?"

"I guess it's true what they say—knowledge is power."

"I could've been shot."

"You weren't. Stop whining."

She dropped the book and rushed to my double. He was still conscious.

"Don't move," she said as she put pressure on his wound. Blood gushed through her fingers.

"Nothing you can do for me," he whispered. He looked at me. "I'm already dead. Around my neck. Take my portal key and Neola's and do what you have to do."

I dug under his shirt and found a chain with a flat rectangle the size of a stick of gum. I slipped the chain over his head. I walked over to Neola and took hers off as well then went back to Jack. On the way, I picked up the gun she'd dropped.

"Neola was right? The conjugator is in Annie's apartment."

He smiled slightly. "Your Annie's, not mine. I got nervous about her. Too many dead."

I knew *her* didn't refer to Annie.

I couldn't resist asking. "In your world…"

"She's dead, too. Car crash. I thought maybe in your universe, she'd be there, but life doesn't work that way, it seems." He coughed, and blood bubbled through his mouth. He wiped it with the back of his hand. "Go. The portal is in the broom closet in the kitchen. Leave me the gun."

I placed the weapon in his fist then got up.

"We're not leaving him here," Claire said.

"Only two people can cross," I said. I stared at Jack. His eyes were closed, his skin already dead white. "There's nothing we can do, Claire."

"Take him to the Thrittene."

"If I do that, you're stuck here. Your job's more important. We're running out of time."

She didn't move for a moment. Then she grabbed the key and marched to the kitchen.

"You're a hardhearted bastard, Jack Meter."

"Yeah," I muttered, without looking back. "I guess I am."

* * *

The portal key brought us back to Garner's house. When we came out, it was still snowing, but the density of the flakes had lessened. Dawn was graying the cloud cover.

"We lost some time again," Claire said.

"Yeah. Can you make it to Annie's apartment by yourself?"

"Faster if I hang on to you."

"Gee, Claire, we're getting to be buddies."

She threw me her killer glare and growled.

* * *

Annie had sublet her apartment until her lease ran out, so, technically, it wasn't her apartment anymore, but that was where my double had said he'd stashed the SC. It would have to be in a place where it couldn't be found easily.

We arrived in the living room. The place was quiet.

"Tenants still sleeping, I hope," I whispered. "You have any idea where it is?"

"Yes."

Claire walked into the kitchen, stopped. I stopped behind her. A woman sat at the table, drinking coffee. She looked hung-over. She raised her head and blinked at us blearily.

"What—"

I dug in my inside jacket pocket and took out my wallet. I flipped it open and closed quickly, flashing my ID.

"Sorry, ma'am, we'll be out of your hair in a minute. If you could be patient." I pushed Claire. "Go ahead, make it quick."

"How did you get in here?" the woman said. She seemed too stunned to scream. She watched as Claire removed the radiator panel to reveal a safe. "I didn't know that was there."

"Me neither," I muttered.

Claire flipped the combination.

"How did the other Jack know the numbers?"

"I guess the other Annie trusted him more," Claire said. She opened the door. The conjugator was inside.

"Let's go," I said as I took her arm.

* * *

"Jack," Claire said, "go pace somewhere else. You're driving me crazy."

I stared at the blank walls of Thrittene. "Two hours, Claire. That's all you have left."

"I'm doing the best I can."

Her best might not be enough. If there was someone bright enough to do this, it was Claire—she could chat with the Thrittene and the Entomons and actually understand what they said—but what she was trying to do now defied even my tendency to expect miracles.

She planned to use the conjugator in the same way she'd used it on Annie, so that all the parts would float back to where they belonged. The trick was not to create another universe by trying to disperse this one, and to avoid making it collapse with ours.

"We don't want another Big Bang," she'd said, her tone dry.

Trebor rose in front of me.

"Your pacing is, indeed, disruptive," he said.

"I need a drink." I paced some more. "Are you sure you can get me in the eleventh dimension?"

"Your friend Winston has provided the coordinates. Leinad has modified the time bubble. You should have no problem."

"Great." At least I'd won that argument. Claire had declared that, to disperse the universe, she'd have to be directly outside of it. She'd come up with the idea of using a version of the Thrittene's time bubble, but I'd been adamant that it would be me who'd go "out there."

"I made that first universe," I said to her. "Even if I didn't do it on purpose, it's only fitting that I be the one to fix the problem. Anyway, it's my case, not yours."

She'd finally relented, more because we were wasting time than because she agreed.

"Got it."

I turned to her. "Are you sure?"

"As sure as I can be. Either it works, or we're all dead and won't care."

I shook my head, picked up the SC. Leinad made me stand in an alcove carved out into the wall.

"Good luck, Jack Meter."

With that, a panel slid in front of me.

Instantly, the bubble became transparent. Streaks of light, from red to yellow, passed by luminous ribbons. Flashing pinpoints of shiny stuff winked in and out. To the sides it was empty black—my brain seemed to stop functioning every time I looked in that direction.

Ahead, an infinite variety of colors swirled. They stretched further out than I could see in all directions. They reminded me of my telecarb. Nasus. It had to be her. I sure hoped she'd survive the universe dispersion.

The universe Neola had created might have been small in comparison to ours, but it loomed in front of me like a tsunami. Through the walls of my bubble, I sensed deep quivers coming from ahead.

My heart thundered. My palms were slick with sweat. I activated the conjugator the way Claire had showed me and pointed it toward the universe. For a while, nothing happened.

She had explained the transfer of people wouldn't take long but that I wouldn't be able to know if it happened. I had to take it on faith she knew what she was doing. I'd silently cursed her arrogance until I looked into her eyes. The terror was still there, mixed with the weight of duty. I'd turned away then, feeling guilty that I'd misjudged her.

After about an hour, the quivers changed to vibrations then to a deep rumble. Small cracks appeared in the universe's membrane. As I watched, awed, the fractures widened; and parts of planets, like small meteors, began to float upwards then sideways in all directions. The farther away from the brane the faster they went, until they became a blur. It was beautiful and frightening at the same time.

Too late, I saw the big chunk hurling toward me. I had nothing to steer with anyway. I shut my eyes and braced for the impact.

*　　*　　*

Someone knocking woke me from deep sleep. I groaned, rolled to the side and fell off the couch. God, every muscle in my body hurt. I got up painfully then stopped.

I was in my office.

That was impossible, though. The house had melted. I blinked, confused. The knocking continued.

"Yeah, yeah, I'm coming," I muttered.

I opened the door. Garner and Winston stood on the stoop.

"Mr. Garner," I said, feeling stupid.

"You know me. Good. Winston here says you can help me." He

pushed past me and sat in the chair across from my desk. I stared at his back then at Winston. His eyes were sparkling, and he was smiling around his cigar.

"I'll only be a minute," I said to Garner. I stepped outside, closed the door. "Don't tell me it's about to start again."

"What, Jack? You need a case, I brought you one." He looked at his watch. "Someone's been embezzling in Garner's company. I'm sure you can wrap it up before Christmas. Sorry, gotta go to court. I have a car waiting."

He winked then went down the stairs. I watched him go, my confusion a thick blanket over my brain. I hadn't dreamt all this. I hadn't. Had I?

Behind me, the door opened.

"Well," Garner said, "do you want the job or not?"

I looked at him. It was the same old Garner—dandruff, stink and all. I walked past him, picked up my coat.

"You'll excuse me, but I just remembered something urgent I have to do."

I left him open-mouthed on the landing.

The cold air outside cleared my head of sleep, if not confusion. I zipped up my jacket—which was minus a bullet hole—and stuffed my hands in the pockets. I felt something in the right one, took it out.

Right there, in my hand, was Karoi's USI.

READ JACK'S NEXT CASE FILE SOON...

ABOUT THE AUTHOR

M. D. Benoit learned to tell stories at her father's knee. His bedtime stories were always full of gadgets, dark doorways and disappearing people. She is continuing the tradition. She lives in Ottawa, Canada, with her husband and her cat (who is really an alien in disguise). Her first novel, *Metered Space*, introduced Jack Meter. *Meter Made* is the second in the series of the Jack Meter Casefiles. M. D. Benoit can be reached at jack@mdbenoit.com, or visit her website at http://mdbenoit.com.